# THE FAMILY JEWELS

## CAIMH MCDONNELL

Caimh McDonnell

Visit my website at www.WhiteHairedirishman.com

First edition: August 2022

ISBN: 978-1-912897-43-8

# AUTHOR'S NOTE

Dear reader,

Let me start this author's note by wishing you and yours a very merry Christmas. I appreciate it may not be Christmas as you read it, but, for better or for worse, this is a Christmas book, so I strongly suggest you get onboard with that idea now.

Previously, I have used these notes to apologise to North Americans for words being spelled the way my mother considers to be correct. I would now like to issue a further apology to Canadians, who, it turns out, insist they don't spell things the same way as the rest of the people on that continent, and they greatly resent the implication. We have received emails. Remarkably polite emails.

Now, I would like to use the rest of this note to issue a heartfelt apology to someone very close to me, namely – myself. You see, this book wasn't supposed to exist. I was writing a novella. A fun, little adventure of about maybe 15,000 words to round out a year where, if I say so myself, I'd worked really hard. I'd sat in my office in the garden for sometimes hours a day, making nonsense up, which, for the purposes of this exercise, we're calling a job. I was due a break from all that 'work'. Instead, this monster developed free will and started rampaging through nearby villages. In other words, it decided it was a full-blown novel without consulting me first. The several months I spent writing it meant I missed out on as many as two trips to the gym, watching all those Netflix shows in foreign languages that everyone keeps telling me are great and, I dunno, being alone with my thoughts. I do have a sneaking suspicion that I have a lot fewer thoughts than I think I thought I had, but we will never know now.

So, I hope you enjoy this book, as thanks to it I still can't speak German, throw a pot or play 'Hey Jude' on the piano, or indeed any other songs. Now, if you'll excuse me, I'm off to attempt to cancel my direct debit to the gym again, which will invariably end up with me signing up for spinning classes I will not be attending.

Merry bloody Christmas,

Caimh

# PROLOGUE

Dave Farrell was a legend.

He had the window of the Granada wound down so that the cold night air could whip through the car and keep him alert. Thin Lizzy was pumping out 'Whiskey in the Jar' on the stereo – the only song you could listen to on this drive through the Kerry mountains. This was living. To his left, a sheer rock face loomed over him as he whizzed past it in the crisp moonlight afforded by the cloudless sky. To his right, a low stone wall was all that separated him from a drive out into wide open space. You'd plummet to your death so quickly that you'd only be able to clamp your eyes shut and it would be over before you knew it.

As far as Dave was concerned, being drunk was not the problem. At this time of night, you'd be a lunatic to drive this road sober. What was life without risk? So many people lived it like they thought that if they were careful enough, they could get out of it alive. Not Dave Farrell. That was what made him a true legend.

Down into third – round the bend, floor it and then back up into fourth for the long stretch.

He was coming from the Christmas do of his soon-to-be ex-employers, Reardon & Sons Engineering. First thing in the morning, he would drag himself out of bed to get in there and resign. He would not give the pricks the satisfaction of firing him. It was a matter of principle and Dave Farrell was a man of principle.

It had not been a good week. For the last couple of years the Christmas party had been held at a hotel out in the middle of bloody nowhere because Sarah Reardon – who, despite the name, had run Reardon & Sons Engineering since her father's retirement two years ago – knew the owner and had got a good deal. The woman was all about the pennies and the pounds. Alright, she had managed to turn the company's finances around in short order, but the place was nowhere near as fun to work at as it once had been. Old man Reardon wasn't perfect, but at least he'd known how to throw a decent bash.

None of the reps had booked a hotel room for the night. Instead, they had relied on Christian Keith to be the designated driver. It was a great system that had worked well for the last couple of years – if you ignored Keith getting the hump when he had to wait around for everybody. Last year he had eventually left Jimmy Laughlin behind when Laughlin had been attempting to get off, and more, with sexy Sasha from Accounts. The idiot had subsequently tried to claim he had been successful, but big John Roberts had brought in a picture of Laughlin a week later, sleeping in an armchair in reception. The piss-taking had been year-long and merciless. Dave had taken particular delight in it, seeing as he and Jimmy were always battling it out for the top spot on the sales chart.

The problem this year was that Christian Keith's wife was up the duff, and even though she wasn't due for another few weeks, Keith had pulled out of going to the party entirely, citing complications, and suddenly, they were all left without a lift home. Efforts had been made to turn Keith around on this, but no luck. Selfish sod. With no other options, the four lads had drawn lots to see who would be the designated driver, and Dave had lost. It was bullshit. He knew for a fact that Jimmy knew how to do card tricks, which meant he was good at that sleight-of-hand crap. They never should have let him be the one to pull the name out.

Still, having resigned himself to having a terrible night, Dave had duly picked up the lads, driven them out to the venue and been at the mercy of the three of them as they spent the journey doing everything in their power to wind him up.

He'd had a solitary glass of wine with dinner. Being stone-cold sober, he'd realised that Christian Keith had been right – the food there really was terrible. Even drowning the turkey in gravy did nothing to hide how dry it was. Then there had been the speeches. The interminable speeches. The bloody things went on for ever, and just when it looked as if they were finally coming in for a landing, up pops old man Reardon to give an unscheduled address.

Renowned for being a man who has never met a drink he didn't like, the whole room had braced itself for Reardon's usual slurred ramble. In previous years, they'd run a book on how long he would go on for. Four years ago, Dave had won with his almost bang-on guess of twenty-two minutes. Against all previous form, this year the old man had gone for the unexpectedly short and sweet "you're all brilliant" option followed by the rapturously received announcement of a free bar. That had been a surprise, especially for his daughter, judging by the face she had on her.

Dave had heard that the two Reardons had got into a row in reception, once the poor mother had left after trying and failing to referee. Everyone else was three deep at the bar. The overwhelmed barman had tried to deal with the unexpected surge in demand as best he could, but eventually, they'd dragged in the receptionist to help out and told people to stop ordering cocktails as they slowed everything down too much.

It was an unrestricted free bar. Shangri-La. Mark Smith from the warehouse had somehow acquired an expensive bottle of Tullamore Dew and had been wandering around, doling out shots. Of course, Dave had accepted one. Everyone knew he loved his whiskey. Alright, maybe it had been more than one. Himself and Mark were the only Leeds fans at the firm and they'd had a few while discussing their team's trials and tribulations, but Dave was still the most sober man in the room.

Then Jimmy had come over and started giving out to him. Whiny little goody two-shoes. Unlike some people you could mention, everyone knew that Dave Farrell could handle his drink. Jimmy wouldn't let it go, and before he knew it, Dave was surrounded by him, Sean and Paschal, all giving him shit for being the designated driver and not staying teetotal. Paschal had kept banging on about how this close to Christmas they were bound to hit a Garda checkpoint on the way home.

Trying to be the bigger man, Dave had offered to see if he could get them a room for the night, but apparently, the hotel was totally booked up. It would be alright, he assured them. He would stop drinking there and then, neck a couple of coffees, and he'd be fine. Jimmy would not let it go, though. Said he wouldn't get into a car with Dave. Started making a big deal about how his uncle had died, like that had anything to do with anything. Eventually, enough was enough, and Dave had told him to go screw himself or, better yet, see if he could shack up with Sasha again.

You couldn't even really call it a fight, although people certainly had. Some pushing and shoving, followed by some grappling, and then they'd fallen over and broken a chair. They'd been split up and, seeing as it was made clear that nobody was getting in a car with Dave, he was no longer the designated driver. Then there'd been no reason not to drink, had there?

After a while, it had become obvious that nobody wanted to talk to him, not even Mark from the warehouse, so Dave had decided to head off. Sarah Reardon and her husband had caught up with him in the car park and demanded the keys to the car. Dave had made it very clear that she wasn't his ma, but she'd responded that she was his boss and, more importantly, it was a company car. He had tried to walk away, but her husband was a big fella who played football for the county back in the day, and he had taken the keys off Dave. Dave could have handled him, but there was no point. He'd stomped off, only to return five minutes later, to take the spare key from its hiding place under the back wheel arch and off he went. You had to get up early in the morning to outsmart Dave Farrell. It actually was early in the morning by that time, but the point still stood.

He'd taken the mountain road because the Gardaí wouldn't have bothered to put a checkpoint up here. Nobody wanted to spend a bitterly cold night just before Christmas standing on the side of a mountain while the wind ripped the skin off you.

All the ridiculous hand-wringing – like he was going to plough into a school trip at 2am on the Ballaghbeama Pass. Well-behaved men seldom made history. Dave remembered hearing that somewhere. It made a lot of sense.

He dropped back into third gear and smoothly guided the Granada around a hairpin bend. It was like being in your own rally. Tomorrow – well, later today – was the first day of the rest of Dave Farrell's life. He'd get a new job. A better job. A job where they treated him with respect. He didn't need Reardon & Sons. He didn't need anybody.

He did need a piss, though. There weren't many places to stop here, but he was fairly sure there was a lay-by in a mile or two. Until then, he would just distract himself.

He joined in with the chorus of 'Whiskey in the Jar' – "Mush-a ring dumb-a do dumb-a da, whack fall the daddy-o, whack fall the daddy-o, there's whiskey in the jar-o." What the hell did that mean? No idea. Great song, though. That's what Dave was now – an outlaw. From now on, he was going to make his own rules and then break them, anyway.

He needed a cigarette. He started flapping about with his left hand, trying to locate his fags on the passenger seat. He darted his eyes downwards. Where the hell were they? Where the ...

Dave's granny had always bored him as a child with stories of how their family had its very own banshee. A woman in a white dress who could be seen wailing on the night a member of the family was going to die. He didn't know how it was supposed to work. Did she just ring the doorbell and start screeching or did you get woken up in the middle of the night by some mad one screaming her lungs out in the back garden?

His right foot slammed down on the brake before his brain could even begin to process what had appeared on the road before him. The woman, her long dark hair blowing in the wind, wore a shimmering white dress, which was picked out by the car's headlights. She was standing in the middle of the road, waving her arms. As the Granada's tyres screeched in protest, there was nowhere to turn – left was a guaranteed collision with sheer rock, right was a *Thelma and Louise* off into the great beyond. All Dave could do was hold down his right foot, keep the steering wheel steady and scream.

The woman stood frozen in the headlights like a deer. Even as he ploughed towards the collision, a part of Dave's brain noticed how stunningly beautiful she was – flowing dark hair, elfin features, olive skin and a glorious body. A glorious body that was about to go flying over the bonnet of a Ford Granada belonging to Reardon & Sons Engineering.

Time slowed to a sickening crawl as the inevitable moment of impact approached. Dave could feel the pull as the back of the car fishtailed. He held on to the steering wheel and screwed his eyes shut. The roulette wheel was coming to a stop and the ball was bouncing onto zero.

He could well have sat there indefinitely, unaware that the car had finally stopped, if his bladder had not decided that enough was enough and voided itself. Nothing brought you back to reality faster than the feeling of warm piss on the inside of your leg. His eyes flew open and there, impossibly, still standing in front of the car in the middle of the road, was the woman.

Dave flung open the car door and stepped out onto the road. The bitter wind hit him like a bucket of cold water. He looked at the woman again, trying to get his head around the idea that she was both real and still alive. "What in the ..."

The car's front bumper was less than an inch from her legs. She turned her head to look at Dave and he realised she was shaking like a leaf. He looked down at his own hand and saw that he was, too. He doubted either of them was doing so because of the cold.

Dave clenched his fist. Now that the adrenaline was beginning to subside, he found himself gripped by anger. "What the fuck were you doing standing in the middle of the road?"

She turned to look at him and her voice came out in a whisper, half lost in the wind. "Help me. Please help me. Help me."

Now that his own – or someone else's – death wasn't taking up all of his mental bandwidth, he vaguely realised that to his left was a parking area, where a silver estate was pulled up.

Before he could respond, the woman collapsed to the ground.

He rushed over and bent down. "Are you—" He yelped as a hand grabbed the back of his neck, pulled him to his feet and spun him around. "What the—"

Firm hands shoved him back against his car. The man was a couple of inches shorter than Dave, with cropped brown hair, an attractive, boyish face and a full mouth that grinned at him in the moonlight. Whatever Dave had been about to say died on his lips as his eyes refocused on the object being held inches from his face. It was a knife.

"Lovely evening for a drive, isn't it?"

Dave barely recognised his own voice as it came out so high and reedy. "I … I don't want any trouble."

"That's good to know. You see—" The man wrinkled his nose in disgust as the smell of Dave's breath hit him. "Jesus." He looked to his left, where Dave was dimly aware of the sound of another set of footsteps. Somebody else was there. "The stench of booze off this prick."

Dave felt the hand tighten around his throat as he watched the tip of the knife move a little bit closer.

The man's smile was gone now, replaced by a snarl. "That's my woman over there and you nearly ran her over, ye drink-driving arsehole. People like you make me sick."

"Bobby," came a male voice from behind Dave.

"Get her in the car," barked the owner of the knife, not taking his eyes off Dave for a second. "I'm going to deal with this scumbag."

"W-w-we need to go."

"Who's in charge here?" the man snapped in response. His eyes flicked away for a moment then refocused on Dave. "Did you piss yourself?"

"Sorry," apologised Dave because he couldn't think of anything else.

The tip of the blade moved closer still to Dave's eye. "You're going to be. Dirty, dirty boy."

Dave could now feel the cold steel against his eyelashes. He had never been more certain of anything in his life – this man was going to hurt him. The barely suppressed excitement in his voice gave it away. This man yearned to hurt him – hurt anyone. Dave was just the fortunate person who'd put himself in his path.

"Lucky you came along." The man sounded disconcertingly cheerful. "We boosted a car, but my associate has poor taste in automotive transport. This is not a place to break down. Can't go calling the AA from here, even if the car wasn't stolen. Then we try to flag down help and some piss-soaked drunk nearly runs over my woman."

The tip of the blade swayed back and forth, caressing Dave's eyelashes. His eyes were watering now. He was terrified to close them in case he never got the chance to reopen them.

"Bobby?" said a soft female voice, breaking the spell.

"For fuck's sake, could you stop using my name?" He nodded at Dave. "Now this dipshit has heard it. It wasn't like there was much keeping him alive before now."

"I didn't hear nothing," babbled Dave. "I swear. Nothing. I ... Please. I'll drive you anywhere you want me to."

The man laughed. "That's hilarious. As if I'd let you drive me anywhere, you pisshead."

"I—"

"You're the second most dangerous thing in these mountains."

The man pressed the cold blade under Dave's right eye. Dave

could feel it poking through the skin, jabbing lightly against his eyeball.

"Guess what the first is?"

Then, because the human body can take only so much from one evening, Dave fainted.

# CHAPTER ONE

It is one of life's inalienable truths that somebody else always seems to be having a better time than you. Often, it is the diners one table over who appear to have ordered from an entirely different menu with much better dishes on it. Occasionally, it's the other patrons in the cinema who seem to be watching a much better film than you are. Inevitably, it will be the people in the hotel room next to yours, who – if the aural collage of grunts, profanities and name-checking of deities is to be believed – are having considerably more fun than one might associate with a stay in a Travelodge.

At that moment, Detective Bunny McGarry felt like the somebody enjoying life more than him was *everybody*. Given that he was surrounded by people struggling to make it home through the arse end of Dublin rush-hour traffic on a dreary late-December evening, that was really saying something. His current location didn't hold *all* the responsibility for his dark mood. His kettle at home had broken, leaving him with nothing but station tea to drink – something that would put a dampener on anyone's day. Dublin had coffee shops and whatnot, but Bunny drew the line at paying for hot drinks. Then he'd managed to find a remarkably deep puddle and had stepped in it, soaking his right foot thoroughly. He'd been so concerned with trying to dry it that he'd left his mobile phone on his desk in the office, meaning he'd have to head back there when his shift was over, wasting more time. It all added up to a steady drip, drip, drip of minor inconveniences that were adding to his rising levels of disgruntlement.

He rested his forehead against the passenger-side window and stared into the gutter, where grey sludge was all that remained of the snowfall from a couple of days ago.

"And then the duck says, 'I thought you were just feeding me funny.'"

The sudden gaping silence in the car left Bunny with a rising sense that he hadn't been paying as much attention to the conversation as he should have been. This was confirmed two seconds later, when he was slapped around the earhole. Slightly too hard to be playful, just soft enough not to be legally actionable.

"Jesus, Butch," he said, sitting upright and rubbing the side of his face.

Detective Pamela "Butch" Cassidy was seated behind the wheel, and had taken the opportunity provided by the tortuously slow-moving traffic of the North Circular Road to lightly assault her partner.

"I was telling a joke, and you weren't paying attention."

"Or maybe I was and maybe I didn't find the joke funny."

"What was it about, then?"

Bunny hesitated. "A dog?"

Butch made a gratingly loud buzzer noise to indicate the guess had not landed.

"Well, it should have been. All the best jokes are about dogs. Besides, since when do you tell jokes, anyway?"

"I'm always cracking jokes."

Bunny rubbed his ear and looked at her sceptically. "Is this still about that thing last week? I feel like I'm going to be repeating this until I'm blue in the face – I didn't say you were no craic."

"I asked you if I was good fun at a party, and you said I wasn't."

"That's not true. I said parties are not your natural environment."

"Same thing."

"No, it isn't, and besides, 'tis the week before Christmas and you volunteered to cover the evening shift, thereby missing party season," said Bunny. "Which sort of proves my point."

"No, it doesn't," Butch replied. "I may not like parties – that doesn't mean I'm not any fun at them. I don't like violence – it doesn't mean I didn't put that twenty-one-stone, coked-up idiot, who tried to bullrush me last month, through the window of a dry cleaners."

"I'm not sure Mahatma Gandhi would tell that story with quite as much relish as you do, o loather of violence. Admittedly, it is your strongest go-to move at parties. Telling the story, not the violence. Although ..."

"Anyway," continued Butch, "I volunteered for evenings to keep you company, ye big cloth-eared idiot, seeing as you got yourself put on the night shift through your own pig-headed stupidity."

Bunny folded his arms as Butch inched the car along the fifteen feet of hard-won road that had opened up before them. "That wasn't my fault."

"Sure, it was. You're the fool who offered to judge the station's baking competition. Did you not notice everyone else running for the hills?"

"I like a bit of cake."

"And you've apparently never heard the phrase 'you can't have your cake and eat it'."

"Which," interjected Bunny, "when you think about it, makes no sense."

"It makes more sense than you offering to pick a winner in the confectionary arms race. Desk Sergeant Geelan has won that thing three years in a row, and you know he and Vinny have that long-standing feud."

"So," said Bunny, "to be clear – I'm being criticised for being honest? Geelan's icing was stodgy, frankly, and Vinny's caramel gingerbread cake was nothing short of a revelation. Three layers of gingerbread paired with caramel buttercream. Santa's sleigh was made from marzipan and placed on top. It was a work of art. I stand by the decision one hundred percent."

"Good. I'm sure the stodgy-icing maker will, in time, come to respect your integrity. If he doesn't, you'll be working every crappy shift until the cows come home. Your partying days might be permanently behind you."

"Ah," said Bunny, waving his hand dismissively, "I don't care. Not in the mood for parties, anyway."

"And, unlike me, you *are* considered great craic at them. The life and soul when the mood takes you. I hear you also declined playing Santa for the kids this year?"

Bunny shrugged.

Butch said nothing for a few seconds as a brief gap in the traffic allowed them to make it through the traffic lights on the third time of asking. When she spoke next, her tone softened. "Look, do you want to talk about it?"

"Which bit? My refined taste in baked goods or how you can't deliver a gag to save your life?"

"Neither, smart arse. I'm not an idiot. There was all that stuff with your team losing the final."

"I don't care about the final."

"No, but you care about the kid. Paul. Have you spoken to him yet?"

Bunny cast his gaze out the window once more. "He's made his feelings very clear on that."

"You could always tell him the truth?"

Bunny turned and gave her a pointed look.

"OK, maybe not. So, there's all that, and it's a year since Gringo's death and, well, you never told me what happened with that nice Simone lady you were seeing, but that ended around then, too. He was your best friend and she, well – I don't know what she was seeing as you never really talk about her, but I remember how happy you were for a while there."

Bunny shrugged and pulled his thick sheepskin coat around him. "You need to get them to fix the heater in this rust bucket."

"Stop changing the subject. It'd do you good to talk about it."

"Would it, though? I mean, what's done is done and all that. Maybe some other time. I appreciate you asking, all the same."

"Well, the offer is always there. Speaking of which – you're coming to mine for Christmas dinner."

Bunny shook his head. "Thanks, but no, thanks. I'm not messing up your great big lesbian Christmas."

"Would you stop calling it that." Butch made no attempt to keep the annoyance from her voice.

"That's what it is, though. How many people are coming?"

"Not including you – five."

"So, five. And how many of them are lesbians?"

"As you well know – all five."

"There you go, then."

"By that logic, are other people having heterosexual Christmases because everyone around the table is heterosexual?"

"Well ..."

"Ha!" exclaimed Butch. "Exactly. Got ye."

"I concede the point."

"So, you're coming?"

"God, no. I've nothing to talk about. I mean, I only know the one Indigo Girls song, and I still can't find that k.d. lang album I bought."

"I know you're trying to wind me up now."

"OK. I'll confess, I amn't wild about the idea of having dinner with you, your ex and her new girlfriend. Sounds like the least relaxing thing imaginable."

"It's fine. We're all being very mature about it. It's totally fine."

"Course it is," said Bunny. "And the fact you've spent the last fortnight trying to assemble a selection of jokes to prove to person or persons unknown how fun you are is a complete coincidence, is it?"

Butch shot him a sideways look. "For a big lump, you can be annoyingly perceptive at times. That's all the more reason I need you there."

"Yeah. Me drowning your turkey in gravy and holding in a sprouty fart for four hours will really help ease the tension."

Bunny noticed Butch's eyes flick briefly in his direction.

"Ara, hang on, there's something you're not telling me here ..." He leaned forward in his seat to look across at her.

"Don't be close-minded."

Bunny walloped the dashboard. "It's fecking vegetarian, isn't it? You're trying to trick me into having a vegetarian Crimbo dinner, aren't you?"

"Like a few vegetables would kill you."

"And you weren't going to tell me beforehand. Oh, ye sneaky so-and-so. A fecking ambush!"

"Oh, for God's sake, it's a vegetarian meal not Pearl Harbour."

Bunny folded his arms. "Thanks, but no, thanks. Turkey is sacrosanct."

"Only last week it was you who said that it's just a crappy dried-up version of chicken and if it was that good, we'd be eating it all year round."

"I did, and what's more, sprouts are dreadful, parsnips are mostly overrated and I prefer big proper sausages to them dainty little pigs in blankets things. Even so, Christmas is Christmas, and on Christmas Day, you eat Christmas dinner."

Butch took the car out of gear and put the handbrake on so she could turn to face Bunny. "Really? And you're going to be having a full Christmas dinner with all the trimmings if you stay at home on your own, are you?"

"Possibly ..."

"Or will you be getting hammered on your own with a microwave meal and a trifle you'll be eating with your hands?"

"What do you—"

"I was round your place last week, remember? I saw the trifle boxes in the bin. Classic comfort eating."

"They were on special offer."

"What was it – buy two, get diabetes free? You need to pull your head out of your arse, Bunny, and start taking better care of yourself."

"I see your softly-softly approach is going well."

She nodded. "Yeah, I've given up on that. You need a wallop up the—" She was interrupted by someone in the car behind honking their horn loudly. "Why is it only criminals can spot an unmarked police car?"

The man honked again and threw in some hand gestures.

Butch glowered out the back window. "Do that again and see what happens," she scowled.

"Yeah," chimed Bunny. "She hates violence, but she will reluctantly jump out of the car and slap the head off you."

The two of them glared at each other – at least as much as it was possible to do so thanks to Bunny's lazy eye.

Much to everyone's relief, the radio on the dash sprang to life. "Car fifty-four."

Butch snatched up the handset. "Fifty-four receiving."

"We need you out in Blanchardstown," came the female voice over the airwaves.

"We're actually headed out that way, Margot, but it'll be a while in this traffic."

"You can whack on the siren. There's been a murder."

# CHAPTER TWO

One of the very first things they taught you down at the Garda Training College in Templemore was the importance of taking down an address correctly. Nothing killed the public's confidence in their police force faster than seeing it fail to locate the scene of the crime. Bunny knew this better than anyone, which is why he'd carefully noted down the details while Butch had whacked on the siren, pausing only briefly to enjoy the horrified expression of the man in the car behind who had been laying on the horn.

In this case the exact address hadn't been necessary. As soon as they turned the corner into Rosepark, twelve minutes later, their destination was clear. The large crowd gathered around number forty-eight, at the bottom of a normally sedate suburban cul-de-sac, was a big clue. Even without the horde of onlookers, the house would have been remarkably easy to locate from space, given the fact it was lit up like a Christmas tree. Although to be fair, thought Bunny, that didn't begin to do justice to the display.

Festive lights and decorations of all shapes and sizes covered the building from top to bottom, so much so that staring directly at it for any length of time was probably medically inadvisable. An eight-foot-tall snowman on one side of the roof waved merrily at four reindeers on the other. Although the quartet was doing a bad job, given that the sleigh they were meant to be pulling was hanging at a precarious angle and appeared to be in danger of careering off the edge of the roof entirely.

A full-sized Christmas tree was also up there, waving alarmingly – it being in possession of more arms than trees were traditionally known for having. In a concerted effort, all remaining areas had been covered with as many lights as possible. It was the type of display the word "festooned" had been invented for. A couple of weeks ago "festooned" had been word of the day on the calendar Bunny kept on his desk – this might be his first chance to use it correctly in conversation.

As Butch pulled up, a uniformed guard rushed to meet them. Bunny called to mind the old cliché that you know you're getting older when police officers start looking young, but the man who waited impatiently as he and Butch exited their vehicle would have looked young to anyone. A big strapping lad he might have been, but he still had acne and a facial expression that said he really wanted to ring his mammy.

"Are you the detectives?"

"What gave it away?" asked Bunny, glancing at the car that'd had blue lights flashing and a siren blaring just a few seconds ago. "Detectives McGarry and Cassidy, at your service."

"Thank God you're here. It's all gone totally mental!"

Bunny looked over the guard's shoulder and spotted his colleague, who appeared to be receiving both barrels from an irate woman in a dressing gown on the property's front lawn. The crowd of onlookers was a mixture of adults and kids. Judging by the prevalence of Santa hats and glasses of mulled wine, a Christmas party had been in full swing somewhere on the road when all this kicked off. Whatever *this* was.

Bunny turned back to the panicked young man standing in front of him and lowered his voice. "What's your name?"

"Boyle, sir."

"Right. Good man. I'm guessing you're still on probation?"

Boyle nodded. "So is Baz. I mean, Garda McCourtney."

Bunny had guessed as much. Two probationers shouldn't be out dealing with calls alone, but the week it was, he guessed somebody had called in sick or just fudged the rotas. "Right so. Do me a favour, Boyle – take a breath, alright?"

Boyle did so.

Bunny placed a kind hand on the man's arm. "These people are looking to you, and the first step to looking like you're in control of a situation is looking like you're in control of yourself. OK?"

Boyle nodded.

"Good man. Now, there's been a death?"

"Not exactly," said Boyle.

"Not exactly?" repeated Butch, from the far side of the car.

"The homeowner rang it in as—" Before Boyle could get any further, the woman in the dressing gown and slippers rushed up to their group. "Are you the detectives?" she demanded of Bunny and Butch. She was in her forties and had a face caked in make-up. Her left calf was an entirely different colour to her right, evidence of a self-administered spray tan having been interrupted.

Butch stepped forward. "We are, yes, ma'am. Our colleague is just bringing us up to speed on the situation."

"Up to speed?" sneered the woman. "I'll bring you up to speed." She turned and waved an accusing finger at the assembled throng. "One of these bastards killed Santa!"

Bunny and Butch stood in the front garden with their backs to the crowd and peered down at "the body".

"What do you reckon?" Bunny asked in a hushed voice.

"Clearly, he's come off the roof, fallen two storeys and had his head caved in, probably by the fall."

Bunny nodded. "Although it also looks like someone had a go at him after. There are definite signs of some kicks having been thrown in."

"Nasty," agreed Butch. "There's some real rage on display here. Who is that angry at Father Christmas?"

"I dunno, but I'd imagine there's a naughty list we need to get hold of."

"Yeah. That'd blow this case wide open."

Bunny jumped as the animatronic Santa Claus twitched slightly and emitted a drawn-out "Ho" that sounded like a death rattle. "Shit the bed!"

"Easy there, fella," said Butch. "The first step to looking like you're in control of a situation is looking like you're in control of yourself."

"Ha, ha. Very funny." Bunny raised his gaze to the roof. "Check this place out, though. The whole thing is fest—"

"What's taking so long?" shouted the woman in the dressing gown, as she was held back from the crime scene by the bright future of Irish policing.

Butch sighed. "I think I'm starting to lose my Christmas spirit."

"I've got some in a hip flask, if you'd like?"

She did a superb job of hiding her smirk as she whirled round to address the crowd. "OK, first things first – who logged the call with 999?"

"That was me," said the woman in the dressing gown. "Margaret O'Malley. The homeowner."

"And can I confirm you told the operator that there had been a murder?"

"Yes," she said, folding her arms. "I wanted to get your attention."

"Oh, you did. It is at this point I should caution you that under the 1976 Criminal Law Act, knowingly making a false report carries a fine of up to five hundred pounds and twelve months in prison."

Bunny noticed how this revelation caused several faces in the crowd to light up with a warm glow.

"What?" asked Mrs O'Malley, her face drawn back in a mask of outrage. "I'm the victim here! That is an outdoor luminous animatronic Father Christmas with motion activation. Do you have any idea how much one of those costs? I had to send away to Canada for it."

"Had to?" said Butch.

"Excuse me?"

"I see," said Butch, in a louder voice. "And I take it that you believe it didn't just fall off your roof?"

"It certainly did not. It was firmly secured up there. It was brutally pulled down in an act of senseless terrorism."

Butch decided to let the terrorism thing go. "And were there any witnesses to this?"

"No, I was in the middle of" – she glanced down in the direction of her unfinished spray tan – "I was indisposed when I heard it come crashing down."

"Maybe the snowman pushed him?" shouted a voice from the back of the crowd, which was subsequently accompanied by an outbreak of widespread sniggering.

Mrs O'Malley's head snapped around. "That's not funny. And, Martin McNally, don't for one second think I don't know that was you."

"Can't be," responded the voice. "I'm not even here."

"OK," said Butch, "let's all just calm down."

"Yeah," agreed Bunny, as he stepped forward to address the crowd with his hands spread out in a placatory manner. "Now, has anyone seen any grinches in the area?"

Butch stood in front of him to prevent the very real possibility of Margaret O'Malley adding assaulting an officer to her potential rap sheet.

"Is this some kind of joke to you?" snapped Mrs O'Malley.

"No, madam," responded Bunny, "but neither is wasting police time. I'm not sure what you want us to do here. There were no witnesses, and besides, why would anyone want to attack your Christmas decorations?"

"Because ..." offered a short man at the front of the crowd. He was dressed in black from head to toe, including a hat, gloves and one of those snood things that had somehow come back into fashion. He looked like the Milk Tray Man, if the Milk Tray Man had also taste-tested the product extensively before attempting any deliveries. "Look at it?" he continued. "The whole place is festooned ..." *Damn it!* "... in gaudy lights. There's more every year. It's tacky. And she leaves it on all night, bright as anything, flashing on and off. It's like living next to the sun." He pointed over his shoulder at a house across the road. "I've had to get a blackout blind installed. Then this year, Santa is ho, ho, ho-ing throughout the night, every time the fecking wind blows."

Margaret O'Malley jabbed a finger at the man with such ferocity that her dressing gown slipped open enough to treat Butch and Bunny to an unwanted flash of boob before she managed to snatch it closed again. "See! I knew it was him. Brian Grayson. Arrest him, officers. Arrest him right now!"

"OK, OK," said Butch. "Let's all just take a deep breath." She made her way towards the man named as Brian Grayson. "Did you have anything to do with this, sir?"

Brian Grayson folded his arms and gave a self-satisfied grin. "I wish to plead the fifth."

Butch sighed. "To be clear, you wish to plead your rights under the fifth amendment of the US Constitution?"

Grayson looked unsure. "Yeah?"

"No problem. Can you prove both US citizenship and that this cul-de-sac has been designated US soil under international law, akin to an embassy? Otherwise, this will not go the way you hoped. I mean, I'm sure you've not just mindlessly repeated something you heard on telly, and that all the above is somehow true?"

He attempted to rally. "She's the one you should be talking to. The council should have banned all this, only her bloody nephew works there. Nepotism."

"That's not what that word means either—"

Mrs O'Malley stepped forward and fixed Brian Grayson with a look of pure hatred. "Look at him. What a sad little man. Trying to ruin Christmas for everyone else."

"Ah, blow it out your arse, Margaret. You're just obsessed with showing off. That's why Derek left you."

His statement was met with a collective intake of breath from the crowd and Bunny noted the wounded look in Mrs O'Malley's eyes.

"What?" he continued. "I'm only saying what you've all been saying."

"Jesus, Brian," said a woman at the front, a tone of horrified reproach in her voice. "Go easy."

"You're one to talk," Mrs O'Malley snarled back at Brian Grayson. "At least I don't have a son with a criminal record for interfering with livestock."

"He was caught cow-tipping!" shouted Grayson. "That's not even a crime."

"It actually is," said Bunny. "But getting back to—"

"There aren't even any farms nearby," smirked Mrs O'Malley. "The little pervert had to catch two buses to go and interfere with cattle."

Brian Grayson gawped at Butch. "Are you going to allow her to say that? He was just pushing cows over. Her suggesting that there was a sexual element is libellous. I want to sue!"

"Firstly," said Bunny, "libel is only when it's written down. That was, at best, slander. Secondly, that's a civil matter. Now, to get back to what we're here for..." He nodded towards the animatronic Santa. "Did you do this?"

"Course he did," said Mrs O'Malley. "He already confessed. They're a family of psychopaths and he killed Santa!"

"Give over," groaned Brian Grayson. "You're a grown woman, Margaret. I hate to be the one to break it to you ..."

Like a car slipping into a skid on ice, Bunny could see the crash coming but could do nothing to prevent it.

Brian Grayson leaned forward and spat the words out. "Santa. Doesn't. Exist!"

Bunny had never seen somebody lose a crowd so fast. The torrent of hissed invectives aimed in his direction as parents belatedly slapped their hands over their children's ears made even Brian Grayson stand back and pause.

Bunny scanned the row of sad little faces looking up at their parents with eyes that spoke of a world crumbling around them. "Whoa!" he called out. "Hang on a second. Messing with somebody's decorations is one thing, but slandering the big man is not something we, the Garda Síochána, will stand for. Rest assured, boys and girls, I happen to know Santa Claus personally, and I can assure you he exists. In fact, I helped him get out of a speeding ticket he received on the M50 last year, because, as we all know, he's a very busy man on Christmas Day, as he has to get around to the houses of all the good boys and girls."

He made his way over to Brian Grayson. "The only reason Mr Grayson here said what he said is because he is on Santa's naughty list as he's been a bad boy. Is anyone else here on that list?" He searched the achingly sincere young faces who were vigorously shaking their heads in answer to his question.

"I'd hope not." Then he looked up. "I should check, though. Mums and dads, I'm ringing Santa this evening because I want to see if he can find Cork a full back. Should I tell him all the kids here in Rosepark have been good?"

His words drew a chorus of relieved assent.

"Alright, then." Bunny put his hand on Brian Grayson's shoulder. "Now, I have to arrest this man for the crime of doubting Santa."

"What?" Brian Grayson's eyes were wide in shock.

Bunny leaned down to whisper in his ear. "Play along and I'll let you out of the car at the top of the road. Either that, or you can stay here and get lynched. Your choice."

He gave a hesitant nod.

"Right, then." Bunny drew his handcuffs out of his pocket. "In which case—"

"Detective McGarry."

Bunny turned to find Probationary Garda Boyle standing behind him. "Not now, Boyle," he warned.

"What are you doing about my Santa Claus?" piped up Margaret O'Malley.

"Enquiries are ongoing," Bunny said with a wave of his hand.

"Mrs O'Malley." Butch moved in front of the woman. "Could I have a quiet word, please?"

"Sorry," insisted Probationary Garda Boyle. "There's an urgent call for you over the radio, Detective McGarry."

"Oh, right," said Bunny loudly. "It might be the Easter Bunny.

Somebody stole one of his big golden eggs and I'm helping him get it back."

A series of titters passed through the crowd.

"Ehm, no, sorry," said Boyle. "The message is about someone called Declan Fadden."

"Christ," muttered Bunny, catching Butch's eye. He lowered his voice. "Speaking of naughty – what has my assistant manager done now?"

"Nothing," Boyle offered. "I mean, the message said to tell you that he's been assaulted and he's in Connolly Hospital."

# CHAPTER THREE

Bunny burst through the doors of the main reception at Connolly Hospital as if the outside world were on fire. The woman behind the reception desk gave him an alarmed look and glanced around for the whereabouts of the security guard.

"Where is Deccie Fadden?"

"I'm sorry, sir, visiting hours are—" She broke off when she saw the Garda ID Bunny produced.

"What was the name again?"

"Declan Fadden."

She consulted her computer and, after a few seconds, came back with, "He's just been moved to a private room on Laurel Ward up on the second floor. The lifts are—"

Before she could offer directions, Bunny was off, taking the stairs two at a time, dodging a couple of nurses and a doctor in his path.

He burst onto the second floor, and had started to run down the corridor when a small man dropped his mop and threw out both hands. "Whoa, whoa, whoa! Stall the ball. No running. Wet floors. Wet floors. I've already had somebody go on their arse today."

Bunny slowed his pace. "You should get one of those yellow signs."

"What do you think the other dipshit fell over?"

Bunny continued on his way, power walking across the wet floor to a backdrop of muttering. He made it to the sign for Laurel Ward and shoved against the door before belatedly realising it required an access code. Bunny lay his finger on the buzzer and watched through the small square window as a matronly woman, who was in fact a matron, glowered at him on her approach. As she buzzed the door open, Bunny produced his ID again to head off the impending stern talking-to before it could get up a head of steam.

"Deccie Fadden."

"He's in room six, down on the left there."

"How is he?"

"OK, considering. Got a very nasty wound on the back of the head, probably concussion and some bruising around the face. Plus, a broken wrist. Somebody worked the poor fella over pretty good. I hope you catch them."

"What exactly happened?"

She drew her head back. "Shouldn't you know that? I mean ..."

"I just got a message he was here."

"Oh, right. Well, from what one of the girls heard from the ambulance crew that brought him in, he got mugged. Couple of lads gave him an awful doing over."

"A couple?" Bunny's hands tightened into fists until his knuckles turned white.

"Yes. Disgusting behaviour," said the matron, shaking her head. "I hope you find them and throw the book at them."

"It won't be a book." Bunny's tone was flat. "Can I see him?"

"Of course."

She showed him down the hall and, after the briefest of knocks, opened the door. "Here we are."

Bunny stepped inside and stopped. "Oh no, I ..."

He'd been expecting someone else – namely, a thirteen-year-old boy – and so, to start with, didn't recognise the man in the bed. His confusion was also partly the result of how small the man now appeared. Never a big man to begin with, Deccie Fadden Senior, grandfather of Deccie Fadden, looked so different without his normal varifocal glasses that Bunny wouldn't have known it was him at all without the substantial clue of the name. He and his wife had been Deccie's guardians for as long as Bunny had known Deccie Junior, and the boy lived with them. The poor man's face was already the site of a nasty hodgepodge of black and purple bruising under the large bandage on his head.

Grandad Fadden squinted. "Who is that? I can't see a thing without my glasses."

"'Tis me, Declan. Bunny McGarry." He moved towards the bed.

"Ah, right," said Grandad Fadden. "We were trying to reach you."

"Yeah, I'm afraid I left my damn phone on my desk. Are you … are you in much pain?"

"Just a few bumps and bruises," he replied, the bravado of the words not carrying through to his voice. "I'll be fine."

"He will be," agreed the matron from the doorway. "As long as he gets his rest. So, if we could keep this short …"

Bunny nodded as he sat down in the chair beside the bed.

"Of course," said Grandad Fadden. "Thanks very much, Nurse." As the door closed, he turned back to Bunny. "They're very good here. Really very good."

Up close, Grandad Fadden's injuries were no easier to look at. The left side of his face was a kaleidoscope of brutal colour, and his right hand was in a plaster cast, but the worst thing was the look in his eyes. Bunny had seen it before, but it didn't get any easier; that expression of residual fear left after an ordinary, decent person has come into contact with the dark violence that festers just under the skin of the world. Once they've been touched by it, they're never quite the same again.

"So, Declan," said Bunny, in a soft voice. "What happened?"

"It was stupid. I blame myself."

"You can cut that out for a start. The nurse said that somebody attacked you?"

"Yeah. I was … I mean we – Deccie and I – were in town, doing some Christmas shopping and collecting stuff."

"Right. Is he—"

"He's fine," said Grandad Fadden quickly. "Thank God. I mean, he was upset and, y'know, wired to the moon. His granny has taken him home. Him swearing all kinds of bloody vengeance. You know how he gets. Bridie will talk him down, though. No one better."

"I'm sure she will."

"He was trying to ring you ..."

Bunny's guts twisted. "Feck it. Sorry. Bloody phone. Today of all days."

"Maybe you could—"

"Oh, don't worry, I'll be heading over to see him straight after I leave here." Bunny didn't want to push things too far, but for Bunny to figure out how he could help, he needed to know what he was dealing with. "So, you were in town shopping?"

"Yeah. We'd just come out of McGrattan's jewellers on Capel Street. My cousin's niece works there, and she got me a good deal. D'ye know it?"

Bunny nodded. He didn't, but it seemed like the best way to move things along.

"So, this girl ... I mean ... I dunno, early twenties. Pretty, I suppose. Had a foreign accent. Hard to place. European but ... Anyway, she rushes up to me and she's all, 'Please help – my friend has collapsed.' And ... I mean, I didn't think. Like, someone asks, and you try to help, don't you?"

"Of course."

"So, she goes round the corner and there's some scaffolding on this building, a skip outside. She nips in this door and we follow her. Only then did I realise that she's led us into an empty shop. Wasn't until the door closed behind us that you think, hang on a sec." Grandad Fadden paused and swallowed. "God! It seems so stupid now. I'm such a fool."

"Here now, stop that," consoled Bunny. "You were trying to help. Nothing wrong with that."

"This woman, she stands back and there's this fella blocking the door, and there's another one. I mean, I didn't even see him. First thing I know his arms are around me. My glasses got knocked off, so it was all a bit fuzzy after that. Blind as a bat without them, so I am. I was useless when that guard was in earlier to take my statement. Everything was a blur."

"Don't worry about that," said Bunny. "You'd be surprised how many victims with perfect eyesight can't describe their attackers. It's the shock."

"Right, well... Deccie roared, 'Leave my grandad alone', and boots the big fella holding me. Gets him right in the shins. Then the other guy grabs Deccie and throws him into the corner. Lucky he didn't get hurt. Rough, like. Jesus ..." Grandad Fadden's eyes filled with tears.

"But he's OK?" asked Bunny. More to reassure the old fella than anything.

"He is, thank God. Anyway, I hear this fella tell Deccie, 'If you move an inch, my buddy is going to really hurt your granddad.'"

"Right."

"And the fella – the one holding me – he said, 'Go easy, cuz.'"

"He said 'cuz'?" asked Bunny. "As in 'cousin'? You're sure?"

The older man's eyes narrowed for a few moments, then he nodded. "He did, yeah. I'm sure of that."

"Great. Well remembered. That'll be a big help. What else did he say?"

"He ... he snapped at the girl. He said, 'You were supposed to get someone on their own.' She said she didn't know he was with me. Deccie had been standing outside because ..."

"If he was with you in the shop," supplied Bunny, "he'd be asking a hundred questions."

Grandad Fadden gave a nod. "Ailish is doing me a favour getting me a discount, and she didn't want her boss to know."

"Right. So, this fella was annoyed you weren't alone?"

"Yeah."

"And did these lads sound foreign too?"

"Oh God, no. Their accents were Limerick. I'd bet my life on it."

Two lads from Limerick, thought Bunny. That'll narrow the pool down a lot.

"So anyway," continued Grandad Fadden, "he tells me to give him everything I have. I empty my pockets. Give him my wallet. He takes it all and asks for my PIN. Says if it's wrong, he's going to hurt Deccie. That fella ..."

More tears welled up in his eyes at the memory. "He wasn't much more than a blur to me, and I'd guess he wasn't that much bigger than myself, but he had a way about him. Something in how he spoke. Y'know, those weren't empty words. I didn't doubt him for a second."

"You gave him your PIN?"

"I did."

"Then you did the right thing. There's no point holding out. 'Tis only money." Bunny looked at Grandad Fadden's face and then down at the cast on his hand. "So, if you gave them everything ..."

Grandad Fadden turned his head away, out of the window where the last light of a crappy day had long since succumbed to darkness.

Bunny resisted the urge to fill the silence. Instead, he left space for the old man to come to it in his own time.

Finally, Grandad Fadden whispered it. "The ring. Bridie's ring."

"That was why you were at the jewellers?"

The older man nodded. "You have to understand – the engagement ring I gave Bridie, it was my grandmother's, and her mother's before her. My great-grandad had brought it home. He'd been a sailor and got it God knows where. Finest ring you'd see round here, I tell you. It's very distinctive – a diamond surrounded by green emeralds. We were always joking that the Fadden family had our very own family jewels.

"Anyway, Bridie was always nervous wearing it. Forty-eight years ago this coming February, we'd just got married and moved into our tiny first place up in the Liberties. That's what it was like in them days – you got married and then got your first home together. Different times now. Anyway, she was doing the washing-up and didn't the ring slip off her finger – down the drain. She was mortified. Me and – I'm not kidding – a dozen of the lads from the factory ended up ripping the pipes apart for the entire building. Took us most of the night but we found it." He gave a sad little laugh. "Hell of a way to meet your new neighbours. Cutting the water off. Anyway, after that, she couldn't be convinced to wear it again. So, for the next forty-eight years it stayed in its box."

"I'd always had it in my head to get it resized but, y'know, she's had a rough year with her health stuff and the rheumatism on top of everything else. All the family – she's got fourteen godchildren, would you believe? – they're all chipping in to get her, well, us, a dishwasher for Christmas. So, we won't be doing any more washing-up. God love her, she does miss playing the piano, so I thought the ring would be something nice for her to see when she looks down at her fingers – y'know, to counteract the sadness. I mean, that was the idea ..."

"So, these fellas took the ring?"

Grandad Fadden nodded. "I had it clenched in my fist, y'see. I grabbed it when I realised something was wrong. But this fella, he goes, 'Where is what you got from the jewellers?' I tried lying."

"But he didn't believe you?"

Grandad Fadden gave an almost imperceptible shake of the head and he looked away. "I even tried explaining how it was Bridie's ring. I wouldn't let it go. The smaller fella threw a couple of digs into me. Didn't see them coming. Then I – well, it's all a blur. I hit the floor." He raised a hand self-consciously to the back of his head. "I think that's when ... It's hard to recall exactly what happened. God, though" – tears were rolling down his bruised cheeks now – "the pain wasn't the worst part. Hearing Deccie screaming for them to leave me alone – that'll stay with me." His voice lowered to a near whisper. "If a man can't protect his family, what kind of man is he?"

Bunny patted his good arm awkwardly. "Stop that now. There was two of them – three of them, really."

"I tried to hang on to the ring, but" – Grandad Fadden raised his right hand encased in the cast – "one of them, I think the smaller fella again, stamped on it."

"Jesus," muttered Bunny, feeling ashamed for reasons he couldn't explain. As if all of humanity had to bear some responsibility for containing such monsters.

Grandad Fadden wiped his free hand over his face to brush away the tears, then he grabbed Bunny's arm. "You've got to get it back." His rheumy eyes were filled with intensity. "Please, Bunny. The ring."

"I'll look into it. You said the Gardaí have already been in to interview you?"

"Yeah. This fella but I don't want him. I want you. You can sort this. You can sort anything."

"I'll do my best, Declan, but—"

"Promise me. Bridie's ring. That's all I care about. They can keep everything else. But the ring, Bunny. The ring. Bridie will ... Get it back. Promise me."

Bunny felt like a rabbit in the headlights, fixed in Grandad Fadden's pleading stare. It was another of those very first things you learned in training – don't make promises to victims. Especially when it isn't your case. "I'll get it back. You have my word."

As he watched the relief wash over the older man he felt the embarrassment rise within him.

"Thank God." Grandad Fadden sank back into his pillows, as if the exhaustion of the day was now overwhelming him. He released his grip on Bunny's arm and patted it instead. "You're a great man, Bunny. A great man."

"I'll get right on it. Is there anything else you can tell me?"

"Actually, there was one thing. The girl. When I was lying on the ground and, well, I was only barely conscious after, y'know. As they were leaving, though, I felt someone leaning down over me. I thought she was trying to check if I'd anything else on me, but she whispered in my ear. I could have misheard, but she said, 'I'm sorry. Please help me.'"

"Really?"

Grandad Fadden winced from a failed attempt at a shrug. "I don't know. Maybe I heard her wrong. Like I said, I wasn't at my best."

"And about these two fellas—"

The door to the hospital room flung open and in stormed Bridie

Fadden, the matron trailing in her wake. Slightly taller than her husband, in Bunny's experience Bridie was a charming, if quite stern and reserved woman. You met her type a lot in Dublin. Working class with little to their names, but what they did have would be cleaned to the point of breaking, and everything would be in exactly the right place.

Today was not her typical day. She searched the room with her eyes, an anguished expression on her face, before visibly sagging. "Oh Lord. Has Deccie been here?"

"I thought he was with you?" asked her husband.

"He was. We went home." She looked pointedly at Bunny. "He tried to ring Bunny and then he ran off. I found his bedroom window open."

"Oh God, no," moaned Grandad Fadden.

Bridie stepped forward and looked across the bed at Bunny. "You need to find him."

Bunny nodded. "I'll get right on it."

"Promise me you'll get him back?"

He found himself locked in Bridie Fadden's penetrating sights. In for a penny.

"You have my word."

# CHAPTER FOUR

Bunny pressed the doorbell and shifted uncomfortably under the piercing gaze of a single glowing red eye. His stare – as in the infamous Bunny McGarry stare – was regarded by some as the most intimidating non-contact experience available to the Dublin criminal community. Many had tried to copy it; few had come close. In truth, if he wanted to be poetic about it, he could claim it was a "gift from God". In reality, it meant he'd been born with a lazy eye and the rest happened by accident early in his law enforcement career while stalling as he tried to think of something to say.

The beam of the one-eyed stare in which he was currently trapped was something different, though. Enveloped in a supposedly festive and cheerful face of a decoration, the eyeball had an ominous red glow to it that made you feel simultaneously uneasy and foolish for feeling so. Bunny was relieved when the door opened and the face was replaced by the considerably more aesthetically pleasing visage of Lynn Nellis.

Bunny liked her. From what he could gather, some mothers of the boys on the St Jude's Under-12s hurling team didn't, but he had a feeling that was mostly jealousy. He had been required to admonish one of the lads a couple of weeks ago for referring to Lynn Nellis as a "stone-cold fox". Bunny had given him a stern talking-to about being respectful. He couldn't fault the lad on the facts, though – she was.

"Bunny," she said, giving him a wary look.

"Howerya, Lynn. Merry Christmas. Can I ask – how come your reindeer decoration thing only has the one eye?"

"Who is it?" came a male voice from the front room. Bunny recognised it as belonging to Lynn's husband, Paddy Nellis.

"It's the Gardaí," Lynn called back. "They want to know why your stupid reindeer only has one eye."

"He's winking!" came the shouted response. The tone of annoyance made it clear that this was not the first time the subject had been discussed.

Lynn rolled her eyes. "Yeah." She pointed at the decoration. "He's a total winker. It really would help if the bulb lighting up Rudolph's nose didn't also light up his eye. I'm having nightmares about the thing. This is what you get from buying Christmas decorations off" – Bunny saw the very moment Lynn remembered who she was speaking to and, as a matter of principle, changed what she'd been about to say to the more non-specific – "some bloke down the pub."

"Right," said Bunny.

"Anyway, you're not here to talk about my husband's eye for a bargain – no pun intended." She raised her voice again. "Although, that is a good idea. I think I will get him an eyepatch."

"Over my dead body," came Paddy's voice.

"Oh, great," Lynn snapped back. "Santa got my letter, then." She gave Bunny a smile. "Sorry. I'm assuming you've not come round to hear us having the same argument we've been having every hour on the hour for a week either. What can I do for you?"

"I was actually looking for Phil."

Lynn's smile fell away. "Oh God, what's he done now?"

"Nothing. I—"

"What do they want?" shouted Paddy. "Have they got a search warrant? This is pure harassment. I'm a legitimate businessman."

While Bunny liked Lynn, his relationship with her husband was rather more awkward. Paddy Nellis was widely regarded by both the criminal fraternity and law enforcement as the finest thief in Dublin. High-end houses mostly, although Bunny wouldn't be surprised if his talents extended into other areas. True, he seemed to have a strict no-violence policy, and he appeared to steal exclusively from the rich – although Bunny noted the Robin Hood principles didn't go as far as distributing his spoils among the poor.

Everyone knew what he was but, aside from one slip-up a few years ago, he'd never been caught. Officially, he did indeed operate a legitimate business as a security consultant. It made sense in a rather perverse way; if you were trying to make a high-end property as secure as possible, having the man most likely to burgle it successfully come in and tell you how he'd do it was invaluable. Plus, Bunny guessed that there was probably an unspoken rule for all concerned that stated Paddy wouldn't subsequently rob a property he'd previously consulted on. There was a not inconsiderable value in that.

"Tell them I'm calling my lawyer," continued Paddy.

"Would you calm down," shouted Lynn. "It's only Bunny."

"Oh, right." Paddy Nellis's tone changed to a more amiable one. "What does he want?"

"He wants to talk to Phil."

"What's he done now?"

"He hasn't done anything, Paddy," shouted Bunny. "I just want a chat."

"He's very popular today," said Lynn. "You're his second visitor. Beating the previous record by a considerable number."

"Who was the first?"

"The short tubby little fella who never shuts up."

"Deccie."

"That's him. Although, he was surprisingly quiet today. Didn't even mention the reindeer."

"Yeah," said Bunny. "I was afraid of that. So, where's Phil?"

"He's out in his lab."

"Lab?" repeated Bunny.

Lynn pulled a face. "Don't." She nodded in the direction of the front room. "My darling husband decided to let Phil have the shed to do his experiments in."

"Experiments?"

"The lad is curious," shouted Paddy.

"That's certainly one way of putting it," muttered Lynn with a shrug. "He's ... he's Phil. At least there's less chance of him burning my house down this way. Tried to invent his own line of aftershave a couple of months ago. People from across the street came over to complain." She turned at a sound from the kitchen and raised her voice again. "Speak of the devil. You'd better not be ruining your appetite for dinner, and keep your grubby paws off them mince pies. They're for guests."

"There's not even mince in them," the voice of Phil Nellis shot back from the kitchen. "They're a total con."

"I am not having that conversation again." Lynn turned her attention back to Bunny. "There's an hour of my life I'm not getting back. Avoid that one if you can." She shook her head. "Eats like a plague of locusts and not a pick on him. Unbelievable." She raised her voice once more. "Bunny is here to see you."

Phil Nellis's pre-pubescent head, accompanied by an improbably large sandwich, appeared around the kitchen door. "What have I done now?"

As Phil tucked into his doorstop-sized sandwich, Bunny sat down on a creaky stool and looked round the shed. The place had a complex smell, featuring hints of sulphur, varnish, oil and something that smelled a lot like cooked fish. A workbench was surrounded by shelves mounted on every bit of available wall, all loaded to the max with mostly electrical items that had seen better days, and possibly the business end of a sledgehammer.

"Where did you get all of this stuff, Phil?"

"Skips, mostly. You'd be amazed what people throw out."

"Does any of it work?"

"Not yet, but it will do. I'll fix it all, eventually."

"Fair play to you. Have you ever watched *The Generation Game*?"

"The what now?"

"'Tis a TV show. They have this thing at the end where there's a conveyor belt of prizes and you've to remember them all." Bunny pointed round the room. "Toaster. Fridge. Portable TV. Four different kettles. Food mixer. Gerbil." He paused. "Phil, why've you got a gerbil? Please don't tell me you're trying to fix it."

"What? No. That's Wilbur. She's a vital part of my experiments."

"She?"

"Yeah. I'd named her before we figured out how you could tell her gender. Gerbils are very hairy down there."

"Right," said Bunny. He didn't want to ask his next question, but felt compelled to do so. "When you say 'experiments' ..."

"I'm trying to see if me and her can develop a psychic link." He reached down beside his workbench and pulled out a large bit of cardboard upon which was stuck every card from a deck of fifty-two. "I think of a card, and if she guesses right, she gets a treat."

"Guesses?"

"I lay the board down and she runs over to a card. She gets it right one time in ten."

"Really? That's very impressive."

"Ah, not so much. She's figured out if she stands just right, she can touch six cards simultaneously. She's just playing the odds."

"Right. 'Tis still an impressive understanding of probability for an animal. Anyway ..." Despite himself, Bunny realised he was getting sucked into one of the infamous Phil Nellis black holes where you came out the other side three hours later more confused and frustrated than when you went in. "We need to have a chat."

Phil held up a hand. "If this is about Paulie, I'm not at liberty to say nothing about nothing."

"It's not." Bunny hesitated. "Seeing as you mentioned it, though. How is he?"

"Like I said, I'm not at liberty to say. He's still furious after you messed up his adoption, and he made me swear to say nothing about him to you. He wants nothing at all to do with you."

Bunny nodded. "Fair enough."

"You need to sort that out."

"I can't. He won't talk to me. How is he liking the new foster place up in Phibsborough?"

"I am not at liberty to discuss that."

"Phil?"

Phil Nellis fixed his gaze on the floor for a few seconds and then looked back up again. "It is what it is. Auntie Lynn asked him round for Christmas."

"That's nice."

"He said no."

"Oh. Why?"

"You'd have to ask him. Only he won't talk to you."

"Right. Well, thanks for the non-update. I came here to talk about Deccie. He came to see you earlier."

Phil's demeanour turned decidedly shifty. "He might have done."

"He did," said Bunny firmly. "That wasn't a question. His grandad got robbed, and he's very upset."

"He was alright, yeah."

"What did he ask you?"

Phil hesitated. "I'd rather not say."

"And I'd rather be on a tropical island skulling drinks with little umbrellas in them, but we're both here and I'm asking you a question, Phil."

Phil abandoned his half-eaten sandwich, got to his feet and began to shift things around on the shelf behind him.

"Phil?"

He examined a toaster intently.

"Phillip Nellis! You answer me right this minute or so help me, I'm going to get annoyed."

Phil mumbled something Bunny couldn't make out.

"What was that?"

Phil turned around. "I said snitches get stitches."

"Snitches get stitches?" repeated Bunny. "Bloody American TV programmes. Yeah, well, gobshites get ..." He paused and scanned the room. "Damn it, nothing rhymes with gobshites." Exasperated, he got to his feet. "Phil, I'm in a hurry here. I'm trying to help get back what was stolen off Deccie's grandad, but before that, I need to make sure Deccie isn't going to do anything silly. Now, what did the two of you talk about?"

"Lots of things."

"Phil!"

Phil looked positively pained. "If it gets out that I talked to the Gardaí ..."

"You're not talking to the Gardaí; you're talking to me. Anyone has a problem with that, send them my way." Bunny spun Phil around and placed a hand on each of his shoulders. "Deccie might be about to do something daft. I need to know what that might be, and I need to know now."

"Alright. He came here, said he needed to find who robbed his grandad. I told him my family aren't criminals, we got in an argument and then he left."

From experience, Bunny knew that Phil was very sensitive about any suggestion that Paddy was a member of the criminal fraternity.

"Did Deccie say where he was going?"

"Stalactites."

"What?"

"Stalactites rhymes with gobshites. Stalagmites too."

"Phil!"

"He said – and you didn't hear this from me – he said that if I wouldn't help, he was going to go ask Flipper."

"Flipper? As in Andy Finn?"

"I cannot confirm or deny that at this time."

"Phil!" Bunny snapped. He pointed at his own head. "Take a good look at my face and have a guess at how much patience I have left."

Phil met Bunny's eyes and nodded. "Yeah, Flipper. Deccie said he's the only other criminal he knows after my uncle." The young lad's face fell. "Not that Paddy is a criminal. He's not. He's a security consultant."

Bunny waved away Phil's protestation. "What the hell makes him think Flipper would know anything?"

"He's big into all the crime stuff, allegedly."

"There's nothing alleged about it," said Bunny. "He gets himself arrested that often we've given him a loyalty card. He gets done for shoplifting one more time, he'll be getting a lovely stay in a nice B & B with bars on the windows."

"Flipper is always talking about crime and all that, though."

"I know. That's one of the many ways we keep arresting him." Bunny knew for a fact that Andy Finn was only out walking around because he was a useful source of information on other criminals. The kind who committed crimes successfully. The other problem with that, though, was that it was only a matter of time before he traded the wrong bit of information. Inevitably, the Gardaí might end up being the least of his problems. "Deccie went to see him? You're sure?"

Phil nodded.

"Alright. Thanks, Phil. You did the right thing."

"You didn't hear nothing from me. No way, never. I didn't say nothing to nobody."

"There's enough double negatives there that I'm going to spend most of the evening figuring out what you just said. Anyway, I should …"

Bunny turned to leave but stopped when something on the top shelf near the door caught his eye.

"Christ on a trike." He felt himself do a double take. "Erm, Phil?"

"Yes, Bunny?"

"What's that up there on the top shelf?"

"The purple thing?"

"That's right. The purple thing."

"I'm not really sure. It shakes, and bits of it spin round."

"I bet they do. How did you get it?"

"Well, you know how poor old Mrs Wilkins over the road died there a few months ago?"

Bunny nodded.

"Well, Auntie Lynn told me to go over and help her son clean out the house as they had to put it up for sale. We took loads of stuff to the charity shop and all that. I found that thing under her bed while we were sorting it all out."

"And you took it?"

"No," said Phil, sincerely offended. "I asked Keith what it was. He got a bit weird – pale-looking, like – and he said he didn't know. So I asked him if I could have it."

"And he said yes?"

"Now that you mention it, he just nodded and sort of ran out of the room."

"I bet he did." Bunny nodded towards the workbench. "Hand me that shopping bag there."

Phil did as he was told. Bunny turned the bag inside out, grabbed the object without touching it and bagged it.

"Here!" said Phil, outraged. "That's mine."

"Not any more. This is one of those times in life you have to just accept something and not ask any questions."

"But you said at practice only a couple of weeks ago that there was no such thing as a stupid question."

"There isn't – at practice. Here – there is. I'm taking this and we will never speak of it again."

"At least tell me what it is?"

Bunny put his hand on the door. "I'll tell you when you're older."

"How much older?"

"As soon as you hit your forties."

"That'll be 2028," said Phil. "I'm going to hold you to that."

"I'm sure you will," said Bunny. "Fingers crossed I'll be dead by then."

# CHAPTER FIVE

Over the course of her policing career to date, in common with all members of the Garda Síochána, Butch had pulled over far more vehicles than she could possibly count. Not only that, but the variety was impressive: cars, vans, caravans, trucks, buses, mobile homes, juggernauts, motorbikes and tandem bicycles.

Once, she'd pulled over an actual clown car; or, at least, a car belonging to a circus. For reasons never fully explained, two of the clowns had still been in full make-up. They'd also all been drunk, which explained how a trailer housing a shooting gallery had ended up stuck in the middle of the N4. A bearded lady had pleaded their case while a team of Polish acrobats held back a ringmaster from kicking the crap out of one or more of his clowns. The whole incident was frequently rehashed down at the station in quieter moments. The odd bit of farce was always a welcome break from the grind, given how much of this job was often mundanity interspersed with tragedy.

Butch could now add "conga line" to the list of things she had pulled over. The fact that the line had consisted of other members of the Garda Síochána, who had roundly booed her as she'd done it, had only increased the embarrassment factor. Bunny hadn't been wrong – Butch had, in part, taken the evening shifts to keep him company, but she couldn't pretend that missing the Christmas parties hadn't been a rather pleasant bonus. They were always drunken affairs and, as a non-drinker, she found them largely tedious – not least because, inevitably, some of her inebriated male colleagues would approach her every year just to "check she was still doing the whole lesbian thing". As if it was likely to wear off. If anything, the yearly parade of drunken masculinity these parties provided acted like a booster shot.

And yet, despite her best efforts, here she was, in the Garda Club on Harrington Street. Not only at the party but pooping the party on official business. Admittedly, "official business" was a questionable term to be used here. Bunny had given her a hurried summary of the events of the Fadden family's awful day and then headed off in search of the grandson. She'd been dispatched to find out who was handling the grandfather's robbery and assault case.

It should have been a relatively straightforward process. Contact Control, find out which detective the case had been assigned to, then get in touch with them, explain the situation and ask about progress. While over the years Bunny had pissed off a fair few people on the force, those individuals were almost all in senior management. He was popular with the rank and file, mostly because of his unpopularity with the higher-ups. Everyone loves somebody who says what needs to be said, as long as they don't have to do it.

One of the core tenets of the police is that every victim deserves the comfort of knowing their case is being dealt with as thoroughly as possible, but the harsh reality is that resources were limited. Bunny's personal interest in proceedings would have an effect.

That had been Butch's theory, anyway – the reality had turned out to be a lot more confusing. She'd been told that the case had been assigned to Detective John Carroll, a slightly odd bloke who was nevertheless good at the job and typically got results. The confusing part was that Control informed her that the case had been designated as No Action Required. Typically, an NAR designation was only issued when there was doubt a crime had been committed at all or if a decision had been reached that it was a matter for the civil courts rather than the criminal. None of that applied to an elderly gentleman being beaten and robbed.

When she'd queried it, she had been transferred to a pissed-off higher-up who she'd never spoken to or even heard of before. She'd been firmly told that no error had been made, the decision had come from senior management and that was that. When she'd pleaded the case, she'd been told her DI would be informed of her insubordination. Insubordination! If they wanted to see a whole lot of that, wait until Bunny found out. Thankfully, he was off dealing with the missing Deccie Fadden Junior, so Butch decided to find out what was going on before she brought him into the loop.

All of that was why she was here, pulling John Carroll out of a conga line. It wasn't much past 8pm and the whole place was already rocking. Someone had made the decision to serve dinner at 6pm, which meant a lot more drinking time. This place was going to be messy when closing time rolled around. Of course, "closing time" for the Garda Club was more of a concept than a reality. Not so much "who watches the watchers?" as "who stops the stoppers?".

After she'd explained over the deafeningly loud ABBA medley that she needed a quiet word, Carroll had followed her into the hall. He now looked at her through what were already glassy eyes.

"Sorry to drag you away, John."

"'S no problem. What's up?"

"Can I ..." Butch knew she shouldn't ask, but she couldn't resist. "Why are you blue?"

"What d'ye mean?"

Butch waved a hand at the fancy-dress costume that Carroll was wearing. His eyes widened as if he'd just remembered he was wearing it. "Ah, this? I'm a Smurf."

"Right." Even as the words were coming out of her mouth, she knew she should leave it there. "Nobody else is in fancy dress, though?"

"What's your point? It's a party!"

"Of course." Now that she thought about it, she had a vague

memory of seeing a photo of a golf day at which Carroll was also, inexplicably, in fancy dress.

"Honestly," said Carroll, puffing out his blue cheeks. "Fella can't get into the Christmas spirit without people making out it's something weird."

"No, I just … I think it's great. More people should wear fancy dress to these things." She could feel her cheeks reddening but for some reason she kept talking. "I might do the same for next year."

Carroll's face brightened. "I've got a Smurfette costume at home if you want it?"

"I'll … I'll certainly think about it." In the absence of any other option, she decided to take the conversation on a hard right turn. "You got assigned a case earlier. Declan Fadden – old guy that got beaten and robbed up off Capel Street."

Carroll nodded. "I did."

"I … I'm just a bit confused. Control says it's NAR and I don't understand why."

He folded his arms and leaned against the wall. "What's it got to do with you?"

"Nothing, but Bunny McGarry is a friend of the family."

Carroll straightened up. "Ah, Jesus. Look, I'm not supposed to talk about it."

"Right," said Butch.

"Not my decision."

"Sure. Can you tell me whose it was?"

"I've been told to say nothing."

"OK. I get it. I do. But … Well, you know Bunny. He's not going to let it lie. He'll be down here within the hour, demanding answers. Charging in like a bull in a china shop."

Carroll flapped a hand in the direction of the party. "I'm on a night off."

"I appreciate that, but I'd imagine Bunny would say that poor Declan Fadden is in hospital with a fractured skull and his case shouldn't be NAR."

"What are you implying?" snapped Carroll. "I'm a detective. If a DI decides on a case, what am I supposed to do?"

"A DI?"

"Look, I'm not supposed to say anything."

"OK."

Carroll bit his lip and Butch stood there, watching the detective's internal struggle play out through his facial expressions. She guessed he was weighing up how much crap he'd get for disobeying an order against the image of Bunny McGarry in full flow coming looking for an explanation.

"Ah, screw it," he said eventually. "I thought it was bullshit, and if they want to come after me for it, then go ahead. He's a nice old man, and I don't understand what the hell is going on either." He leaned towards Butch and lowered his voice. "It was Grainger."

Butch drew back in surprise. "DI Grainger?"

"Yeah."

"Isn't he ... Didn't he get transferred to whatchamacallit?"

"The Interpol liaison team, aka the Suntan Gang."

"What's international crime got to do with a mugging on Capel Street?"

"I've no clue," said Carroll. "And believe me, I asked. He said he and his team were on their way back up from Limerick and they would handle everything."

"What?"

"Look, it didn't make any sense to me either. If I recall correctly, the pompous arsehole said it was a matter above my pay grade and to not worry about it. If you need anything else, you can go talk to Grainger. In fact, be my guest."

"But ..."

Before Butch could ask any more questions, a group of people passed by them on their way into the party.

"Evening, Detective Carroll," one of them called. "You're looking a little blue."

"Ah, piss off," snapped Carroll, killing the laughter from the group.

Butch grimaced as the party-goers hesitated for a moment before continuing through the doors into the main room. When she looked back at Carroll, he'd clenched his eyes shut and was holding his hand to his forehead.

"Did I ..." he moaned. "Did I just ..."

Despite him not being able to see her, Butch nodded. "Tell the Assistant Commissioner to piss off? Yes. Yes, I'm afraid you did."

Carroll turned and headbutted the wall repeatedly. Not with enough force to do any damage to it, but he'd left a noticeable blue smudge.

"I'll ... I'll leave you to it," said Butch, backing away awkwardly. "Merry Christmas."

# CHAPTER SIX

Niall Duggan was seated on the couch, holding Björn tenderly in his hands. Björn was his pigeon. He was deeply regretting having taken him out of his crate because Cousin Bobby was now in one of his moods. Experience told him that the best thing he could do was shut up and hope for the black cloud to pass sooner rather than later. He dearly wanted to remove Björn from the firing line but any attempt to put him away would only make things worse.

Bobby was standing in the centre of the room, his shirt off, flapping his arms about as he spoke. He loved to take his shirt off, to display all the hard work he had done in the gym. Niall was a lot bigger than his cousin but not in that sculpted way. One of Niall's schoolteachers had once referred to him as a big graceless lump and he'd subsequently been known as Lump for years – up until the point he reached six foot three at the age of fifteen and suddenly nobody felt brave enough to take the mickey to his face any more.

People still never believed that he and Bobby were related. Bobby was all suave and handsome whereas Niall's ma used to say straight after a haircut that he always somehow looked like he needed another one, and that he walked hunched over, like a gorilla trying to fit into a Mini. Niall would just have to sit there, grinning along as the rest of the family laughed.

"What the hell were you thinking?"

Thankfully, the question wasn't directed at Niall or Björn. It was aimed at Sofia, who was sitting at the other end of the couch, hugging her knees to her as she watched Bobby with big, fearful eyes. When he raged like this, she always looked so tiny.

"I'm sorry, baby," she said, pleading. "I thought the man was on his own."

"Well, he wasn't," snapped Bobby. "It's lucky it was only a kid and I was able to control the situation. He could have blown the whole thing."

"I know," she said, her face barely visible from beneath a cascade of long, dark hair. "I'm sorry."

He took a few steps until he was standing over her, then reached down and grabbed her wrist. "Stop telling me you're sorry!" he roared, as she looked up at him fearfully. "That's not going to do me any good when I'm sitting in a prison cell because you couldn't follow simple instructions."

"I'm ..." She broke down in tears. "I'm ... I don't know what you want me to say."

Niall cleared his throat. "Alright, Bobby. She gets it."

Bobby let go of Sofia's arm and redirected his ire towards Niall. "And as for you, you big, dumb ape ..."

"What did I do?"

"You referred to me as your cousin, you moron."

"I n-n-never." Whenever Bobby got like this, it brought out Niall's stutter.

Bobby began to speak in the exaggerated, stumbling drawl he used when impersonating Niall. "Take it easy, cuz. Take it easy, cuz."

"That doesn't mean you're my cousin," protested Niall. "People refer to each other as 'cuz' all the time."

"Would you listen to him? Black fellas in America might, but nobody around here does."

"He wouldn't have noticed. He was scared. I could feel him sh-sh-shaking."

Bobby sneered down at him. "Ah, was he sh-sh-shaking?" he mocked. "Christ – for such a big lad you're soft as shite. Maybe we need to toughen you up a bit?"

Bobby made to grab Björn, but Niall had been anticipating the move and tucked the bird away, shielding him with his body. "No."

"No, what?"

"Leave B-B-Björn alone," said Niall softly.

"Björn? What kind of name is that for a pigeon?"

When Niall had bought the four birds, he'd decided to name them after the members of ABBA. Agnetha had not come home last year and Benny had died of a heart attack when next-door's cat had leaped up at the coop. Anni was hopefully back home in Limerick by now. He'd let her go a few days ago.

Before he'd left for Dublin, he'd asked his friend Mark to stop by and feed his birds, and he felt confident he would. Niall really liked the guy. He'd moved into the area a few years ago to live with his granny. He was deaf and didn't speak, but that was alright. Niall didn't talk much either, and weirdly, that made things a lot easier. Plus, Mark was one of the only people he'd ever met who didn't either take the piss out of his stammer or treat him like he was an idiot because of it.

Niall opened his mouth to speak then closed it. What he wanted to say was that Bobby hadn't needed to be so rough with the old man. The cracking noise when he'd stomped down on the poor fella's arm had made Niall feel like throwing up. He elected to say nothing on this occasion because when Bobby got like this, there was no talking to him. Instead, he concentrated on shielding Björn.

At the far end of the sofa, Sofia continued to sob softly.

And then, as quickly as it had come on, Bobby's tantrum was over and charming Bobby was back. His unpredictability was weirdly predictable. He went over to Sofia, swept her hair back and cupped her face in both hands. When he spoke again, his voice was as smooth as silk.

"Come on now, beautiful," he said gently. "No need for that. You know I'm doing this for you, right?"

She nodded.

"And we are so close now, but we're running out of time, and we can't afford any mistakes."

"I know," she said. "I really am sorry. I didn't see the kid."

"That's alright. Let's move on. I've got to go meet this guy about the thing. You need to get yourself ready for your date tonight. Wear that dress I like."

She looked up at him warily. "Are you sure?"

"Yeah. You look hot in that." He glanced at his watch, or rather the watch he'd acquired a couple of days ago when they'd robbed that bloke down in Skibbereen. Rolex. Niall noticed that Bobby got to wear one, but he didn't.

Bobby slid his hand into his pocket and drew out the ring they'd stolen from the old man. "Tell you what," he said to Sofia, taking her dainty little hand in his, "why don't we slip this on here." Sofia sniffed and smiled as Bobby slipped the ring with its single diamond surrounded by emeralds onto the ring finger of her left hand. "That way everybody knows you're my girl."

She held her hand out and admired it. "It is beautiful."

"And so are you. Nothing but the best for my girl." Bobby threw a glance at Niall as he stepped away. "And you – stay here and cook some food, would you? And keep out of that hot tub. You and your stupid bird are not on a romantic weekend away."

They were staying in a nice holiday home they'd rented up in Wicklow. Niall had thought it was a mad expense, but Bobby had explained that they needed somewhere to lie low where nobody would come looking for them. Sofia had been able to pay the landlord in cash and they'd been delighted – undoubtedly thrilled to have some money coming in that the taxman didn't need to know about. There was one enormous bedroom that was Sofia's and Bobby's, and two smaller ones, each with a single bed. Niall spent his nights trying not to fall out of the bloody thing while listening through the walls to Bobby and Sofia going at it.

Bobby snatched up the car keys and slammed the door behind him. A few seconds later came the sound of the scattering of gravel as Bobby floored it and zoomed off down the long, winding road as if he was a rally driver. Even if he and Sofia had wanted to go anywhere, they couldn't. The house was miles away from anything.

Niall looked across at Sofia. "Are you OK?"

She bobbed her head. "He scares me when he gets like that."

"His bark is worse than his bite."

It wasn't. Niall knew that better than anyone. When Bobby really lost it, you did not want to be anywhere near him.

Sofia shuffled along on the sofa until she was sitting beside him. Her sweet smell filled his nostrils as she slipped her tiny hand inside of his. When she spoke, it was barely above a whisper. "You will keep me safe, won't you?"

As he went to speak, he could feel his mouth tensing up as if he were about to stutter. He took a deep breath. "Course."

She leaned her head against his arm. "My hero."

# CHAPTER SEVEN

Bunny stood in front of McGrattan's jewellers on Capel Street – the scene of the crime. To be precise, Deccie Fadden Senior had been led around the corner to a vacant sandwich shop, and that was where the assault and robbery had occurred, but this was where they had identified their target. The gang. Or was it a gang? Traditionally, gang members rarely whispered apologies to their victims as the girl had done, and never asked for help. That was the confusing element to all this.

Not that Bunny had had much of a chance to take a step back and look at the bigger picture. He'd been running around like a blue-arsed fly trying to find Deccie Fadden Junior before he did something stupid. Seeing as the lad's last reported whereabouts was looking for Andy "Flipper" Finn, the odds of that had only increased. Bunny, having now retrieved his mobile from the office, had already received two anxious calls from Bridie Fadden and he was expecting more. He couldn't blame her. Deccie's granny was a strong woman but a husband in the hospital and a grandson off seeking ill-judged revenge would have anyone at their wits' end. Bunny had already been everywhere he could think of and contacted anyone who might know anything, but so far, nobody knew where Deccie was.

In the absence of any better idea, Bunny had come to Capel Street. It was a logical place for Deccie to start his search, assuming he was thinking logically. Meanwhile, Bunny had to try to be patient. He had put the word out and he had to give it time to work. He was owed a lot of favours in this town. Fingers crossed, by the end of the night, he'd be owed one less.

Butch appeared beside him.

"You said you'd be here in five minutes, twenty minutes ago," chided Bunny.

"I know," she replied. "Even after late-night shopping's finished, it's a nightmare to find parking round here. I drove by this place twice. Any word yet?"

"Nothing," said Bunny.

"He'll turn up. I mean, he's only a young fella. How much trouble can he get into?"

"That question, when asked about Deccie Fadden, is a very dangerous one. The lad is plenty smart enough to find a way to do something really stupid."

Butch pointed at the window of the jewellers. "I think I saw some movement at the back of the shop there."

"Yeah," agreed Bunny. "Even though they're closed, I'd imagine there's some staff inside getting stuff ready for tomorrow. This'll be their busiest time of the year."

"Have you tried knocking?"

Bunny shrugged. "I was considering it, but I'd imagine anyone in there is going to ignore it. I mean, nobody working in a jewellers after hours is going to open the door to a bloke they don't know, regardless of how much ID he waves about. Can't say I blame them." He glanced down at Butch. "Besides, I'm assuming whoever is in charge of the official investigation has already been in to check the CCTV and all that?"

"About that ..." Something in Butch's tone of voice made Bunny turn and face her. "And this seems an appropriate time to remind you of the phrase 'don't shoot the messenger'. I went and found John

Carroll, who was assigned the case originally, because it's been marked NAR."

Bunny's eyes widened in disbelief. "No action required? Are you shitting me? A defenceless old man gets beaten and robbed and we sit on our hands and do nothing? That's bullshit!"

Butch put a hand out. "I know. And for what it's worth, so does Carroll. It wasn't his idea. It took some doing, but he eventually told me that the instruction had come down from on high."

"What in the shitting hell! From whom?"

"From what he was told, it was something involving your old friend DI Grainger."

Grainger and Bunny went back a long way. They'd been in the academy at Templemore together. They hadn't got on then and things hadn't got any better. Earlier that year, Grainger had been in charge of a high-profile task force to find a couple of individuals who'd been attacking homeless people. Much to Grainger's chagrin, Bunny had solved the problem while being on sabbatical, something that had done nothing to warm up their frosty relationship.

"That shit-sipping bucket of ineptitude?" asked Bunny. "What the hell has this got to do with him?"

"I don't know," said Butch. "But you need to calm down so we can find out."

"Calm down? With God as my witness, I'm going to find him and feed him his own arse."

"I don't think even God wants to see that."

"Hang on a sec, didn't I hear something about him being moved to head up that Interpol liaison office?"

"Yes," confirmed Butch. "The latest step in a career that shows there's no limit to how far you can fail upwards when your uncle is Minister for Justice."

"And what in the hell would the Suntan Gang have to do with this —" Bunny stopped himself. Of course. "The girl! Deccie Senior said she sounded foreign, and she asked for help."

"What?" asked Butch. "You've not told me any of this."

"Yeah, he said she leaned over him when they were leaving, whispered 'sorry' and said she needed help."

"Oh dear, sounds very Patty Hearst."

"Grainger can worry about that. My interest here is getting justice for the Faddens, and that's what is going to happen."

"OK, but..." Butch's face drained of colour. "Oh God."

"What?"

She licked her lips nervously and grabbed Bunny's arm, urgency in her eyes. "This is really important, Bunny. For your own sake and for the sake of the Faddens, I need you to stay calm."

"What do you mean st—"

She squeezed his arm. "Promise me?"

"I—"

"McGarry." The voice came from behind him, dripping scorn. "What are you doing here?"

Bunny whirled round to see DI Grainger standing in front of him, swathed in the permanent air of unearned entitlement he wore. The man had a square jaw, slightly piggish nose, and a hint of baby fat around his face that meant he could never be described as thin, despite more or less being so. It was a reasonable collection of features when considered individually and yet, somehow, they collectively coalesced into the most punchable face imaginable. It was the look, thought Bunny. Something in the eyes. Like he knew better despite all historical evidence clearly indicating that he didn't.

"I should ask you the same thing," said Bunny. "Why the hell are you interfering in the investigation of the violent robbery of Declan Fadden?"

Grainger lifted his chin slightly. "That is none of your concern."

Bunny heard Butch groaning behind him.

"None of my concern? I'm a member of the Garda Síochána and it is a serious crime. That's the kind of thing we're supposed to take an interest in, or have you been at so many conferences and symposiums now that you've forgotten that?"

Grainger's eyes widened. "I am your superior officer, and you will address me with considerably more respect than that."

"Superior?" repeated Bunny. "Let's just go with 'higher-ranked' so that we're not stretching language to its breaking point."

Bunny noticed a slight tilt to Grainger's head, as if he wanted to look around but was resisting it. It was at that moment that Bunny belatedly realised there were several people standing behind the detective inspector who were considerably more than curious bystanders. Bunny recognised one of them as Robbie Farmer – Detective Sergeant, to give him his full title. Farmer was a dumpy fella from Roscommon with a twitchy air, who could crease a suit by looking at it.

The other three men were strangers and Bunny would bet his salary that none of them were guards. Two of them were Mediterranean-looking and, in stark contrast to Farmer, knew how to wear the hell out of a suit. They were large slabs of manliness who had the air of hired muscle. Behind them stood an older, bald black guy with a white goatee, who was dressed in a more casual jacket and trousers. He looked uncomfortable, and not, Bunny guessed, because he was underdressed relative to his companions.

Bunny pointed in their direction. "And who are they?"

Grainger straightened up. "That is on a need-to-know basis, and you do not need to know. Now – what are you doing here?"

Bunny narrowed his eyes and focused his attention back on the detective inspector. "As it happens, I'm a friend of the family. Deccie Fadden Senior is the grandfather of one of my boys."

"What?"

"The lads from my hurling team."

"Well, rest assured, this case does not involve any hurling." Grainger gave a smile, as if he'd said something funny. If he had, nobody else within a half-mile radius had heard it.

"No," said Bunny, taking a step towards him, "it involves a serious assault and the robbery of a highly valuable piece of jewellery with great sentimental value."

"Of course," said Grainger dismissively, flicking invisible lint from one shoulder of his suit. "And you can assure Mr Fadden that the matter is being looked into."

"Is it, though? It's been marked as NAR on the system, which would imply it's being hushed up rather than investigated."

Grainger wound his neck in, as if dodging a jab. "It is being treated with the utmost urgency."

"Why isn't it being logged properly on the system, then?"

"That is an operational decision," responded Grainger.

"Is that right?" said Bunny, aware that Butch was trying to make a warning noise behind him. "So you're in charge of the investigation, then?"

"I am."

"And you're only turning up at the crime scene now?"

"Not that it is any of your business, but we had to drive up from Limerick."

"Sorry for your trouble. As luck would have it, we have Gardaí in Dublin now too – why not let us handle it, and you and the League of Nations here can get back to sightseeing?"

Grainger jabbed a finger in Bunny's face. "You are drifting dangerously close to insubordination."

"I'm actually driving straight for it; you must not be picking up on everything I'm saying. Not that surprising given your investigative prowess. To be clear, I have zero confidence in your ability to investigate your way out of a wet paper bag and I'm not leaving this to you." He waved a hand towards Grainger's entourage. "I don't know what this is – but it stinks. A good man is lying in a hospital bed out in Blanchardstown, having taken an awful kicking and having had his world turned upside down, and nothing you have said has explained why the investigation into it got halted."

Grainger's face was now a shade of red not normally seen unless accompanied by a heart attack or heat stroke. "Enough is enough. Are you going to leave, or will I be forced to take steps?"

"I didn't really think taking action was your thing. Shouldn't you call a meeting first?"

Grainger's eyes widened. "Oh, I'll take action."

"I'd love you to," Bunny responded, jutting out his chin and pointing at it. "In fact, I'll give you your first action for free."

"Bunny!" exclaimed Butch, placing a hand on his elbow.

"That does it, McGarry. You're an embarrassment to this force. Consider yourself on report, and I'm having you suspended from active duty."

"You can't do that!"

Grainger looked over his shoulder and noticed the shorter suit smirking. He took a couple of steps forward, squaring up to Bunny. "I can and I am. Keep going and you'll be off the force completely."

Butch appeared between the two men. "OK, let's just ..."

"Keep out of this, Cassidy," snarled Grainger.

Butch placed a hand on Bunny's chest in an attempt to guide him backwards. "I'm just trying to defuse the situation, sir."

"Are you being sarcastic?"

"What?" asked Butch, genuinely confused. "No, I'm just trying to dial down the testosterone levels here."

"Right, you're suspended, too."

Butch gawped at him. "What did I do?"

"You attempted policing," said Bunny. "DI Grainger hates that."

"Get out of here now, or this will be so much worse for the both of you. This is a crime scene."

"Yeah," grumbled Bunny while trying to shake off Butch, who was now putting her back into pushing him away, all attempts at subtlety gone, "what's going on here is criminal, alright. You useless bag of donkey shite ... Ow! Ow! Ow!" The unmanly ow-ing was because Butch, keen to get Bunny's undivided attention, had resorted to a vicious nipple clamp. "Butch, what the hell are you doing?"

"Stopping you destroying two careers, one of which happens to be mine."

"But—"

"How is anything you're about to do going to help anyone? Most of all the Faddens?"

Bunny looked down at Butch and then back at Grainger. After a long moment, without saying a word, he turned and walked away.

. . .

Five minutes later, Butch and Bunny were crouched in the doorway of the now-closed-for-the-night Ilac Shopping Centre, sheltering from the rain that had started to pelt down. Butch stood with her phone pressed to her ear.

"Seriously, Sarge – suspended? You're kidding me. How does Grainger have enough sway to get us taken off duty, and in a week when resources are stretched, too?"

As she paused to listen to the response, Bunny thought there was a real risk she might hurl her mobile into the rainy night.

"So that's it, then?" she said flatly. "He's got some powerful friends, Bunny gets into an argument with him and both of us – BOTH OF US, mind – get suspended? And he can get it approved, in what, ten minutes? This is the first efficient thing Grainger has done since he's been on the force. This is—" She looked at her phone in disbelief. "He hung up on me!"

"Unbelievable," said Bunny.

"Bloody idiot," responded Butch.

"He certainly is. You can say that again."

"Not him. You! Ye big dumb gorilla." She waved a hand back in the direction of Capel Street. "What the hell was the point of all that? You don't like Grainger – what a massive shock. I'm glad you went to such great lengths to show it – now we're both suspended. Great lot of use we can be to the Faddens now."

"Well—"

"Shut up," snapped Butch, slipping her phone into her pocket. "You've done more than enough talking. You may be half in, half out of being a member of the Gardaí, but I like the job and I worked damn hard to get to where I am. Harder than you or any other man had to work to get to the same spot."

Bunny made to speak again but didn't get the chance.

"And don't say how Grainger got where he is. We know. You're not the first one to bloody notice that either, Columbo. We get it. I'd call him an arsehole only those have a practical use, so the comparison is grossly unfair to arseholes. He's a moron and you just let yourself get outsmarted by him. How clever do you feel now?"

Bunny looked down at his feet and then back up at Butch. "I'm sorry."

"Don't take the piss."

"I'm not. I'm sincerely apologising."

"Well then, stop trying to be reasonable. It's too late and I'm still angry at you."

"If it's any consolation, my nipple is still really sore."

Butch narrowed her eyes. "And don't you dare try and make jokes."

"Who's joking? It's proper killing me," he said, rubbing his palm over it. "That's a medical fact. Where did you learn to do that?"

"Back when I didn't know I was a lesbian. Came in handy on the dating scene."

"I never knew you ... I have so many questions."

"Good. Well, I won't be answering any of them. You can sit at home while you're on suspension and contemplate them to your heart's content, though. I guess I've not got an excuse to do Christmas shopping now." She clenched her fist. "I should knock you out."

"You could do, or ..." Bunny left the suggestion hanging in the air.

"What?" snapped Butch.

"You could help me find out what Grainger and his little international task force were up to in Limerick. Because whatever this is, you can be damn sure that they won't be worried about the Faddens seeing any justice."

"You're unbelievable! We just got suspended."

"I know," agreed Bunny. "Means we've got some free time on our hands. Want to use it by seeing if we can get a little justice and piss off Grainger at the same time?"

Butch held her head in her hands. "Why do I listen to you? I'm starting to think our friendship is really some form of elaborate self-harm. I need to forgive myself."

"If it helps, I forgive you."

Butch's head jerked up. "You forgive me?"

With impeccable timing, Bunny's life was saved by his phone pinging. He fished it out of the pocket of his overcoat. "Finally."

"Deccie?"

"Not quite, but someone has a location on Flipper. You coming?"

Butch hugged herself against the cold night air. "Sure. Why not? It's not like I've got anything else to be doing."

Bunny gave her a big smile. "Excellent. And cheer up, will ye? It's Christmas!"

# CHAPTER EIGHT

Andy "Flipper" Finn exhaled a smoke ring into the inky night sky, pulled his coat around him to fend off the winter chill and passed the joint to Davey Hannigan.

"That's some seriously good gear."

"It is," agreed Davey. "It had want to be to have me sitting out here freezing me bollocks off."

Flipper tsked. "Here we go, always moaning."

"I'm just saying – we could go round to Damo's and sit in his conservatory. His ma is working nights, and she kicked his dad out last month after she caught him getting his end away with that hairdresser."

"Didn't they have a big fight in the street?" asked Flipper.

"They did," confirmed Davey gleefully. "Our Yvonne saw it. Said Damo's ma pulled your one's hair extensions out. It was quite the to-do."

"Jesus. I wouldn't have thought Damo's da was worth all the effort."

"I don't think his ma would disagree with you. It was more the principle of the thing. Damo says she's never been happier." Davey exhaled and, despite his best efforts, failed yet again to form any kind of smoke ring. "So, we could go round Damo's gaff."

"Absolutely not," said Flipper.

"You're seriously going to keep this going?"

"He knows what he said."

"But you told me you can't remember what he said. You were both stoned at the time."

"It doesn't matter that I can't remember exactly what he said. I remember it was bad, and I know for a fact he remembers exactly what it was. Now, until he A – tells me what it was, and B – apologises for it, Damo is out of the circle of trust. Besides," Flipper continued, spreading his hands wide to indicate the canal they were sitting next to, "this is perfect. Here we are, communing with nature, enjoying some top-notch gear, without a care in the world."

Davey looked up and down the path glumly. "Communing with nature. That's one way of putting it."

"Are you still worried about that bleedin' swan?"

"I'm telling you – they can break your arm."

Flipper rolled his eyes. "Some gangster you are. How are we going to run this town if you're scared of a jumped-up duck?"

"It's not a duck. It's a lot bigger than a duck. And it's owned by the Queen."

"What, like the Queen queen?"

"I don't mean the band. Your one with the crown, all that. She's married to Prince Charles."

"No, you muppet. He's her son."

Davey crinkled his nose. "Ugh. That's messed up, even for royalty."

"Never mind." Flipper sat up slightly. "Are you telling me that English swans are over here breaking people's arms? And give us that joint back."

Davey duly passed the aforementioned back to his colleague and wrinkled his brow in concentration. "Now that you mention it, yeah – that doesn't seem right at all, does it?"

"No," agreed Flipper. "It most certainly does not. You'd want to tell your cousin Johnny and his mates about this."

"Did I not tell you? Johnny says he's now left the IRA."

"Is that right?"

"Yeah. Philosophical differences."

"How so?"

"He thought they were going to be fighting a war against the oppressor to free the six counties from the yoke of British imperial rule, but after two years, all he'd done was hand out a load of leaflets and got taken up to the mountains a couple of times to shoot an old rifle at a tree. He said it was like being in the Scouts, only you had to sit through more boring speeches. Besides, the wool in the balaclava was setting off his eczema something rotten."

Flipper fired a rapid series of smaller smoke rings into the night air. It was annoyingly impressive. "And so, the cause loses another brave foot soldier."

"Yeah. He's gone back to playing five-a-side football out in Finglas. He says the scraps are a lot better." Davey shifted in his seat. "I tell you what, I need to get laid in the worst way."

Flipper turned to look at his friend and raised his eyebrows. "That was quite the segue."

"Sorry" said Davey, accepting the return of the joint. "It's weighing on my mind."

"Clearly. I thought you were going steady with Fat Mary?"

"Ah, would you stop calling her that," snapped Davey irritably. He paused, as if remembering a line from a script. "It is dehumanising, disrespectful, and body-shaming at its worst. It's also not true. She's lost all the weight."

"She has, to be fair. She looks great. But we've called her that since we were kids. You can't change it now."

"Try explaining that to her. She said if I loved her, I would get people to do exactly that."

"How are you supposed to make that happen?" asked Flipper.

"That's what I said. She said that Mary Gibson was fatter than her now and she wanted me to get people to call her it instead."

"Mary Gibson?"

"Aka Squinty Mary."

"Sure, she already has a nickname."

"I know," agreed Davey morosely. "Believe me, I tried to explain all that."

"And what did Fa—What did your Mary say to that?"

"Not much. Let's just say that certain privileges were withdrawn. The woman knows how to send a message."

"So, what did you do?"

"Exactly what you think I did. I went around and started referring to Squinty Mary as Fat Mary."

"Did anyone go for it?"

"Course they didn't. Least of all Squinty Mary. I thought she'd have been happy."

"She is very self-conscious about the squint."

"Exactly. You'd think she'd appreciate somebody drawing attention to another feature instead."

"I take it she didn't?"

"Booted me in the knackers incredibly hard, right in the middle of the dance floor in Fibber's. I mean, talk about excessive force – I was still feeling it several days later."

"What did you do in response to that?"

Davey threw up his hands in exasperation. "What could I do? I'm not gonna hit a woman."

"You're a gentleman," said Flipper.

"I am."

"Not enough of them about."

"And what did being a gentleman get me? I'll tell you what – my Mary makes a big show of dumping me the next day, and now her and Squinty Mary are best buddies."

Flipper shook his head as Davey took a large drag on the joint. "There is no justice in this world, my friend. No justice."

Davey leaned his head over the back of the bench and looked up into the now almost clear night sky. "Let's talk about something else. This is wrecking my buzz. I'll tell you what – that rain earlier really emptied the clouds from the sky, didn't it? It feels like one of them metaphors."

Flipper leaned his head back too. "It does. That could be our lives. Like, all the recent shit we've been through, that was the rain. And now, this lovely clear sky" – he waved a hand at the stars above – "this could be our bright future."

And then, because God enjoys a well-timed line as much as anyone, Flipper's view of his star-filled future was blocked out by Cork's version of the Death Star drifting ominously into view.

Bunny McGarry gave a smile to chill the soul. "I wouldn't bet on that, lads."

# CHAPTER NINE

Five minutes later, Davey Hannigan was still on his knees on the path beside the canal, hacking and spitting after having thrown up. He took a final sip from the plastic bottle of water then tried to hand it back to Detective Pamela Cassidy.

She pulled a face. "Yeah. You can keep that."

Bunny, who was standing beside the bench, his hand resting casually on Flipper's shoulder, shook his head. "I still don't understand what the hell he thought he was doing."

"I think," started Flipper - Bunny could see the strain of thought on his face as he attempted 'clever,' - "he swallowed his cigarette, because you startled him by sneaking up on us like that."

"Sneaking up on you?" repeated Bunny. "You're on the path beside the canal. Look at it. There's barely enough room for two people to pass each other. All we did was walk down from the bridge. There was no sneaking involved."

"That's not possible," countered Flipper. He glanced at the railway line behind him. "You must've gone down onto the tracks and snuck up behind us."

Bunny looked at Butch and laughed. "Mr Finn here thinks that we hopped down onto a dangerous railway line, then scaled an eight-foot electric fence before climbing the embankment through head-high brambles so that we could gain advantage on him and his associate here."

Butch nodded. "To be fair to him, normally we would have parachuted in, but the Gardaí's B-52 bomber is in the shop."

Bunny tapped Flipper on the forehead a couple of times. "I hate to be the one to break it to you, Flipper, but people in several surrounding parishes can smell your joint. You're that stoned, I'd imagine there is a good chance a brass band would be capable of taking you by surprise."

After a moment's hesitation, Flipper offered, "I wish to plead the fifth."

Butch threw up her hands. "For Christ's sake, is there a new series of an American cop show on telly or something?"

Bunny looked over at her. "Butch?"

She shook her head. "Don't mind me. Mr Finn here was attempting to talk his way out of an arrest for possession of drugs."

"I don't know what you're talking about," objected Flipper, sounding suitably outraged.

"Yeah," agreed Davey. "I've never taken any drugs in my life. My body is a temple."

"Is that right?" asked Butch, wrinkling her nose and indicating the erstwhile contents of Davey's stomach with her foot. "Would you care to explain how, amidst the entire bucket of KFC that you just coughed up, there is half of a large joint?" Despite herself, she leaned down to take a better look. "Jesus," she said, with a glance across at Bunny, "the thing is still lit. How is it still lit?"

"I've never seen that before in my life," said Davey, in a tone that suggested even he didn't believe he was saying it.

"Yeah," agreed Flipper. "We are just two honest citizens, sitting here and enjoying a bit of nature. We're not harming anybody."

"Too right. You should be going after them royalist swan bastards," said Davey. "They are the real criminals here."

"Run that by me again?" asked Bunny, genuinely confused.

"As it happens," said Butch with a grin, "Detective McGarry has a colourful history with swans himself."

Bunny shot her a look, which Butch met with a sarcastic eye-roll. "Never mind that," he added quickly. "We were discussing how you two gentlemen are bang to rights."

"You got nothing on us," said Flipper with an unlikely air of confidence.

"Actually, what we have is probable cause, given the potent smell of wacky-baccy in the air. That's enough for us to legally search you."

Flipper's eyes widened, then he looked pointedly at Davey. As Davey casually attempted to move his right hand towards the pocket of his bomber jacket, Butch used her foot on his back to nudge him to the ground. He threw his hands out in front of him to prevent an unhappy reunion with his recently liberated dinner. "Hey!"

Butch reached her hand into his pocket and pulled out a large lump of hash. "Well, would you look at that? Looks like somebody had plans for a very mellow Christmas."

Davey's eyes were full of hurt. "I thought you were supposed to be the nice one?"

She grinned down at him. "I am, but everything is relative."

"That it is," agreed Bunny, turning to Flipper. "And while this is obviously a career-defining bust for both me and Detective Cassidy, it's not actually what we are here about. Deccie Fadden came to see you."

"I don't know who that is," said Flipper quickly.

Bunny gritted his teeth and scratched his forehead irritably. "Jesus. You can't even lie well. We both know that you know who Deccie Fadden is. He grew up four doors down from your house. Now stop pissing me about and tell me what he asked, and what you answered."

"And what exactly is in it for me?"

Bunny leaned down so that he was inches from Flipper's face. "What's in it for you?" He left a long pause so that even Flipper's drug-addled brain could register that the conversation was heading down a dark road. "Well now, depending on what you told Deccie, who is in a very fragile state, I will be annoyed. Keep in mind, this has already been a very bad day at the end of a very bad year and my patience is running thin. So, if I was you, I'd tell me quickly before my temper can get up a real head of steam.

"The good news for you is that Detective Cassidy and I were suspended from the force about an hour ago, which means we're not going to arrest you. The bad news for you is that Detective Cassidy and I were suspended from the force about an hour ago, which means that I am here in a personal capacity, and I am about to take this *really* personally. You see, one of my boys is in trouble and I think that you may have contributed to that state of affairs, so believe me when I say, one way or the other, I'm going to find out where Deccie is. So, to reiterate, my advice is – start talking fast and don't leave anything out."

To put it kindly, Andy "Flipper" Finn was not a smart man. Now nineteen years of age, he had spent most of his life to this point being not a smart boy. While his school reports had been damning, nowhere in them had anyone used the phrase "not living up to his potential". Flipper had been dim from birth. The worst kind of dim. The dim that thinks it is smart and unlucky, as opposed to consistently stupid. For all of that, it is still a fact of life that all living creatures require a base level of intelligence to remain alive. Near the end, even the slowest of the dinosaurs looked at the large red ball in the sky hurtling towards them and thought, "Ohhhh, that's probably not a good thing." In that moment, Flipper could feel his face growing warm.

"Alright," he said, "but I need you to remain calm."

"Talk," said Bunny. "Fast."

"So Deccie comes to us—"

"You," interrupted Davey. "Leave me out of this."

Flipper glared at Davey. "Dude! Circle of trust."

"Ah, fuck off. Circle of trust. I was the one that said not to mess with him."

Bunny pushed Flipper back on the bench as far as he could go.

The big man's face grew steadily redder as he held the guy in place. "How exactly did you mess with him?"

Flipper shot Butch a pleading look.

"Don't look at me," she said with a shrug. "You made your bed. It's time you noticed it's on fire. Answer the man."

"Alright. Look, he was saying his grandad had been mugged, and he kept asking me who did it. How would I know that? And frankly, I resent the implication that I hang around with criminals."

Bunny spoke through gritted teeth. "How did you mess with him?"

"It was a joke," said Flipper weakly. "Anybody would have sussed I was clearly joking."

"So, tell us this joke, so we can all have a good laugh."

"He kept demanding a name ..."

"And what did you give him?"

"Gerry Lamkin," blurted Davey, unable to take the tension any longer. "He told him that Gerry Lamkin was running a crew that was robbing people like that."

"Gerry fecking Lamkin," spat Bunny in an ominous growl.

"Who is Gerry Lamkin?" asked Butch.

Bunny gave her a confused look for a moment before righting himself. "He's probably been in prison most of the time you've been stationed in Dublin. Grade-A violent loon. An entire picnic short of a picnic. Luckily for this idiot, he's still in Mountjoy."

At this, Flipper tried to shrink down on the bench, as if attempting to become small enough to disappear completely. "Actually ..."

"He can't be," said Bunny. "Nobody is letting Gerry Lamkin out early."

"Good behaviour," confirmed Davey.

Bunny shook his head in disbelief. "Only because anyone with an ounce of sense wouldn't go within six feet of him." He turned back to Flipper who was clenching his fists so tightly that it was becoming painful. "And you sent a vulnerable kid looking for him."

All bravado gone, Flipper was now cowering before Bunny. "It was a joke," he repeated in a hoarse whisper.

"Do you see me laughing?"

Butch moved over towards her partner and placed a hand on his arm. "Easy," she said in a soft voice, before raising it to speak to Flipper. "And did you tell him how he could find this Gerry Lamkin?"

Flipper spoke to the ground in front of him. "I said he could be found either up at Phelan's pub or over at Shotz – the snooker club."

"Right," said Butch. "The roughest boozer in Dublin or the underworld's snooker establishment of choice. Course you did. Is there anything else we need to know?" She looked between Flipper and Davey, who both shook their heads.

"OK, Bunny." She was alarmed to see that he was still staring fixedly at Flipper. "Bunny," she repeated. "We don't have time for this idiot. Deccie – remember?"

After a couple of long seconds, Bunny nodded. "Right. Flipper – you are now officially in my bad books. In fact, I'm opening a new book just for you. You have two choices; one, I can leave here right now and, at some point next year, you won't know how, you won't know when, but I will exact my revenge on you for your funny little joke that has put a young lad in danger. And believe you me, it'll be worth waiting for ..."

"I just—"

"Or," continued Bunny. "You can get it out of the way right this minute. Tonight. Y'know, so you can enjoy Christmas."

Flipper looked up at this. "Really?"

"Really," Bunny confirmed. "We are walking away now. If you'd like to call it even, by the time we've travelled the one hundred or so feet back to the bridge there, you will have leaped – not slowly climbed in, mind, leaped – into the middle of the canal."

"But it's freezing," said Flipper.

Bunny's voice came out in a guttural snarl. "I wasn't suggesting it because I thought it would be a pleasant experience. The choice is yours."

Before anyone could say anything else, Bunny turned on his heels and strode back towards the bridge with such purpose that Butch had to hurry to catch up with him.

She gave it a couple of seconds before speaking. "Christ, Bunny, I'm getting a bit sick of feeling like the clown whose job it is to distract the rampaging bull. Do you want to get a grip on that temper of yours?"

"A nice old man is in hospital and a young lad is in danger."

"I get all that, but you going off like a Roman candle isn't going to help anyone. First Grainger and now that idiot. Dial it back, OK?"

Bunny gave a half-nod as he strode.

"Great. I'll take that as an emphatic, 'Yes, Butch. Sorry, Butch. Won't happen again, Butch.' Do you want to split up?"

"Good idea. You can drop me back at my car."

"Right. So, snooker club or pub?"

"I should probably take the snooker club. Jacinta Phelan isn't my biggest fan right now."

"Look at you, winning friends and influencing people all over town."

They were a few feet from the footpath on top of the bridge when they heard the loud splash followed promptly by an expletive roared with such ferocity that birds flew out of nearby trees.

As Bunny turned left to head back to where Butch's car was parked, he shouted over his shoulder without a backwards glance, "It was just a joke, Flipper! Just a joke. You're still in my bad books."

# CHAPTER TEN

Detective Inspector Fintan O'Rourke approached the door of the most powerful office in Irish policing and paused.

In his earliest days living in Dublin, as a wet-behind-the-ears probationary garda, O'Rourke had briefly shared a room in a rented flat with a fellow probationary officer by the name of Seamus Geraghty. Seamus came from a tiny town in Clare where everybody knew everybody else and, more importantly, everybody else's business. It was fair to say that moving to the bright lights of the big city was a dream come true for young Seamus. He subsequently spent every waking hour, that wasn't taken up with law enforcement, attempting to meet, greet and bed members of the opposite sex. His single-minded dedication to this goal was, in its way, impressive, although it must be said that quality control was ... variable.

This meant that young Fintan O'Rourke would often come home from a long shift to be greeted by the sight of a sports sock hanging on the door handle of the bedroom, the system the industrious Seamus had come up with to signal when he had company. Usually, the animalistic grunting noises were enough of a clue, but it was good to have a fallback. Sick to his back teeth of sleeping on a two-person couch several nights a week while glaring at the door to the room he was paying rent for, O'Rourke had moved out to his own place as soon as possible. The last he had heard of Seamus Geraghty, he was back home in Clare, having left the Gardaí to go into politics. He was now a proud father to a whopping seven children, having married what his bio amusingly described as "his childhood sweetheart".

What made O'Rourke think back to those heady days was the fact that something was hanging on the door handle to this particular office. It was not a sports sock in need of a wash but rather what appeared to be a white false beard. Commissioner Gareth Ferguson had a reputation for being many things, but nowhere on that list was "philanderer". O'Rourke regarded the beard for a moment, before clearing his throat and knocking.

"Come in," came the barked response from within.

He entered to find the head of the Irish police force sitting with his feet up on his impressive mahogany desk, holding a large whiskey in one hand and a cigar in the other, while dressed head to toe in the red suit that went with the beard.

Commissioner Ferguson regarded O'Rourke with hooded eyes over the rim of his whiskey glass. "I appreciate that, given the circumstances, Fintan, you may have an urge to make some remark about wanting to sit on my knee and tell me what you'd like for Christmas. I strongly suggest you resist that urge."

O'Rourke stood to attention. "The thought never crossed my mind, sir."

"Superb lying as always, Fintan." He nodded towards the chair opposite. "Take a seat."

O'Rourke did as instructed.

"And for what it is worth, I feel moved to apologise for calling you in, given the time of year. Did I derail anything significant?"

"Dinner with my in-laws, sir."

"I see. Should I be thanking you, or should you be thanking me?"

O'Rourke gave a tight smile. "A bit of both." The reality was it depended greatly on how much umbrage his wife was going to take at his unscheduled departure. The initial look she had shot him over the table as he left had not been encouraging.

"If it's any consolation," continued the Commissioner, "I guarantee your night has not gone as badly as mine. The reason for that we will get to presently, but then there is this" – Ferguson waved his cigar-holding hand at his outfit – "utter disaster. As I assume you know, given the spontaneous and much-appreciated show of largess that led to every senior garda in the country independently purchasing tickets for its annual raffle, my wife is the patron of a well-known children's charity."

O'Rourke nodded. He'd bought three.

"Every year they have a large fundraising dinner where the great and good – by which I mean anybody who can afford two grand for a table – get fed and watered while patting themselves on the back for being philanthropists. This year, it was being held at the National Gallery, where there is currently a highly prestigious collection of touring art from the Louvre."

"Yes," offered O'Rourke, as there had been rather a lot about it in the media. "I hear the exhibit is very good."

Ferguson shrugged. "Possibly. I don't know. I consider myself a cultured man, but I'll be honest, most such art leaves me cold. I mean, portraits and all that. Seems to be all aristocratic men staring deep into the eyes of their horses, and partially clad women gazing wistfully into the distance – possibly contemplating how to get the men to look at them instead of the horses."

"Still," said O'Rourke, trying to be diplomatic, "I'm sure they made a wonderful backdrop for the meal."

"I wouldn't know. You see, as part of the fun – and I use the word under duress – every year at this do they have a 'celebrity'" – the amount of disdain Ferguson packed into the four syllables of the word was quite impressive – "Santa Claus to hand out pressies, take photographs, et cetera, et cetera. Formerly, it had been entertainers, politicians, journalists – a weatherman last year, which went down particularly badly for understandable reasons – and, this year, it was supposed to be a certain former member of an eighties boy band. I take it you can guess which one?"

"Ah."

"Yes, that one. The one we are currently investigating because him surrounding himself with teenage girls in 1988 was cute, but him attempting to do the same in the year 2000 is at best grim, and at worst, well, enquiries are ongoing."

"I see the problem," said O'Rourke.

"I thought you might. Unfortunately, you're looking at what was the proposed solution. The committee, in their infinite wisdom, thought the most highly ranked member of the Garda Síochána fulfilling the role would be a hoot – especially since, let's be honest with ourselves here, options were very limited, given the notice."

"I'm sure people would be understanding."

"Oh," said Ferguson, "that was not the problem. Quite the contrary, in fact. The announcement of yours truly led to a surge in ticket sales."

"That's good," said O'Rourke, instantly regretting his choice of words as the Commissioner's scowl told a very different tale. "That's not good?"

"No. As well as bankers and property developers and whatnot, do you know who else has a couple of grand in disposable income lying about the place?"

O'Rourke winced.

Ferguson nodded. "Now you're getting it. I turned up and the front three tables alone were all populated by subjects of ongoing investigations. It seems organised crime are particularly adept at organising themselves a fun night out. I would imagine they were considering it money very well spent if they could get a nice picture of themselves sitting on the head of the police force's knee, telling him what they would like for Christmas."

"Did you—"

"I got the hell out of there. I was really hoping for some suitable cover, like an armed uprising or the assassination of the taoiseach but, much to my regret and ongoing disbelief, neither of those things have transpired. This means I am in for the most ice cold of Christmases, have no doubt of that."

"Most unfortunate, sir. I'm sure if you explain the circumstances, your wife will understand."

Ferguson knocked back the rest of his whiskey and pulled a sour expression that may have had nothing to do with the taste of the drink. "If you honestly believe that, Fintan, then you're not half the detective I thought you were." He drew his legs off the table and sat upright, flicking the ash at the end of his cigar into a handily shaped award that sat on his desk. "So that explains what I'm doing here, but rest assured it does not explain why you are here. While misery does indeed love company, even I am not callous enough to call you in just so you can sympathise with my awful night. We have a problem. Actually, we have two problems." The Commissioner pursed his lips and scratched his chin with his free hand. "Indeed, you could present it as three interlinking problems." He glanced at the bottle of whiskey sitting on his desk. "Before I get into that, I feel obliged to ask if you would like a drink, Fintan?"

"No, thank you, sir."

"Yes. I shall also refrain. The last thing I need is to be pulled over by one of the many drink-driving checkpoints that I banged the table for. The irony alone could prove fatal." He sat back in his chair. "Problem number one.... Does the name Accardi mean anything to you?"

"Should it?"

"Not unless you're a student of continental politics, but I always like to give my officers the chance to impress me. As I'm sure you are aware, Italy traditionally has more elections in the average year than most countries have bank holidays. I suppose we should not be surprised that the people who gave us opera have a rather dramatic disposition. Amidst that perpetual chaos, as a rock in a storm-thrashed sea, stands one name – Accardi. Flavio Accardi. A man who has been head of Banca d'Italia, or the Italian central bank to you and me, for nigh on two decades.

"Politicians come and go but, much to the relief of Brussels, old Flavio is there, day in and day out, a steadying hand on the economic tiller. A fiscal conservative entirely above corruption for the simple reason that the man already has more money than God. Or, to be exact, he's married to it. His wife, Marta Accardi, is the eldest daughter of the Caputo family, who are the closest thing the modern day can offer in terms of Caesars. I'm told they own most of everything worth having, and a lot more besides. Whole industries. Large chunks of cities. And art, of course, because it seems to exist primarily to allow the filthy rich to keep score. The Accardis are about to be announced as the proud patrons building a state-of-the-art something or other at our very own University of Limerick, where, entirely by coincidence, their youngest daughter is studying. You may be wondering why I am offering you quite such a detailed back story?"

"The daughter?" asked O'Rourke.

"The daughter," confirmed Ferguson. "As of two weeks ago, she disappeared."

O'Rourke raised his eyebrows. "How is this not a massive story?"

"Well now – asking the pertinent questions as always, Fintan. 'Disappeared' is probably the wrong word. The more precise phrasing would be that she has 'gone off the reservation'. She is believed to have fallen under the spell of one Bobby Walsh, a young lothario from Limerick with a cheeky glint in his eye and a heart full of criminal intent. As a side note, you have to be a little bit proud that, as a country, we are producing the kind of Don Juan that can sweep an Italian heiress off her feet. Clearly, what they say about the accent is true. The problem is, for the last few weeks Bobby and, we believe, his witless cousin, are on quite the little crime spree, and they've taken the young Ms Accardi along for the ride."

"Now," he continued, taking a puff on his cigar, "you may be thinking that this is the kind of thing that we, the police force, traditionally take a dim view of. In fact, I've given you most of the pieces. As a political animal yourself, Fintan, would you like to fill in the rest?"

"The Accardi family don't want the embarrassment?"

Ferguson jabbed his cigar in O'Rourke's direction. "Ding, ding, ding! If I had not left my bag of pressies behind when I had to flee the

National Gallery, you'd certainly be getting one. As far as they are concerned, she is a young girl bamboozled by the silver tongue and high cheekbones of criminal elements. And when I say that is what the Accardi family believe, I mean it is the story that their government, our government, and everybody in between, is going with."

"Which you don't agree with?"

"It's not that I don't believe it," said Ferguson. "I have every sympathy for someone young and foolish getting themselves swept up in something they don't understand. I wore a tie-dye poncho for two whole weeks in the sixties. It's just that, as an officer of the law, I don't care. By which I mean, it's not my job to care. Call me old-fashioned, but when crimes are being committed, what I think we should do – the 'we' here being, you know, the Garda Síochána – is arrest those involved and let the lawyers deal with the whole punishment side of the crime-and-punishment fandango. But they don't want that to happen because of – join in for the chorus ..."

"The embarrassment."

"The embarrassment," confirmed Ferguson. "Instead, what we have is an unofficial task force run by your friend and mine, not to mention the nephew of the sainted Minister for Justice, DI Grainger."

"Oh dear."

"Yes. An embarrassment to the force running an embarrassment to the force while being aided by a bunch of Italians because, oh yes, our political masters also agreed to that defecation on the concept of jurisdiction. Up until this point, our intrepid trio's little crime spree comprised non-violent crime, as far as we know – or rather it did, up until today. An elderly gentleman was robbed and violently assaulted on Capel Street by a gang whose description matches that of exactly who you think it does. Prior to this, they'd been operating down in Limerick and Cork, but it seems they have now decided to hit the capital – with 'hit' being the operative word."

"So, we're now turning a blind eye to violent crime?"

Ferguson moved his cigar round in his mouth so vigorously that it looked as if he were about to chew the end off it. "Yes. And believe me" – he held his thumb and forefinger half an inch apart – "I am this close to throwing my toys out of the pram. The only reason I haven't is that they half want me to. There are those in our government who favour a new, more forward-looking form of policing. What that means in practical terms is instead of working for the people, we should work for the politicians. They wouldn't phrase it like that, of course. I've been in plenty of meetings, and believe me, the abuses of the English language they come up with *not* to say that exact thing should literally be criminal."

"I am a dinosaur. A relic. A roadblock to progress, and that progress takes the form of my recently anointed assistant commissioner." Ferguson narrowed his eyes. "The ability for your face to remain completely expressionless, Fintan, is a genuine talent. Don't worry, I am not expecting you to express any opinion on the snivelling little weasel who would step over my still-warm body to get into this chair. I didn't call you in to curry your support as, quite apart from anything else, the people who make such decisions do not care one jot what the rank and file think. No. You are here because of problem number three."

O'Rourke, sensing where this was heading, held up his hand. "Excuse me, sir. Would I be right in assuming that somehow problem number three involves Detective Bernard McGarry?"

"What gave it away?"

O'Rourke resisted the temptation to let his body sag, his worst fears having been confirmed. "I'm honestly not trying to be unhelpful but, as I have mentioned previously, I hold no sway over Bunny McGarry and have absolutely no ability to control him. Frankly, sir, I'm not sure what you expect me to be able to do."

Ferguson puffed on his cigar. "Feel better for getting that out, do you, Fintan?"

O'Rourke held his tongue.

The Commissioner leaned forward and stubbed out the remains of his cigar and left it resting on the award made from Waterford Crystal. He picked up his gold-plated lighter and placed both his elbows on the table. "Don't worry, I'm not expecting you to fly the aeroplane. I'm just looking for your opinion on whether it's going to hit the mountain."

O'Rourke licked his lips. "I'm afraid you've lost me on that one, sir."

Ferguson settled back in his chair and flicked his lighter into life, before running the fingers of his left hand absent-mindedly through the flame. "It seems, through a truly bizarre twist of fate, given their recent history, that Grainger's and McGarry's paths were destined to cross again. God does indeed enjoy loading the dice. I don't have the full whys and wherefores, but it would seem McGarry knows the poor man who was assaulted and robbed, and he has taken an interest in proceedings. He and DI Grainger had a coming-together a couple of hours ago, which resulted in McGarry – and Detective Pamela Cassidy, for some inexplicable reason – being suspended from duty."

O'Rourke raised his eyebrows. "Grainger hasn't got that kind of power."

"No, but my second-in-command does, and they are two peas in the same shitty pod."

"The Garda Representative Association will not be happy."

"Of that I have no doubt. Come to that, I'm not happy either. The question is, what am I going to do about it?" Ferguson wound his neck back in. "Did you just smirk, O'Rourke?"

"Sorry, sir."

"Is there something funny here that I'm missing?"

"Well, I think the word 'funny' is probably inappropriate, given the situation, but ..."

"But?"

"DI Grainger wants Bunny out of his way so he can't interfere with his investigation?"

"Yes."

"And he thought the best way to do that was to suspend Bunny."

Commissioner Ferguson looked up at the ceiling and the hint of a smile played across his lips. "Ah, I see your point. The last time that happened, when he found the homicidal pyromaniacs behind the homeless attacks that Grainger's then task force could not ..."

"He was on sabbatical," finished O'Rourke. "And DI Grainger has just given him quite a lot of free time ..."

"Not to mention a considerable amount of additional motivation," continued Ferguson.

"Indeed, sir. Bunny McGarry, when he is on the force, is difficult to keep in line at the best of times."

"But now he's temporarily off the force, placing him completely beyond my control. So, as Commissioner, I am not responsible for anything he does."

"Yes, sir. In his attempt to maintain control of the situation, DI Grainger inadvertently unleashed the forces of chaos."

"'Cry "Havoc!", and let slip the dogs of war.'" A broad grin spread across Commissioner Ferguson's face as he reached across the desk and grabbed the bottle of whiskey. "I think I shall treat myself to a taxi home and have another drink. Would you care to join me, Fintan?"

"Just the one, sir."

"Good man," he said with a waggle of his eyebrows. "It is Christmas, after all."

# CHAPTER ELEVEN

On the surface, Shots snooker club could be seen as an excellent example of nominative determinism, the pavement outside the front door having seen not one, but two shooting incidents in the last three years. Those who knew better knew that it was owned by Patsy Clark, a bloke from Donegal who had now "retired" to Spain. Before that he had enjoyed a criminal career that had been remarkably light on time served, if even half the rumours were to be believed.

Regardless of what Patsy Clark may or may not have done, his known-associates list read like a *Who's Who* of Irish crime. Unfortunately, some of the aforementioned "who's" didn't get on, hence the occasional outbreaks of gun violence. In those circumstances, most people would have either shut the establishment or at least rebranded. To be fair to Patsy, he had taken the second option – technically. As Bunny crossed South Great George's Street and made his way towards the unremarkable door that sat between an Indian restaurant and a plumbing-supply store, he noticed that the second S in the word "Shots" on the small sign above the door had been replaced with a Z. Normally, Bunny would have found that immensely annoying, but there was currently no available space on his list of irritations.

He'd heard that a growing school of thought believed that women made superior door staff to men as they were far better at de-escalating confrontations. This notion stood in stark contrast to the old-school idea that door security was best handled by finding the most immense human being possible, sticking him in a monkey suit, and plonking him on the doorstep to glare at people while obsessing about what was and was not classed as a trainer.

Patsy Clark, it seemed, subscribed squarely to the second school of thought. Bunny was still a few feet away when the iceberg in a tuxedo guarding the door held up a shovel-sized hand.

"Private members' club."

"I know," said Bunny. "Hello, and Merry Christmas by the way. I just need to nip inside for a mo, as I'm looking for a friend."

"The gay bar is back over the road there," said the gorilla with a self-satisfied smirk, amused by his own well-worn line.

"It is. And the stand-up comedy club's down in Temple Bar. Best of luck in your next career. In the meantime, Patsy knows me." This was technically true. Bunny had, after all, arrested his brother for being a violent pimp. That particular collar had earned him an official warning on the excessive force front. He had considered having it framed. "I will just be inside for about one second."

"It will be about one second," said the bouncer. "It'll be within one second of one second. It'll be zero seconds, Detective McGarry." Bunny guessed the man didn't own a mirror as he had the type of dental work that was not designed for the broad smile he now gave. "Yeah, I know who you are."

Bunny nodded. He had been deliberately avoiding going down the police line. Shotz was not the kind of place that would welcome the Garda Síochána with anything less than a search warrant. "Lovely to know my reputation precedes me. Look, I'm not here on business. There is a young fellow I know, only thirteen years of age, and I've been told he might be in here."

"Well, he's not, and for what it's worth, when you do see him, tell 'im that trying to convince people he's actually thirty-six years old with a wasting disease is in poor taste."

"Hang on, he's been here already?"

Despite the absence of a neck, the man managed to nod. "Only a few minutes ago. I mean, I'm assuming we're talking about the same fella. We don't get many kids trying to get in here. When his first story didn't work, he also tried to claim he was an undercover representative from Guinness. He told me if I didn't let him in, we were going to lose our licence. Like Guinness give out the liquor licences."

"Yeah, that sounds like him alright. Did he say where he was going?"

"What am I? His babysitter? I just told him to bugger off and away he ran with his tail between his legs."

Bunny shook his head. "If only. I'm afraid he's not the run-away-with-his-tail-between-his-legs type. How long ago was this?"

"I dunno. Ten, maybe fifteen minutes."

"And is Gerry Lamkin in there?"

The bouncer hesitated.

"I'll take that as a yes."

"I didn't say that."

"No, but if you ever start playing poker, let me know. I could do with the money. Now, I strongly suggest you let me in, because I guarantee the young fella is inside by now."

"What? Are you drunk? There's only one way in – and he didn't get by me."

"Ah, but there is never just one way in, is there? There will be a deliveries entrance, or a fire escape, or a something. He can be alarmingly resourceful when motivated, and believe you me, he is motivated."

This caused the bouncer to wrinkle his immense brow momentarily before laughing out loud and wafting Bunny away. "Yeah. Get out of it. You're more full of shit than he is. There is no—"

He was interrupted by the sound of shouting, breaking furniture, and then something large and heavy shattering. It was coming from upstairs.

Bunny cocked his head. "That'll be him now."

Bunny was lighter on his feet than people expected, and he dodged the bouncer with ease to make it to the top of the stairs first. What greeted him could best be described as a tableau of frozen chaos.

The L-shaped room contained nine full-sized snooker tables complete with tent-like overhead lights that illuminated the baize while casting the rest of the room into puddles of murky darkness. Eight of them were arranged to Bunny's left on the long side of the room, while one stood under a fancier-looking series of lights in the stubbier end of the L-shape. The area also contained Shotz's one lone pool table, which sat beside a jukebox that had been plugged out in the last century, just after it was last dusted.

Two of the tables on Bunny's left were in use, although the quartet of players were looking towards the corner of the room, dumbfounded. The corner was home to the establishment's bar, behind which stood a red-headed woman of about thirty who was sporting an eyepatch over her right eye. In stark contrast to the rest of the room, the woman was calmly cleaning glasses. In front of her, on the near side of the bar, two men lay groaning on the ground, holding their hands to their bloodied faces. One of them was failing to staunch the flow of blood from his injuries as a large red stain was forming on the carpet beneath him. Deccie, wielding a cue, was standing atop the particularly fancy-looking snooker table.

"Declan Fadden," hissed Bunny, "get down this instant."

"No can do, boss. Got to retain the high ground."

"You're in a fecking snooker club, not the Battle of Iwo Jima. Get down!"

Deccie ignored him. Instead, he kept his attention focused on where the rest of the room was also looking.

He had a couple more tattoos than the last time Bunny had seen him, but the figure of Gerry Lamkin was unmistakable. The hard-to-fathom part of the picture was that he was on his knees in front of a now-empty plinth, an unhappy assortment of lumps of plaster of Paris scattered across the floor in front of him. He kept picking up various pieces, holding them side by side in the hope that they would magically fit back together, before discarding them, muttering disconsolately to himself as he did so.

"Ah no, ah no, ah no."

The remains of a bar stool lay to one side.

"Jesus, Hazel," said the bouncer. "What the hell happened?"

"Well, Deano," began the barmaid, calmly setting down one glass before picking up another to continue cleaning, "since you ask, it's been an eventful couple of minutes." She spoke in a bizarrely flat monotone. "The young fella over there appeared out of the ladies' toilets, which struck me as strange as I'm the only lady on the premises. I was in there ten minutes ago and I'd have noticed his presence while taking a pee. If men, even little ones, are climbing through that small window, Uncle Patsy is gonna have to brick it up. Having the ladies' to myself is one of the few perks of this job. But I digress ..."

She put down the glass and began work on another one, holding it up to the light for a second of critical regard, before commencing polishing it. "The young lad walks up to the bar and asks is anybody here Gerry Lamkin. Gerry duly identifies himself, at which point the young fella demands his granny's ring back. Gerry says he doesn't know what he's talking about. The young fella says he knows for a fact that Gerry was behind it getting stolen, and he demands its return in no uncertain terms. This does not go over well with Gerry, who stands up to direct the young fella to leave the premises immediately. The young fella then – in a move that was high on bravery if low on common sense – escalates matters dramatically by sucker-punching Gerry right in the bollocks."

Hazel nodded towards one of the bleeding men lying on the floor in front of her bar. "Karl there, in a monumentally poor assessment of the situation, laughed. Gerry wasn't ready to see the funny side of things." She tipped her head towards the other bleeding man. "Donal – he was just in the wrong place at the wrong time. The two boys dispatched, Gerry then turned his attention to his attacker. He picked up his bar stool and threw it at the young fella. He missed."

"Oh dear God," said the bouncer, in the kind of ominous tones concomitant with having been told that nuclear weapons have just been launched and the odds on soft-boiling an egg before the apocalypse were, at best, fifty-fifty.

"Yeah," continued Hazel, "he missed his target, but he unfortunately hit Uncle Patsy's most prized possession – the signed plaster cast of the hands of the snooker legend Alex 'Hurricane' Higgins. Patsy is mental for the man. It's verging on the homoerotic if you ask me – not that anybody does."

Hazel noticed Bunny looking at her. "In case you're wondering, and I can see that you are, I've got this thing called Creutzman Belling Syndrome." She pointed a finger at her own forehead. "I had a whack on the head when I was sixteen and it did some damage. Now I'm unable to lie. It's a very rare condition. They did an article about me in the *Independent*."

"Right," said Bunny, only half focused on what she was saying as he tried to figure out how to manage the situation. "You can only tell the truth? That must be awkward for you."

She nodded. "Well, let me put it this way – I used to have two eyes."

"Oh."

"Yeah. I work here because I'm Uncle Patsy's favourite niece. I used to be the second most untouchable thing in this place." She looked down at Gerry. "But I think I've just received an upgrade. It turns out his nuts getting Pearl Harboured is nowhere near the worst thing that happened to poor Gerry tonight."

Gerry took a last look at the shattered remnants of the Hurricane Higgins shrine and stood up, patting the dust off his jeans. "This is going to go very badly for me. Very badly." The man's voice was disconcertingly soft and melodious. He shook his head wistfully. "Serves me right for throwing things about."

The one time that Gerry and Bunny had met previously, Gerry had taken exception to one of his neighbours mistreating a dog. He had strong opinions on such things. The Lamkin family were very well known to the Gardaí by that point, so much so that a plan had been in place. A dozen guards had shown up. Gerry represented the kind of call any law enforcement official on the planet hated. The man had only ever known violence, and he was terrifyingly good at it. Most criminals had more sense than to throw a punch at a member of the Garda Síochána, given how the courts took a poor view of such things. Gerry didn't think like that. When the red mist descended, there was no control. Men such as Gerry got treated as if they were a one-man riot, and were met with overwhelming force for the safety of all concerned.

Thankfully, on that occasion, Gerry had come peacefully, and Bunny had been in the patrol car that'd taken him in. Gerry had chatted amicably about his love of animals in general, and how he'd never met a dog he didn't like. The memory that had stayed with Bunny was of him using the phrase "there are no bad dogs, only bad owners". He'd wondered if there had been any self-awareness in it.

As Bunny had heard it, the Lamkins were one of those families blighted by violent men who begot more violent men. Even with that low bar, Gerry's father, Gerry Senior, had been the worst of the worst. A pure sadist. Teachers had reported young Gerry turning up to school, when he turned up at all, with bruising and worse. By all rights, he should have been taken into care, but the fear Gerry Senior engendered had allowed for a shameful lapse whereby several people had not done their jobs. Gerry Lamkin Junior was what happened when those in a position of authority let a worst-case scenario play out rather than deal with it.

After the incident regarding the mistreated dog, Gerry had been let go without charge. When he'd kicked the door in, the neighbour had leaped out of his own window rather than face him, and had broken his leg upon landing. Not only did the man refuse to press charges, he'd pleaded with the Gardaí to assure Gerry that, going forward, that dog would eat nothing but steak.

People who heard such stories before seeing the man in person were always surprised to realise that Gerry Lamkin stood at only five feet eight in height. His shaven head took nothing away from the almost childlike dimpled grin that could often be found across his

94

face. As he looked around the room and saw Bunny, there it was again, every scintilla of it genuine.

"Ah, Bunny McGarry – is that you?"

"It is, Gerry."

"Long time no see. How've you been?"

"Up and down – yourself?"

"Ah, incarcerated mostly. Only got out last week. Good behaviour." Gerry gave a little shrug and another flash of that weirdly childish grin. "I'm as surprised as you are. Turns out the meds they had me on were doing the job. Unfortunately, what with the cutbacks and everything, they didn't give me any of them to bring with me. I've been trying to use the drink but it's not the same."

"Is that right?" said Bunny. "Seems like a false economy, alright."

"Always the way, though, isn't it? Are you here to play some snooker?"

"Nah," said Bunny, "not my game."

"Mine neither," agreed Gerry. "I only come here because it's quiet. Or at least it was. Speaking of which, nice seeing you, but if you'll excuse me ..." He sounded oddly resigned, as if it was his turn to put the bins out. "Now I'm going to have to beat the shit out of that young fella."

Bunny glanced at the bouncer, who noticeably took a step back.

"Whoa, whoa, whoa," said Bunny. "No need for that. You wouldn't hit a kid, Gerry. He's only eleven years old."

"As of last Wednesday, I'm thirteen," protested Deccie.

Bunny glared at him. "What did I tell you about shutting up?"

"Thirteen is plenty old enough to catch a beating," said Gerry, his tone cheerful. "So is eleven, for that matter. I got hit regularly when I was younger than that – never did me any harm."

"Sorry to interrupt," said Hazel the barmaid. "I'm doing a part-time degree in psychology at UCD. Do you mind if I use that quote for a paper I'm writing?"

Bunny fixed his glare on her.

"What?" she objected, tapping her forehead. "Creutzman Belling, remember? Don't blame me, blame the half-blind prick driving the forklift."

"Anyway," said Bunny, turning back to Gerry. "I'm going to have a very strong word with that young man, and trust me, he will offer an incredibly sincere and grovelling apology."

The look Bunny shot in Deccie's direction was thankfully enough to stop whatever words were about to come out of the lad's mouth.

"He accused me of stealing his granny's ring," said Gerry. "I greatly resent the implication. I've never been a thief, Bunny – you know that."

"I do. He's a young fella, he's had a very traumatic day, and some gobshite sent him your way as a stupid joke."

"OK," said Gerry, scratching at his chin. "You're an honourable man, Bunny. Just tell me who it was who gave him my name and I'll deal with the situation."

Bunny paused for a few seconds then shook his head. "While I'm tempted, I can't do that, Gerry, but you have my word – I will deal with it."

Gerry sighed. "That's a shame. I'd like to help you out, but it's a matter of principle. My character has been maligned and my testicles assaulted. Somebody must catch a beating for that. Rules are rules."

Out of desperation, Bunny considered threatening to arrest Gerry, but he dismissed the thought as a non-starter. The Gerry Lamkins of this world didn't care a jot about such things. In their messed-up heads, reputation was the only currency that mattered.

"I know you're a reasonable man, Gerry. Now, given the circumstances, I'm willing to look past all of this ..." Bunny jerked his head towards the two men in front of the bar, who had both managed to sit upright again, but were wisely staying put in case standing up was misinterpreted.

"Oh, thanks very much," said the man previously identified as Karl, speaking while clutching his shattered nose.

"But," continued Bunny. "The madness stops now." He eyeballed Deccie. "Like I said, the young lad will be happy to apologise."

"My arse I will!" shouted Deccie, still clutching the snooker cue. "This gobshite has granny's ring."

"He doesn't," hissed Bunny through gritted teeth. "Now, shut up, Deccie. That's an order."

"Apologies don't matter now," said Gerry. "A line has been crossed. Steps must be taken. And afterwards, if the young fella tells me who gave him this bad information, you can be certain I will deal with them too. I'm a very reasonable man."

"Fair enough," said Bunny. "In which case, would it be acceptable if I stood in for the young fella?"

"What?"

"Consider me his second, if you want."

"Really?" said Gerry.

Bunny nodded.

Gerry ran his tongue around his mouth as he considered the proposal. "That's very good of you, Bunny. I'll be honest, and no offence intended, but I would be happier fighting yourself. Much more sporting. I wouldn't like to feel like a bully. I hate bullies."

Bunny had no doubt Gerry Lamkin meant every word he said. In his mind, such things made perfect sense. He bobbed his head in assent and scanned the room. "We should probably clear a bit of space, though. You know, so we don't damage anything." Bunny pointed at the remains of the Hurricane Higgins shrine lying at Gerry's feet. "Patsy is already going to be upset."

"That's very true," agreed Gerry. "I'll probably end up in an unmarked grave in the Wicklow Mountains for that one."

"I'm sure you won't," said Bunny, making a conscious decision to ignore Hazel, who was stood behind Gerry, nodding in agreement with Gerry's original statement. Instead, Bunny pointed at Deccie. "I reckon if we shift that snooker table over to the corner, that'd give us a good open space. Declan, get off there now."

"But," said Deccie, eyeing Gerry suspiciously, "he's going to batter me."

"Course he won't," said Bunny. "We've come to an understanding."

"Absolutely," concurred Gerry, sounding positively cheerful. "And I hope you find whoever nicked your granny's ring. That's an awful thing. My granny was the only person who was ever nice to me, God rest her. In fact, if you find this thief, send them my way and I'll be happy to deal with them for you."

Deccie's face lit up. "Brilliant. Thanks very much." And with that, he hopped down off the table.

"OK," said Bunny, walking over and positioning himself on the shorter side of the snooker table facing away from the bar. "I'll grab this end – Gerry, you take the other." He pointed at two of the spectators from one of the other tables. "Do me a favour, boys, and grab a side each there, will you?"

After exchanging a worried glance, the duo set down their cues and took up their positions as requested.

Gerry trotted over to the far side of the table, slapping Bunny amicably on the back as he passed. "Many hands make light work." Once in position, Gerry looked at the other three men. "And remember to lift with the knees," he began earnestly. "I wouldn't want to see anyone injure themselves."

From behind him, Bunny heard Karl of the broken nose make some kind of remark that thankfully went unheard.

"Here we go," said Bunny, taking a firm grip of the underside of the table. "And one. Two. Three. Lift."

All four men heaved in unison. The thing was even heavier than it looked.

"Right," Bunny said through gritted teeth, "I'll go forward. You go back, Gerry. We'll get it into the corner over there."

They began manoeuvring as instructed. Bunny upped the pace.

"Careful now," said Gerry cheerfully. "More haste, less speed."

Bunny sped up more and Gerry threw him a shocked look. The two other men also looked at him in confusion.

"I said, go easy. You'll have me over—"

"Sorry about this, Gerry," muttered Bunny as he surged forward with all his might. The table hurtled into Gerry, slammed him into the wall and pinned him there. The two other men yelped and dropped the table as if it were burning hot.

As Bunny turned to run, he clocked Gerry's expression, which was a mix of physical and emotional hurt, before he grabbed Deccie by the scruff of the neck and charged for the exit as fast as he could.

As the duo darted past the bouncer at the top of the stairs and fled, the last thing Bunny heard was the roar of Gerry Lamkin.

"I'll get you for this, McGarry, ye lying bastard. We had a deal! A DEAL!"

# CHAPTER TWELVE

Stephen McGilloway pursed his lips and considered the large charcuterie plate in front of him warily. It was enough for eight people according to the lady in the shop – what with all the cured meats, plethora of cheeses, fruit, dried fruit, three different types of crackers and half a dozen types of chutneys, quince, and jams. Almost certainly far too much but he had panicked. After all, what were you supposed to feed a hooker?

There was no guide for such eventualities – he'd checked. When he'd started to panic earlier in the evening, he had done an internet search for the phrase "what to feed an escort", but all it had given him was a list of things not to eat, which, worryingly, included cheese. Most people didn't have this problem, but then, most people probably took their escort out for a meal. Stephen couldn't do that. He knew people in this town and, more importantly, people knew him. Insurance may have the image of being a dull industry, but it was something everybody needed, which meant you ended up knowing everybody. Besides, Dublin was a small city, and there was nowhere he could have gone for dinner with a young woman who was very definitely not his wife and felt relaxed.

This had all seemed like such a good plan last week. Samantha had taken the twins to New York with her sister for a pre-Christmas shopping trip. It had been his treat. She and he had not been getting on very well lately and the mini-break was an olive branch, albeit an expensive one. She had all but accused him of having an affair, which was completely untrue, and he had been, as far as he was concerned, rightly outraged by the accusation.

Had he considered an affair? Absolutely, but the concept of holding people responsible for what they were thinking about doing was an Orwellian nightmare. People think about killing other people all the time, but you can't lock them up for that. Had he been tempted? Sure – but quite aside from any other considerations, the opportunity had not arisen. As the saying went, it took two to tango. Seeing as Samantha had used his snoring as an excuse to sleep in separate bedrooms, Stephen had been dancing on his own for quite some time now. A man has needs. As far as Stephen was concerned, if he was going to do the time, he might as well do the crime.

When he'd thought of this plan last week, it had felt as if everything was falling perfectly into place. That little Chinese woman was coming in tomorrow to do a deep clean – whatever the hell that was – of the entire house, in advance of Samantha's mother coming for Christmas. That meant that any and all evidence would be removed before Samantha's return. It did also mean that he would need to get his visitor out of the house by 9am. He was rather nervous about navigating that. Of all the professions, escorting didn't seem like one that would attract early risers.

In fact, that was a small part of the big problem with all of this that he now felt immensely nervous about. He had made the booking while drunk after coming back from his firm's Christmas do, and he may have been overly ambitious. For a start, he'd booked the girl for the entire night. On sober, nervous reflection, a whole night felt like an awful lot. Aside from the expense, which had been considerable, there was the matter of how you filled the time. He'd dug out a jigsaw puzzle before thinking better of the idea. He knew what was supposed to take up most of the time, but he was a little out of practice, and feeling less and less confident about his abilities to entertain a guest in that manner.

Oh God, what if he couldn't do it at all? He had spent most of the afternoon at work thinking just that, and then trying not to think that, which made him think that all the more. It was like a golfer getting the yips. Trying not to think about something was impossible – like if somebody tells you not to think about zebras. Suddenly, all he could think about was zebras – all of them staring judgementally at him and his flaccid penis.

His solution had been to focus on dealing with other elements of the evening. He'd spent a lot of time selecting music, picking out his outfit – a rather fetching silk jacket that Samantha didn't like – and, of course, the catering. He had considered ordering in a meal from a restaurant, but after a couple of phone calls he'd abandoned the idea as, it being Christmas week, everywhere was run off its feet.

Stephen made himself take a deep breath. Relax. It was just like riding a bike. A 23-year-old hot-bodied brunette bike called Yvette. He'd picked her because her pictures on the website had been most alluring, although they hadn't shown her face. It did of course make sense when he'd thought about it. Discretion was important. Still, it would have been nice to know exactly what he was buying.

Oh no – what if she had a squint? He'd had to change his dentist because that nurse had been cross-eyed and it had been really off-putting. People with wonky eyes really freaked him out. Had done since he was a child. Stephen gulped down a large mouthful of his sauvignon blanc. Get a grip, man. He was just catastrophising now. The girl was a highly skilled professional, undoubtedly good at her job. Why was he worrying about making her comfortable? Surely, her making him comfortable was the whole point. He patted the envelope of cash sitting in the inside pocket of his blazer. This wasn't romance, this was commerce – and he was damn good at that.

He felt reassured. He glanced again at the sports bag on the chair beside him. That at least had been a good idea. If romantic comedies had taught him anything, it was that adulterers were invariably caught out by the discovery of carelessly discarded underwear or jewellery. When the moment was right, he was going to ask his female companion to place all such items into the sports bag for retrieval at a later point. The idea had come to him while he'd been considering the larger issue of venue. In braver moments he'd considered a carnal tour of the entire house, taking in the kitchen, the shower, the gym equipment in what used to be his study, even that bloody greenhouse Samantha had demanded and never used. Those options had been abandoned as the inner insurance man came to the fore. What if the young lady injured herself while in the throes of passion on the kitchen island, or while doing something acrobatic amidst the unfilled potting benches? No, best to stick to more conventional arrangements.

He had considered using the marital bed as a sort of screw-you-if-you-don't-want-to-screw-me to Samantha but had decided against it. He'd also thought about going for the bed in the spare room that he had been "temporarily" sleeping in for the last nine months, which, come to think of it, now held a wardrobe with all his clothes in it. Instead, he'd settled on the idea of using the nanny's bed. Something about that, which he couldn't quite put a finger on, was really working for him.

The hiring of a male nanny had unquestionably been a calculated insult to him. As if he couldn't be trusted with a young nubile female living under the same roof. Stephen had been tempted to make a big deal out of Samantha hiring a twenty-something Swedish male to have at her beck and call, but he'd held off and been glad he had. In hindsight, it was an obvious trap. Andreas was a short, dumpy gay man whom the children admittedly adored, but who wasn't anything that would interest Samantha. He had gone home for Christmas via a knitting convention in Frankfurt, of all things. Still, his bed would do nicely. He could pretend that Yvette was indeed their nanny, which was a rather hot idea.

Stephen took a deep breath. He was feeling better about things now. He looked at his watch – almost time. The front room looked good. Fresh bottle of white wine in an ice bucket on the table beside the charcuterie plate. He'd dimmed the lights, finally getting some use out of the dimmer switches Samantha had decided every room needed, bright lights being one of the many things that gave her a headache.

Oh God – Samantha. Stephen looked around the room. Everywhere his eyes fell, his wife was looking back at him. So many pictures. Would the sight of his wife be a turn-off for Yvette? Or for him, for that matter? Instantly, he was struck by the idea to turn all the pictures around or place them face down. As he raced over to the shelves to do this, he realised just how weird it would look. Would it make him appear nervous? Maybe if she got the impression that he feared his wife, she might think that he would be open to blackmail? Come to think of it, both of those things were correct.

Dead!

That was it. He would tell Yvette his wife was dead. He nodded to himself. Yes. That worked. She had died recently – after a long harrowing illness which he had nursed her through selflessly. Her dying wish had been for him to get back out there. Not to spend his life alone. To find love.

Oh yes – this was brilliant. Women loved shit like that. A man coming to terms with grief after being a steadfast rock in a sea of tragedy for the woman he loved. That sounded exactly like the type of book that Samantha would read on holiday. Grief porn. Yvette could be so turned on, she might not even charge him. Could this be the start of a beautiful relationship? As soon as he had that thought he was reminded of the inconvenient truth that his wife was still very much alive and in remarkably good health. She should be – the woman did that much Pilates and yoga, it was amazing she was as inflexible and uptight as she was.

He briefly considered the idea that New York was a dangerous place but dismissed it. Not that he wanted his wife to be murdered by a gang of knife-wielding delinquents, it was just that the idea in that very moment held a certain appeal. Plus, there was the matter of the twins, and of course he loved them with all his heart. Still, though, they were often fighting with their mother. Maybe they would get on better with someone closer to their own age? Yvette could be not just a stepmother but also a friend.

Stephen was pulled out of his reverie by the sound of the doorbell. Christ, she was here. Suddenly this all felt very real. He was a portly man of nearly fifty who was paying some woman half his age to come round to his house and have sex with him. Dirty, naughty, nasty, things-you-wouldn't-dream-of-asking-your-wife-to-do sex. He took a step towards the living-room door and stopped. He reached down and cupped his meat and two veg then spoke directly to it. "You can do this. You deserve this. Don't let me down."

The doorbell rang again. "Coming."

Stephen drew a deep breath and opened the door. Standing on the other side was a stunningly attractive brunette wearing a fetching red overcoat beneath which he could see a flash of fishnet tights and matching red heels.

The woman favoured him with a dazzling smile as she tilted her head. "Hello, you must be Patrick."

For a couple of seconds he looked at her, confused. "Yes, shit," he managed finally. "Yes. That is me." He had given a fake name. Of course he had.

"Very good," she said in her rather sexy accent that sounded less like the advertised French, and more like Italian. He didn't care. It was working. "I am Yvette."

She reached out her hand and he shook it. It occurred to Stephen in that moment that, in the same way that he wasn't Patrick, she was almost certainly not really called Yvette.

She waited for a couple of seconds and then asked, "Can I come in?"

"Right. Yes. Of course. Sorry." He released her hand, stepped to one side and opened the door fully, only then clocking the car on the other side of the large, pebbled driveway. What looked like a Granada was parked beside his Jag, Samantha's Range Rover and the Ford Fiesta that they had got for Andreas to run errands in.

Yvette followed his gaze. "Ah. That is my driver."

"I see," said Stephen. "Of course. Makes sense. Can't be too careful in your line of work. I mean, in any line of work."

She moved past him into the hallway and, with a last glance at the unfamiliar car, he closed the front door. When he turned around, she had removed her coat and, in that moment, Stephen felt very reassured that he could definitely keep up his end of the bargain. She was wearing a simple black dress that emphasised what a terribly wonderful decision this was after all.

She smiled and held out her coat. "You have a lovely home."

"Thank you. My wife does it. Did it. I mean, past tense. She is dead now. Dead. Yes. Very dead." Stephen was conscious he was babbling, but that awareness didn't seem to allow him to stop. "She died. Not here. Hospital. In a hospital. Terrible disease."

Yvette held a hand to her mouth. "I'm so sorry. What was it?"

Stephen's mouth was suddenly dry. Weirdly, he became acutely aware of the coat rack beside the door, upon which hung several coats belonging to his not-dead, dead wife. He ignored the question, snatched Yvette's coat away with a bit too much force and hung it up. He guided her in the direction of the sitting room. "Charcuterie?"

She paused. "Sorry?"

"You know – cheese, olives, lots of different meats. I'm afraid I'm not much of a cook. My dead wife did all the cooking." Oh Lord, why could he not let the dead-wife thing go?

"I see," she said, in a tone of voice used by someone who was trying to weigh up how mentally unstable the person they were dealing with was. "That sounds fantastic. May I use your bathroom?"

Stephen's hand, which was apparently smarter than the rest of him, automatically pointed down the hall, which made it even more surprising when his mouth caught up and chipped in with, "What for?"

Yvette seemed suitably stumped by the question.

"I mean – number one or number two? Downstairs toilets in some houses don't have the flushing capacity for large loads. I mean – ours does, I mean – mine. Sorry, I haven't got used to referring to the toilets as just mine yet. Grief does terrible things to the mind. Anyway, just down there. Feel free to have a shit if you'd like."

He watched her walk down the hall and then went into the sitting room where he could quietly thump his head against the wall repeatedly. It had started badly and got worse. There were many lowlights, but "feel free to have a shit if you'd like" was going to take quite a lot of beating. One of the photographs he had turned around fell off the shelf beside him. He looked down to see Samantha on a holiday in Greece beaming up at him, her smile seemingly mocking him.

He picked up the picture frame and shoved it behind a cushion on the sofa. He needed a drink in the worst way. Wine would not cut it. He headed over to the drinks cabinet and fixed himself a large vodka tonic. He gulped down a mouthful and winced. OK – on the bright side, it couldn't get any worse. Come to that, she was the professional here. Of course he was nervous. This was his first time doing anything like this. From her perspective, maybe he was just a very nice man who was struggling with the memory of his dead wife for whom he was admittedly unable to come up with a cause of death at short notice.

He should have got some cocaine. He had also been thinking about that. He never used it much – only the once, but it was the kind of thing that hookers liked, wasn't it? When he said he'd only had it the once, that had been at a company retreat. He had walked into the disabled toilets in search of somewhere to alleviate the pressures of an excessively carb-heavy meal without being overheard, only to find Danny and Amir from actuaries doing lines off the cistern.

It had been awkward. He didn't know them well, and they had been caught bang to rights. He had laughed it off, wanting to appear cool to the younger men. Amir had then offered him a line and, not wanting to look like a square, he had done some. For a while he had felt nothing, then he had felt fantastic and, for some reason, explained to Cathy from admin for thirty minutes how he was going to open his own scuba-diving business despite not being able to swim. Then his chest had grown tight, and it had felt like he was having a panic attack. He'd ended up going back to his room early, claiming a headache, and had spent the entire night sitting up, paranoid that he was about to be drug-tested by the suspicious-looking man down at reception.

Overall, it had not been a great experience, but then, maybe he hadn't done it right. If it helped to relax Yvette, he would have been fine with it. Amir had since moved on to another company, but Danny was still with them. Stephen had dropped over to his desk yesterday but, after some rather awkward football banter, he had left again. It turned out slipping the phrase 'where would I get hold of some class A drugs, please?' into casual conversation was not as easy as he'd thought it would be. He had gone back to his office and ordered the bloody charcuterie plate immediately after. He looked at it again. Somebody had better eat the stupid thing, otherwise it would go to waste.

He was just wondering where Yvette had got to, when he heard the bifold doors in the kitchen being opened. Christ, what the hell was she up to?

Still clutching his drink, Stephen rushed out into the hallway and down into the kitchen. As he pushed open the door, he was greeted by the sight of Yvette, cigarette in hand, standing beside the open bifolds.

"What are you doing?"

"Sorry," she said, looking nervous, "I was just going to have a cigarette."

"Jesus, don't do it in the house. The wife will kill me. I mean ... Cancer!" he shouted, sounding bizarrely pleased with himself. "Cancer. She died of cancer. So, you know – no smoking in the house."

"Of course," she said. "I'll just step outside."

Stephen nodded. "Right. Good. Yes."

He took a step towards the doors to follow her, and then thought better of it. Instead, he turned around and, for no reason he could fathom, opened the fridge. Now that he had done so, there had to be some intent behind the action, so he started randomly removing items and studying their best-before dates. Those prawns hadn't even been opened, and they'd gone off two days ago. What an absolute waste.

He heard a noise behind him. "Would you like a sandwich?"

He yelped and spun around as a male voice answered, "That'd be lovely." The man had short brown hair, a broad smile and the hint of a scar under his left eye. "I'll have the sandwich, thanks, along with every valuable in the house." The man shoved Stephen back against the still-open fridge, causing the shelves to dig into his back, then held up a blade in his free hand. "Don't worry about slicing it, I brought my own knife."

Stephen went to speak and found he could think of nothing to say.

"Yeah," said the man, a mocking lilt to his voice. "You're not the first person to order something off the internet and get more than he bargained for." He leaned in. "My advice is to lie back and take it – which was probably what you were expecting my girl to do, ye dirty, dirty mongrel. Some things are not for sale."

"I ... I ..."

"Whatever, fella. I'm not here to judge, just to take. Now," – he leaned in further, so close that Stephen could feel his stale breath on his face, followed by the cold steel of the blade against his cheek – "are you going to be a good boy, or do I have to carve you a permanent reminder of this evening?"

"I'll be ... I'll be good."

"Glad to hear it," said the man, flicking the blade away in a single motion, before slapping Stephen on the cheek. "Good man yourself."

Stephen nodded meekly, and then ...

He never saw the punch coming as it slammed into his stomach and made him double over. He heard what might have been another set of footsteps coming in from outside, but he was distracted by his body attempting to remember how to breathe.

As he lay crumpled on the ground, tasting the spilled remnants of his gin and tonic on the tiled floor, he felt a soft hand on his back and the scent of perfume as Yvette moved closer. She spoke in his ear in a whisper. "I'm so sorry. You have to help me."

# CHAPTER THIRTEEN

Bunny pulled his car over in front of Deccie's house and turned off the engine. They had driven here in near silence, which was worrying, given that Deccie Fadden was to silence what three-toed sloths were to top-level gymnastics. Initially, the lack of conversation had been because they were both out of breath, having run flat out from South Great George's Street up to Aungier Street where he had parked his car. There had been no sign that Gerry Lamkin was giving chase, but Bunny had not hung around to confirm that. You don't slow down to check if the volcano has changed its mind.

At a certain point, though, trying to recapture their breath had turned into an awkward silence that had lasted for most of the twenty-minute drive. Bunny had been tempted to break it, but he was very aware of the fact that they were about to have a tricky conversation, and he needed the time to figure out how best to approach it. It didn't feel like he'd come up with anything, but it was now shit-or-get-off-the-pot time, as the Americans would say.

He turned to face Deccie. "Right—"

"I tell you what," said Deccie, before Bunny could get any further. "Whatever new air-freshener thing your garage is using when they return your car is a big step up. It smells lovely in here. Like a hot-cross bun."

"Why is it every time somebody sees this car," said Bunny irritably, "they assume it has just come from the garage?"

"Because it breaks down that much, there are icebergs that have done more mileage in the last couple of years."

With all his heart Bunny wanted to refute that claim but, as it happened, he had picked up the car from the garage yesterday evening, following its latest visit. It was a 1983 Porsche 928 S LHD and his most beloved possession. It had also been declared a write-off by two different insurance companies now – the last time because Bunny himself had driven it off a cliff and into the sea. The first time was when Bunny had found it. Owning such a car had been his life's ambition since he was a kid. He had bought it for just above its scrap value, and had then attempted to get it up and running. Or, rather, he'd paid others to do so, having no mechanical abilities himself. Not that all the professionals were doing much better. The only thing now harder to come by than the required parts to fix it, was a mechanic willing to try.

He had deliberately avoided running the numbers, but he had a strong suspicion that by this point he had spent so much money on it that he could have just bought a new sports car. For better or for worse, Bunny McGarry was not a man to give up on something, no matter how much of a lost cause it appeared to be. Which brought him back to trying to talk sense into Deccie Fadden.

"Don't you mind about my car. It's you I'm worried about."

"I had the situation under control."

"Really? Please tell me you're not daft enough to believe that?"

"That Lamkin fella wasn't even that big."

Bunny sighed. "Fellas like that never are. Trust me, he's plenty big enough. And where did you get the idea of punching people in the knackers?"

"From you!"

"I never—"

"You bleedin' did!" protested Deccie. "Remember a couple of

years ago when there were reports of a weird fella hanging about? You told all the lads – if in doubt, go for the knackers and leg it."

"I ... That was entirely different. For a start, I didn't say go looking for trouble. And you also didn't do the running-away bit, which was the most important part of the plan. Violence is no way to solve your problems."

"Says the man who hit him with a snooker table."

"And then I did the bit you didn't – I made a tactical retreat."

"Is that not a bit cowardly?"

"That was not cowardice," said Bunny, trying to keep the edge of annoyance from his voice, "any more than not running into a wall isn't cowardice. You need to understand, Deccie, that in this world there are men like Gerry Lamkin who are nothing but bad news."

"I know. And the people that hurt Grandad work for him."

"No," said Bunny, exasperated, "they don't."

"How do you know that?"

"Firstly, because while Gerry Lamkin has been in trouble with the law his entire life, none of it has been because of stealing. Use your brain. Did he strike you as a leader of men?"

Deccie shrugged. "People seem to be afraid of him."

"That isn't the same thing, although some fools seem to think it is. More importantly, I talked to that idiot Flipper Finn, and he told me he made the whole thing up just to mess with you."

"He wouldn't."

"Of course he would. He's a know-it-all gobshite pretending he's some kind of gangster, but ask yourself, would a real gangster spend his time sitting around bragging to young kids?"

"I dunno."

"You do, Declan. You're smarter than this, and you need to start listening to the right people."

"Well, I had to do something."

"And that was to ring me."

"I tried that, and you didn't answer," said Deccie angrily.

"Jesus," exclaimed Bunny, grabbing a fistful of his own hair, "I left my phone on my desk for a few hours. Me not being able to answer your call straight away does not mean that you should go all Charles Bronson."

"Who?" asked Deccie.

"He's an actor. Starred in the *Death Wish* films."

"Never heard of them."

"They were big in the seventies and the eighties. This guy goes off looking for violent revenge all the time."

"They sound great. I'll check them out."

"You will not," said Bunny. "You're not old enough to watch them."

"Don't worry about that. Liam Brophy's brother knows a guy – he can get you any film you want, no questions asked."

"You're still not allowed to watch them. I forbid it."

"Well, why are you recommending them, then?"

"I wasn't recommending them. Look – we're getting off the point."

"Were you ever on a point?"

"Mind your manners, Deccie," warned Bunny.

"Sorry," he said, folding his arms and looking disconsolately out the window.

There was a lull in the conversation. This wasn't going well. Bunny needed to start again. He took a deep breath and made a conscious effort to sound calmer as he spoke. "Do you know who Gerry Lamkin is? He's the reason I started St Jude's. I mean, not him – people like him. Or at least poor unfortunate kids who find themselves in a situation like the one he grew up in. Mother dead. Father a right bastard. Nobody to turn to. Nobody looking out for him. He sees the world in terms of violence because that's all the world has ever shown him. Me trying to fight him wouldn't have proven anything and it wouldn't have made anything better for anybody – believe me."

"I don't think he agrees with you about the fighting thing. He was screaming a lot as we left."

Bunny shrugged. "You're right, but that is a tomorrow problem. Look – I know you're understandably upset because of what happened to your grandad, but you going off like that doesn't help.

You won't enjoy hearing this, but you're still young. It's not your job to fix everything."

Deccie wiped his nose messily on the sleeve of his coat. "If a man can't protect his family, what kind of man is he?"

Bunny paused. Deccie Fadden Senior had used the exact same phrase earlier in the day. He certainly hadn't meant it to refer to his grandson. "That's true," said Bunny. "But there's more than one way to do that. You're getting older now, and I think it's time you and I had a chat about some stuff."

Deccie raised a hand. "Let me stop you there – no need. We did a class in science where they showed us some weird pictures. Apparently, a woman's foo-foo looks like a goat, and you can stop having a baby by putting a balloon over a banana. Mr Calhoun showed us that, but he said not to tell the Christian Brothers, so I assume it was their banana he had nicked. Anyway, we were curious, so we all chipped in and got a blue movie off Liam's brother's mate."

Bunny struggled to process all of that. Eventually, he managed, "You got a fucking video?"

"Yeah. That was exactly what it was."

"I think I'm going to have to have a word with Liam's brother's mate. He shouldn't be giving that kind of thing to young lads."

"I agree," said Deccie. "I'll be honest, I didn't like it at all. Sex is disgusting. The whole thing seemed very unhygienic and a lot of effort for very little results."

"Right," said Bunny, entirely unsure of what else to say. He remembered the object he'd taken off Phil Nellis earlier that day. It was still in a shopping bag in his boot. The problem with twelve-year-old boys is that at some point they all became thirteen-year-old boys. "I think we're getting off the point again. What I was trying to say was – the thing that happened with your grandad today was terrible, but it is not your job to try to fix it."

"Whose is it, then?"

"The Gardaí."

"The Gardaí," scoffed Deccie.

"I am a member of the Gardaí, Declan," he said pointedly.

"Yeah," Deccie conceded, "but not really."

Bunny toyed with the idea of admitting he was currently suspended, but he couldn't see how it was going to help his case. "You know my friend Pamela?"

"Pamela?" echoed Deccie, shaking his head.

"You do. Her nickname is Butch."

Deccie's eyes widened. "Oh yeah, her. We all remember her. She's the short woman who does all the karate and stuff. She can punch through a brick wall, and she dumped you on your arse at training that one time."

"That was supposed to be a demonstration of how a smaller opponent can use a bigger opponent's strength against them, if they are intelligent about it."

"That's not what any of us remember about it, though, is it? It's also why now, before every practice, we have to check the whole field to make sure there's no dog shit on it."

"So you remember Butch. Do you remember that she's a guard too?"

Deccie nodded begrudgingly. "Suppose."

"So that's two members of the Gardaí who I am going to assume you have the highest respect for. Well, she and I are now on the case about your grandad's mugging, so you don't need to worry about it any more."

"And Granny's ring?"

For the second time that night, Bunny was reminded of why he didn't like making promises. Still, if it meant that Deccie would stay home and stay sensible, it was a risk he was going to have to take. "Yes. You have my word. We will get it back."

Deccie extended his hand solemnly. "Swear?"

Bunny shook it. "Swear."

"And don't go thinking that if that Gerry Lamkin fella finds you and kills you it means you don't have to get it back. You have to do what you promised. You do that and, on my honour, I shall avenge your death."

"On your honour?" Bunny repeated.

"Liam's brother's mate got us a pirate copy of *Gladiator* too. Now *that* was a film. I don't know why anyone bothers with all that sex stuff when they could be fighting with man-eating tigers on chains and big spike things."

"I'm guessing you might think differently when you're older."

"I doubt it." Deccie looked out the window and up at the front door of his house. "Is Granny mad at me?"

"Oh, absolutely livid. I'll let you in on a secret, though – she's going to be so over-the-moon delighted to have you back that she's going to have a really hard time staying angry. If I was you, I'd apologise and accept whatever punishment is going, then go upstairs and clean your room. Give it a couple of days and odds are she'll have forgotten whatever sentence she passed."

Deccie opened the door. "You've not seen my room, boss. It will take a lot longer than a couple of days to clean that up."

"Good. It'll give you something to focus your considerable energies on. Now, go on – I think I can see your granny looking out the window."

Deccie got out of the car and was about to close the door when he stopped. "Hang on a second." He dug his hand into the pocket of his anorak. When he pulled it out again it was holding a snooker ball. "I should probably give this to you."

"What the hell are you doing with that?"

Deccie handed it over. "I was going to feint at the guy with the snooker-cue thing then chuck that at his head. You've got to have a plan for these situations, boss."

"There is something deeply worrying about you, Deccie. Do you know that?"

"You have to improvise using what you can find. I learned that in the Cubs."

"Didn't they throw you out?"

"It doesn't make it bad advice. Obviously, you shouldn't try that. Your aim is not very good. I suggest you stick it in a sock and use it as a cudgel."

"Or," said Bunny, "I could try to resolve disputes by peaceful means."

Deccie shook his head. "Do you know what your problem is, boss?"

Bunny laughed. "Let me guess ..."

"You have no—"

Deccie was interrupted by the sound of his grandmother roaring from the doorstep. "Declan Fadden, you get into this house this instant!"

Deccie slammed the car door and ran up the path. Bunny watched as Bridie Fadden glowered at her grandson as he approached, then dragged him into a bear hug and dissolved into tears.

She waved at Bunny, who nodded and then started up the engine.

It took three attempts to get going. Bloody stupid thing.

# CHAPTER FOURTEEN

Mark Dillon lay in his bed and attempted to ignore the lights as they flashed on and off above his head. The council house that had been his gran's before she had passed last year, and which was now "under review", was not possessed by some vengeful spirit. At least, not unless you stretched that definition to cover the kids from the estate who had realised a while ago that ringing the doorbell made the lights flash on and off. He'd assumed they'd get bored of doing it, but it had been going on for several months now and there appeared to be no end in sight. He could, of course, disconnect the bell or rewire it. He was good with electrics, and it would be easy to change it so that he could turn it off before he went to bed. However, for reasons he couldn't quite articulate, he didn't want to. Maybe it was an admission that nobody would be ringing his bell except for the annoying little scrotes, and that was a depressing realisation.

Some part of Mark knew that the walls were closing in, and that his world was getting smaller and smaller. He had been diagnosed as profoundly deaf since birth, so it wasn't like his was a great big world to begin with. Now Nana was gone, his only remaining family was a couple of uncles he rarely saw. His best and only true friend was Niall Duggan, who was on the run from the

Gardaí now, his inability to get away from his idiot cousin Bobby having finally got him into something he couldn't just walk away from.

The guards had been around earlier that day, asking Mark what he knew. They'd brought a sign language interpreter with them, despite Mark being able to read lips perfectly. The woman's signing had been quite poor. Mark had enjoyed correcting her while answering the questions, while the rest of the room had been unaware of the conversation within the conversation.

Still, he'd been thinking about it all night. Niall wasn't coming back. He'd either get away or, as was a lot more likely given the involvement of Bobby Walsh, he'd end up in prison. Maybe even dead. Mark enjoyed taking care of Niall's pigeons, but it was a lot more fun when they did it together. He had been teaching Niall sign, and his friend had been getting pretty good at it. He was actually a pretty smart guy. Everyone just assumed he wasn't because he was big and wasn't much of a talker. The world was full of people all too willing to shove you into their little boxes and leave you there, and Mark was getting royally sick of it. The council were going to take the house and put him god-knows-where. Niall would be gone anyway and, odds on, whatever crappy flat they found for him, there'd be no room for the pigeons.

He'd been trying to get a job. Mark was good with electrics and engines, and he had qualifications, but he couldn't ever get past the interview stage. One garage had told him they were worried he'd get run over while working there. How the hell did they think he made it to the interview in the first place? He was so damn sick of his life as it was, and he could only see it getting worse. Increasingly, he'd found himself looking for ways out.

He had shoved his head under the pillow to block out the flashing lights, which was why the first thing he knew about the intruders was when the hands grabbed him. Two big men – one shaven-headed with an earring and the other with slicked-back blond hair, both wearing suits. Mark kicked and fought as hard as he could, getting a few digs in, but they overpowered him by pinning him down, and restrained him by wrapping the sheet from his bed around him. Then he was marched downstairs.

A man was sitting at his kitchen table, having made himself a cup of tea and found the biscuits. Mark recognised him. He'd been with the Gardaí earlier that day, standing back as that DI Grainger bloke had led the interview. Mark was a hundred percent deaf, but even he could tell that Grainger had been shouting his questions at him. Idiot. The previous interview had taken place in Mark's kitchen too. One of the main differences had been that he'd not been bollock-naked at the time.

He was shoved into the chair opposite the guy he assumed was the boss. Hard to tell with him being sat down, but he seemed a lot shorter than the two goons. His eyes were lively and green, he had a hawkish nose, and a crooked grin played across his lips. As his smile widened in greeting, Mark could see that one of his front teeth was gold.

He calmly finished his biscuit before speaking. "I didn't think this country was warm enough to sleep naked." Then he pointed at his own mouth. "You can understand what I am saying?"

Mark bobbed his head.

"Good. My name is Inspector ..." Mark didn't get what followed.

He shook his head and shrugged.

"You didn't understand?" asked the man, before nodding. He picked up the pen that was on the table and wrote on the pad that always sat there. After a second, he held it up to show the words "Inspector Schillaci".

Mark indicated the pad and Schillaci spun it around and handed him the pen. Mark wrote on it and passed it back.

Schillaci laughed and held up the page to the two men standing behind Mark. "Look at that – he wrote 'Fuck off Inspector Schillaci'."

Mark was jerked forward by someone punching him hard in the back of the head. After a couple of seconds, he straightened himself up and looked defiantly across the table at Schillaci.

"You Irish, always trying to be funny." Schillaci's grin faded. "So boring. Now, I know you spoke to the police earlier, but I think you know more than you said. I am here to ask you again."

Mark looked at the pad, which Schillaci duly spun around and pushed back to him.

Schillaci read the note out loud as soon as Mark had finished writing it. "'Like I said earlier, I don't know anything.'" He nodded. "You did indeed say that, but you may have noticed who isn't here this time. It's just you, me and my men. I don't work for the guards, as you call them. I work for a man – you won't know him, and I won't write his name. He is a well-respected man. A powerful man. A man who is a ..." He looked behind Mark. "What is that phrase again? Yes!" he said, slapping the table and turning his attention back to Mark. "A pillar of the community. He is also the most absolutely ruthless man I know."

"Your friend and his cousin have taken that man's daughter, and he sent me here to get her back. You see, I am the most ruthless man he knows. If I were you, I would tell me everything you know, and then we can be friends. Trust me, you don't want me as an enemy."

Mark picked the pen up in his left hand and drew the pad back to him. He underlined the words "I don't know anything" and held it up.

"You are left-handed?"

Schillaci nodded to one of the men standing behind Mark. Mark tried to pull his right hand away, but he wasn't quick enough. Strong hands grabbed his right arm. The other goon leaned heavily on his shoulders, pinning him down in the chair. Schillaci reached forward and gently took Mark's right hand. He tried to keep it balled in a fist, but Schillaci prised it apart and took a firm grip on his index finger. Mark struggled, but there was no getting away.

"Look at me," ordered Schillaci. "Look at me." When he was satisfied he had Mark's undivided attention, he continued talking. "Do not test me. That will go badly for you. Now, where is Niall Duggan?"

With difficulty, Mark turned the page on the pad and wrote "I have no idea".

Schillaci read it and shook his head. "Wrong answer."

Mark groaned in frustration.

"OK," said Schillaci. "Let us try this. I do not believe they are just robbing people for the sake of it. What are they up to?"

Mark wrote on the pad again, his normally neat handwriting becoming increasingly ragged due to the angle and physical pain of having a large man leaning on top of him.

Schillaci read it out. "'Do not know'."

He shook his head in frustration. "If you are holding on to the hope that I am bluffing, you are going to be proven very wrong." Schillaci locked eyes with Mark then altered his grip on his finger. "I know you need this. For your sign language. I am aware of what I am doing and I don't want to, but my boss, he wants his daughter back, and he does not care what I have to do to make that happen. I have no choice, so you have no choice."

Mark did not know much, but in that moment, he was entirely certain of two things. One, Schillaci was not bluffing, and two, no matter what, he was never ever going to betray his friend. Pain would not be a novel experience for him. Life being unfair did not come as a surprise, and whatever happened, he wasn't telling this arsehole a thing.

"Last chance," said Schillaci. "Where is Niall Duggan?"

Mark did not know the answer to that question, so he couldn't have answered it even if he wanted to. With difficulty, he wrote on the pad and held it up.

NO IDEA

He screamed when the first bone broke.

# CHAPTER FIFTEEN

If Detective Inspector Vanya Coyne turned her head sixty degrees to the left, she could have enjoyed a rather spectacular view of the light from the rising sun glistening on the surface of the Shannon as it lazily wound its way through Limerick. She didn't, though. She had seen it before and she wasn't in the mood for beauty, scenic or otherwise, this morning. Instead, she pulled her coat tightly around herself, slid a cigarette from the pack and cupped her hands as she attempted to light it.

The sunrise may have brought light and beauty with it, but it carried bugger all heat. As someone who became a wheelchair user late in life, one disadvantage, apart from the obvious massive one, was that being in an electric wheelchair meant that your body generated very little heat for itself. In other words, it didn't matter what Vanya Coyne wore at 7:30 in the morning as she moved around Arthur's Quay Park, the city coming to life around her, she was invariably bloody freezing. Added to that, the wind off the water could cut right through you if it caught you just right.

She had never been a big fan of the great outdoors, but she didn't have a choice. As her cigarette finally took light, she drew her hands away and turned her head in the opposite direction to the spectacular view to stare daggers at the large St Bernard dog that was still not taking a shit.

"For God's sake, Clancy, just pop one out, ye big hairy eejit."

Clancy responded by shooting her the big brown puppy-dog eyes that let him get away with murder.

Vanya took a drag on her cigarette. "If anybody else disobeyed as many direct orders as you did, they would long since be out on their arse."

When she looked back towards the main gates of the park, she saw the unmistakable figure of Bunny McGarry striding towards her with a short woman in tow. She took a drag on her cigarette and then exhaled. "Bernard McGarry," she said, her delivery dry. "What a massive shock this is."

Bunny gave her a slightly awkward smile. "Vanya. Good to see you. You're looking well."

She shook her head. "For feck's sake, McGarry, the last time you saw me I was walking upright unassisted. That charm of yours would sweep me off my feet if I wasn't already in this fecking chair."

He shuffled his feet awkwardly. "I was sorry to hear about your—"

She cut him off with a dismissive wave of her cigarette. "Oh Lord, it's too early to do all of that now. Let's cut to the chase. You are sorry to hear about my accident, I'm sorry to hear about Gringo, and you are sorry to hear about the untimely death of my husband while out jogging, of all bloody stupid things." She turned her attention to Bunny's companion. "It's been a real gangbusters couple of years." She narrowed her eyes. "Pamela Cassidy?"

The woman looked taken aback for a moment before she nodded. "That's right."

"I saw you doing the whole martial-arts thing at that cross-border cooperation games thingamajig a few years ago. Didn't you slap seven kinds of shite out of that massive northern woman after moving up a few weight divisions?"

Butch shrugged. "I got lucky."

"And you can cut that nonsense out for a start. You're a woman in the Garda Síochána – there'll be enough people dismissing your abilities without you doing it too. Cassidy," she repeated, looking thoughtful. "Given the lack of imagination shown by most of our male colleagues in uniform, am I right in guessing that your nickname is exactly what I think it is?"

"I'm afraid so."

Vanya nodded. "How tediously predictable. Well, if it's any consolation, Butch, I'm sure somebody would have tried to give me the nickname Wheels, or something equally tedious, if I hadn't nipped that crap in the bud immediately." She flicked some ash off the end of her cigarette. "Anyway, it was great to see the two of you so unexpectedly but, seeing as you must've got up at, what, four o'clock in the morning to get here from Dublin, so taken were you with the urge to go for a casual stroll in one of Limerick's fine parks at this ungodly hour, I should really let you get back to it."

"You knew we were coming?" asked Bunny.

"Of course I knew you were coming, because while Dinny might be your old drinking buddy, he actually works for me. He belatedly realised that telling people how to find senior members of the Gardaí was probably not the greatest idea in the world."

"I did think about ringing you directly."

"But you rightly assumed that I'd probably slam the phone down on you."

"I'm sorry that—"

Vanya cut him off again. "Please, don't insult the both of us by pretending you are sorry for what you did."

"No," said Bunny. "I think we both know I'd do it again. But I really am sorry that it damaged our friendship. I wanted to come to Michael's funeral, but I didn't think you'd like it."

Vanya looked away. "Well, seeing as you didn't take that chance, we will never know, will we?"

"For all that, I can't help but notice that you knew I was coming and yet you're still here?"

She shrugged. "If the dog needs to take a shit, the dog needs to take a shit." She looked across at where the St Bernard was still sniffing the grass while pointedly failing to achieve the previously stated objective.

"Since when are you a dog-lover, Vanya?"

"Since never," she answered. "Clancy here was found half starved and abandoned with a nasty wound on his back leg, out near Mary Immaculate College. Michael, the big softie, convinced me we should take him in, just until he got better. Then, six weeks later" – she left it to Bunny and Butch to fill in the gap – "and for reasons past my understanding, I can't seem to bring myself to get rid of the massive hairy lump."

She gave a rueful shake of her head. "What a ridiculous pair we make. Look at the size of him. Occasionally on a walk, the big eejit just decides he's sitting down and not moving and there's nothing I can do about it. He is supposedly bred to save people up mountains, and yet he hates when it rains, and the wind scares him. He is the bane of my existence."

As they all looked at Clancy, the dog met their gaze with his big brown eyes. Then, as if on cue, he hunched over and produced the goods.

"Miracle of miracles," said Vanya with a sigh. She turned back to Bunny. "Seeing as you're here, you might as well buy me breakfast. But first, you can make yourself useful." She pulled a poo bag out of her pocket and held it out to him.


As soon as they entered the greasy-spoon café, the waiter nodded his hellos and removed the reserved sign from the table in the corner. Judging by the absence of chairs on one side, DI Vanya Coyne was a regular. Bunny ordered the full Irish and Butch a bowl of porridge while Clancy slurped happily at the dish of water that had been left out for him. Bunny noticed a man in a suit two tables over, looking horrified at this scene before making his feelings known to the waiter. Judging by the stroppy face he was left with after their brief conversation, his position in the pecking order in relation to Clancy had been explained to him in no uncertain terms, and he was not happy with the result.

As the trio made awkward small talk while waiting for their food, the dog placed his massive head on Vanya's lap and looked up at her adoringly. She rested her hand on top and scratched behind his right ear as his tail wagged contentedly. When the food arrived, they all ate in silence for a couple of minutes, save for the sound of Clancy's jaw smacking contentedly as Vanya slipped him two rashers of bacon from her plate. Only once the dog had slumped heavily onto the floor did Vanya place her fork down and look across at Bunny. "Alright, then – let's hear it."

Bunny, having demolished his full Irish in record time, set his cutlery on his plate and wiped his napkin across his lips. "I have been led to believe that this fair city has been favoured with a visit from one DI Grainger?"

Vanya looked up at the ceiling and shook her head. "Nothing was more certain than that you would come all the way down here to ask about something I have been specifically told not to talk about."

"So, you met him, then?"

"I did," she confirmed. "He's even less impressive in person than his reputation would have you believe."

"Oh," agreed Bunny. "You have no idea. Did he happen to have some international guests with him?"

"Before I answer anything about that," said Vanya, "do you want to explain why any of this is of interest to you?"

Vanya listened as Bunny recounted what had happened to Declan Fadden Senior the day before, including a full description of his injuries and an explanation of the importance of the ring to the Fadden family.

Vanya took a sip of tea and set her mug back down on the table. "Good God. Was there ever anything more certain than that this shit show was going to get more and more out of control?"

"I knew nothing happened in this city without you knowing about it," said Bunny.

"And you can save your cheap attempts at flattery, McGarry."

"Flattery?" he asked. "It's fact and we both know it. You could be running the entire force if you were ever inclined to leave here."

"And yet I'm getting a bollocking from our assistant commissioner instead, for interfering in a – and I'm quoting him directly – highly sensitive investigation with an international angle."

"Speaking of unimpressive people ..." ventured Bunny.

"No argument from me," said Vanya.

"So, you could tell us exactly what's going on here?"

"If I was willing to ignore a direct order to keep my mouth shut."

Bunny nodded. "Would you like a list of the times when I know for a fact you did exactly that?"

In spite of herself, a smile spread across Vanya Coyne's lips. "I think we might have found the other reason that I'm not commissioner of the Garda Síochána."

Bunny said nothing and paused to take a slurp of his tea.

"Screw it," said Vanya. "The whole thing stinks to high heaven. I'm not giving you the lot, but I'll steer you. The two lads from your story I can identify as Bobby Walsh, a nasty piece of work with a baby face, and his cousin Niall Duggan, the kind of big dim unit that was born to be a henchman."

"I'm guessing their involvement," said Butch, "is not what has got the higher-ups all aflutter?"

"Well surmised, Detective Cassidy. Sofia Accardi – youngest daughter of some very high-up political types in Italy and, until recently, student of music and dance at the world-renowned University of Limerick. Only, she disappeared a few weeks ago after having been seen in the company of the bold Bobby. They've not been home, and the trio have been on quite the alleged spree. I don't know the exact details because they are being hushed up, but the group have been linked to several robberies of various forms, although your poor friend marks an escalation in the violence stakes. I heard a whisper they carjacked some guy a couple of nights ago up on the Mullaghanish mountain roads after a car they'd nicked broke down. He only came in to report it yesterday."

"Why?" asked Bunny.

"At a guess, the idiot was pissed while driving and had to sober up after he eventually got home."

"Christ," murmured Butch.

"Yeah. He said that the man we're assuming was Bobby Walsh pulled a knife on him and he fought him off. I'm calling bullshit on that part, but the fool was very shook up, by all accounts. That's not even my favourite of Bobby Walsh's misdeeds, though," said Vanya. "They set Sofia up as an escort on some dodgy website and then the two boys robbed the punter. We know this happened once, but by the nature of the crime, there's every possibility it's happened a number of times and the victims have decided to keep quiet, for obvious reasons. That one case only came to light because, I kid you not, the wife of the idiot victim knew he was up to something and was having him followed by a private investigator. The guy got footage of the whole thing."

"Really?" said Bunny. "Any chance we could see that?"

"None. Grainger impounded it."

"Did this investigator not think to intervene when the guy was getting robbed?" asked Butch.

"As the gumshoe in question said to me, not long before my entire investigation was shut down by the arrival of DI Grainger and the goon squad, it isn't his job to go saving horny gobshites. As someone whose job it is, I can't say I hold it against him."

"So, they think this Sofia Accardi is being held against her will?"

Vanya shrugged. "That is the impression I'm getting, or at the very least, it suits everyone to believe that. Mind you, here's a weird little wrinkle – the john mentioned that while he was being relieved of all his valuables, Ms Accardi apologised and asked him for help."

"Now that you mention it," said Bunny, who had forgotten to include that detail in his summary of Deccie Fadden Senior's experience, "she said the same thing to my guy. So, these boys with Grainger are Italian police?"

"One of them is," said Vanya, "but at least some of the others – and I'm not sure how many of them there are – are private contractors."

"What the hell does that mean?" asked Butch.

"It means they have even less oversight than the scant amount their boss is getting. I don't mean Grainger there, by the way – there is some little Italian prick with a gold tooth who is police. Inspector Schillaci."

"Like the footballer?" asked Bunny.

"I'll take your word for it," said Vanya with a shrug. "There have been several jokes around the station that I've not understood. I do know that little gold-toothed poser had a couple of his boys drive his Porsche all the way here from Italy and, I shit you not, one of them guards the bloody thing in the station car park. I mean ... Anyway, Schillaci, Grainger and the boys from the Interpol liaison office went around and conducted some standard interviews, but I heard some noise that Schillaci's boys were also doing some stuff on the side."

Bunny drew his head back. "You're kiddin'!"

"No," she responded, "I'm not. We've got these whatever they are running around on the edges of a Garda investigation, doing whatever the hell they're up to with no oversight. I did bring it up with DI Grainger, which is why I got the phone call. Officially, of course, the individuals are private investigators hired by the Accardi family and are in no way directly linked to blah, blah, blah, blah, blah."

"Unbelievable."

"Actually," said Vanya Coyne, pouring herself another cup of tea from the pot, "it's not just Italians. There was one fella with them who was French. He's a *juge d'instruction*. You know, from their weird legal system. Like a district attorney in America, only he investigates stuff and directs police. I've no clue why he's here. I heard him on the phone in the hall once. For what it's worth, judging by his body language and the little bit of French I retained from school, he is not enjoying being associated with Grainger, Schillaci or his goon squad any more than you and I would be."

"I think I saw him," said Butch. "Last night, while Bunny was busy getting us both suspended. He's a Black man?"

Vanya nodded. "That's him."

"And what did Bobby Walsh and his merry little band get off these victims of theirs?" asked Bunny.

"Cash, watches and jewellery – the big trifecta of easy-to-move swag. They took the guy's bank cards too, after squeezing his PIN out of him, and grabbed what they could from his accounts before dumping the cards. We found them in a bin beside the bank, and we got a lovely action shot of Niall Duggan at the ATM doing the business. What are the odds Bobby is smart enough to get the dense lad to make the withdrawals for him so he's not the one getting his picture taken?"

"Could this be drugs?" asked Butch.

Vanya shrugged. "Always a possibility, but I can tell you that from all we know, Bobby Walsh wasn't a user before now and Niall Duggan's sole addiction appears to be to pigeons."

"Excuse me?"

"He races pigeons, or whatever the hell they call it. Mad about them. If I was overseeing the investigation, I'd have installed surveillance on his coop at the end of the garden. Their little gang is off somewhere in hiding but I'll bet the only thing big Niall is missing is those bloody birds. I once caught a guy with a wife and three kids who didn't contact them in any way for the three years he was on the run but who couldn't resist coming home to try and see his dogs. People get weird about pets."

On cue, Clancy made a contented little grumbling noise to himself.

"Anyway," she concluded, withdrawing her purse from her coat pocket and dropping a couple of notes on the table in front of her, "that's definitely all I can tell you without losing my job."

"Right," said Bunny, "only I could do with a bit of a steer on where we go from here?"

"Back to Dublin would be my advice. It was nice meeting you, Detective Cassidy."

"But—"

"You never did learn how not to push your luck, did you, Bernard? Don't forget to leave a good tip." Clancy lumbered to his feet as Vanya grabbed his lead and nodded at the waiter. "See you tomorrow, Marv."

―――――

Bunny and Butch watched in silence as the waiter held the door open and DI Vanya Coyne deftly manoeuvred herself and the St Bernard out the door and into the early morning pedestrian traffic.

"Shite," said Bunny. "I was really hoping for a bit more information than that."

"Bunny?"

"Although I suppose there was every chance she was still going to be mad at me."

"Bunny?"

"I don't know who else to try with— Ouch!" The "ouch" was because Butch had just bopped Bunny on the knuckle with her spoon. "What the hell was that for?"

In lieu of an answer, Butch nodded to where Vanya had dropped the £10 note on the table. Bunny pushed it aside and looked at the scrap of paper on which two names and addresses were written in narrow handwriting, identified in turn as being for Bobby Walsh's brother and a woman identified as Sofia Accardi's flatmate.

"Holy shit," said Bunny. "She really is a hell of a lot smarter than I am."

# CHAPTER SIXTEEN

Butch stood to the side of the room and tried to ignore the nauseous feeling in her stomach. She had been in a dance studio several times during her childhood and had hated every last second of those occasions. This was back when her mum, under pressure from her interfering mother-in-law, had tried to get her daughter out of her obsession with martial arts and into more "ladylike pursuits". After a couple of months of misery, Butch's mother had, thankfully, finally snapped, having picked her daughter up in tears one too many times.

Butch focused her attention on the floor. If she looked in any other direction, she was confronted with the sight of pre-teen ballerinas, or their reflections, twirling in the ubiquitous mirrors and it was making her stomach twirl unhappily in unison. She was aware that this was some form of low-level PTSD but she doubted there was a support group for it. It was bad enough that she had had to get up at 4am that morning to accompany Bunny to Limerick; if she had known that this gut-wrenching trip down memory lane was part of the deal, she would have stayed in bed.

She was at the dance studio because a trip to Sarah Kennedy's home address – a rather fancy-looking apartment building overlooking the Shannon – had found the woman in question not at home, but the building's concierge had informed Butch that she was probably off teaching at the Amanda Blake-Jones School of Ballet. A text from Bunny had confirmed that his trip to the University of Limerick campus in order to check into Sofia Accardi had drawn a blank too. The administration was clearly under strict instructions to refuse to answer all questions about their missing student. While Bunny refocused his energies on looking into the Walsh family, she had drawn the short straw and come here.

When she had approached the rather pinched-faced woman behind reception, who wielded a smile like it was the only thing stopping her from killing again, the greeting had not been warm. The woman had not been keen to let Butch speak to Sarah Kennedy at all. Only Butch's assertion that her enquiries related to a missing female student got her rather reluctantly on side. Butch guessed she was the eponymous Amanda Blake-Jones. She was informed she'd have to wait twenty minutes until Sarah's current class had finished, but after that, Sarah was due a short break – with a rather heavy emphasis given to the word "short".

Butch now watched as the class came to an end. While she hated being there, Butch had to admit that Sarah Kennedy was quite clearly a good teacher. She seemed genuinely committed to making it fun for her pupils, which was very different to how Butch remembered the whole thing going back in her day. Her teacher had been a crook-backed woman with an alarming wart who thumped her cane on the floor and gave the definite impression that all the joy had been squeezed out of her back in the 1950s. In stark contrast, Sarah Kennedy had a cheerful demeanour, short black hair in a bob and the kind of lean figure you'd expect from a professional dancer.

As the class broke up, Sarah found herself surrounded by her giddy pupils looking for more of her attention and handing her brightly wrapped Christmas presents that she insisted were not necessary. She dealt with it all good-naturedly – mirroring the children's excitement and telling them all with kind words of encouragement how much better they were getting. Butch manoeuvred her way through the crowd, introduced herself and explained the reason for her visit. Sarah Kennedy did not look pleased, but she guided Butch towards the back of the studio, her arms now filled with gifts.

"A peculiar kind of torture, this," she told Butch. "Most of these will be boxes of chocolates that I can't bloody eat. Got a showcase in January." She placed her armful down on top of an even larger pile. "I don't have much time and Amanda will kill me if I'm not ready to go for the next group."

"I won't keep you long," promised Butch.

Sarah nodded and indicated a fire exit. "Would you mind if I sneak a smoke while we talk?"

"No problem."

Sarah led her into an alleyway and quickly sparked up a cigarette. As she took her first drag, Sarah noticed Butch's facial expression. "Sorry about the smell. The Thai restaurant we back onto is considered really good, but I have to admit, after smelling how bad their bins stink, I won't be eating there again." Her expression fell abruptly. "Sorry. Listen to me jabbering on. Has there been any news on Sofia?"

"Not as such," said Butch, "but investigations are ongoing." Her words made her uncomfortable, although technically she wasn't lying. Investigations were ongoing, it's just that she was not part of any official one. "I appreciate you covered this before with other officers, but I'm a fresh pair of eyes. Could you give me an idea of what Sofia is like?"

Sarah took another drag. "I don't know her that well. We were only flatmates for a couple of months."

"Is this the apartment over on the Riverside? Very fancy student digs, if you don't mind me saying."

"Oh. You don't know?"

Butch shook her head.

"It's ... This will probably sound weird, but a couple of weeks before I was supposed to start, a woman from the university approached me. They explained that there was this Italian girl who didn't know anybody in Limerick and was joining the course at the same time as I was – I'm in my first year of a BA in music and dance – and they asked if I'd like to share an apartment with her. When they told me it was rent-free, I couldn't believe it. They said that she comes from a wealthy family, and that they were worried about her being on her own. I mean, I'm on a part-scholarship, so this was a dream come true."

"And the first time you met was when you moved in together?"

"Yeah," said Sarah. "To be honest, I was expecting her to be a shy girl, maybe with not much English. You know, seeing as the family were so concerned and all, but that wasn't what she was like at all."

"What do you mean?"

"For a start, her English is superb. Mind you, she told me about the various schools she'd been to as a kid. The kind of money you spend on that sort of education, you'd expect your child to be conversant in several languages, and possibly be making up a few of their own. I mean, look, I grew up on a farm ten miles outside Athlone. Sofia didn't have a different life from me, so much as she might as well have come from a different planet. She has handbags that cost more than my entire education."

Butch nodded. "So did you two not get on, then?"

"No," Sarah said quickly. "I mean, to be honest, I was expecting to have to take this girl under my wing. It actually ended up being the other way round. She's a bit of a party girl and I come from a fairly sheltered background – certainly compared to what she was used to. We got on great, though. I thought so, anyway."

"Did she have any boyfriends?"

Sarah flicked some ash away, and Butch caught the hesitant look on her face.

"Look," Butch said. "I'm not writing anything down, and I'm certainly not here to pass judgement on anybody. I just need to know as much as I can about Sofia. My only interest is in finding this girl and getting her home safe. I'm not going to quote you directly or get you in any trouble. Trust me."

Sarah looked slightly reassured by this and nodded. "Let me put it this way; you know that Pulp song 'Common People'?"

Butch nodded.

"It felt like I was living in a pretty full-on version of that. Sofia was ..." She licked her lips, trying to find the right words.

"Sexually active?" suggested Butch.

Sarah gave a little laugh and nodded. "Don't get me wrong. If she was a bloke, nobody would bat an eyelid. In fact, they'd be calling her a legend. But yeah – she's a very pretty girl, and she got a lot of male attention. Let's just say she enjoyed it to the max. She seemed to have a particular thing for lads who are a bit rough around the edges. One of them nicked my iPod on his way out the door."

"Oh dear. Did you tell Sofia about that?"

"I did. She thought it was hilarious. She just gave me a couple hundred quid to buy a new one."

"Right."

"I don't ... Look, I'm making her sound bad there. She just ... She comes from a world where money is no object, so I guess she sees these things differently to how I would. And she wasn't just chasing after boys from the estate, as my mum would refer to them. One evening she didn't come home, and I was worried. I tried ringing her mobile and got nothing. Midday the next day, I was this close to ringing the police when she rolled in. Told me she'd slept on some guy's yacht. You know – as you do." Sarah shook her head. "She wanted me to go to a party on it with her the next night."

"Did you?"

"Nah," said Sarah. "I faked being ill. I saw the guy picking her up, though. Older dude in a sports car that screamed raging mid-life crisis. I had a suspicion about how many people might be at this little soirée. Like, I might end up on a double date with his even creepier mate." Sarah stuck out her tongue and gave an exaggerated judder.

Butch laughed. "Sounds like she's quite the wild child."

"I suppose. I mean, between you and me, I got the very definite impression that she doesn't get on well with her parents. Like, serious daddy issues in particular. We all go through our rebellious phase, but she's been having hers for quite some time now. She didn't talk about her past much, but I got the impression her home life was rather chaotic. And then there was all the stuff in Paris."

"Paris?"

This earned Butch an assessing look from Sarah. "Did they not tell you anything?"

She decided to bluff. "Obviously, I know the official version of events, but I was just interested in how she described it to you."

"Right. Like I said, she didn't go into a lot of detail. All I know was she was studying at the Sorbonne, and she got kicked out. Didn't say what it was but, given the kind of money her family has, it must have been pretty bad that nobody was willing to look the other way."

"She sounds like a nightmare to live with," observed Butch.

"No, not at all. She can be really lovely. For a while there, I honestly thought that Sofia was gonna be my lifelong best friend."

"For a while?"

Sarah started to look cagey again. Butch watched as she clearly weighed up how much she wanted to say. After a couple of seconds, she took a final drag on her cigarette and tossed the butt away. "OK. Full disclosure – I guess I sort of got wrapped up in Sofia's world. We were out partying most nights. Then, one morning, after she'd convinced me to go out when I really didn't want to, I had a recital in front of a few lecturers and the class. I was hungover, and it was an absolute disaster. Like, I got pulled aside afterwards and my tutor had a serious word with me about how I was in danger of throwing away all the hard work I'd done to get here."

"Oh dear."

Sarah nodded. "I was mortified. I went home, told Sofia all about this and she laughed it off. Then I said I wasn't going out any more for a while and she flipped. I mean, she lost it. All of a sudden, I was betraying her. I mean, where the hell did she get that from? I was stunned. She started throwing stuff around. Absolute madness. I'll be honest with you, I'd never seen anything like that in my life."

"And what happened after that?"

"What happened was, she didn't speak to me for two whole weeks. We were still living in the same apartment, and she refused to offer a single word any time I saw her."

"Wow," said Butch.

"I know, right? Who does that? I was feeling really bad, wondering if she'd misunderstood what I said. I get she has some serious trust issues with her family or whatever, but this had sent her completely off the deep end."

"So, had you spoken to her before she disappeared?"

Sarah gave a rueful look. "Sort of. Out of the blue, this guy turns up at the front door. He's evidently been sent by her parents. He was there to do a random drugs test."

"Oh boy."

"Yeah. First thing I know about it, Sofia comes charging into my room and demands that I pee in a cup for her."

"And did you?"

"No! I was freaking out. I thought being involved in anything like that could mean I lose my scholarship or something. When I said I wouldn't do it, I honestly thought she was going to attack me. It was terrifying."

"So did she fail this test?"

"I don't think she ever took it. She started arguing with the guy in Italian and then he left. Next thing I heard about it, I came back from college the following morning and she told me that, thanks to me, she'd been cut off by her parents. By that point I'd had enough. I asked about and found a room I could share for a couple of hundred quid a month. I don't really have the extra cash, but living with Sofia was doing my head in. I told her I'd be out of there the following week."

"But you're still there?"

Sarah shrugged. "Three days after that, she didn't come home. I left it one more day, but when there was still no sign, I thought I'm gonna have to say something to somebody. I spoke to the tutor, who talked to the college, who contacted the Gardaí and her parents, and well ... here we are."

"You've had no communication from her since?"

She shook her head. "Nothing, and I wish I had. I mean, she's got a lot of shit going on, clearly, but I reckon she's got herself in far too deep with the wrong people. And now, for whatever reason, she can't get herself out of it. She must be terrified."

Sarah rubbed her hand over her forehead and Butch placed a hand gently on her arm. "Are you OK?"

"To tell you the truth, I've been talking to the university about taking the rest of the year off and coming back next year. This whole thing has my head wrecked."

Butch nodded sympathetically. "Sounds like a lot, alright."

"I was just ... Ye know, I'd been working towards making it here for years and" – she gave a shrug – "let's just say I thought it'd be a bit different." She looked at her watch and her face fell. "Shit. I need to be back inside." She turned back towards the door.

"Sorry. Yes. Of course," said Butch. "Really quickly – did you ever meet Bobby Walsh?"

"Sort of. I only know that's his name because the other gardaí showed me his picture. He was in the apartment a couple of times when I came home, but this was when Sofia wasn't talking to me. He didn't say anything to me either. He just ..."

"What?"

"Looked at me. You know, one of those guys that looks at you a certain way and it makes your skin crawl? Like that. I started locking my bedroom door at night."

Before Butch could ask anything else, the fire exit opened to reveal the figure of Amanda Blake-Jones glaring at them.

"Sorry, Amanda. Coming right now."

"And spray some perfume on yourself. I can't have my teachers stinking like an ashtray." After shooting Butch one last dirty look, Amanda Blake-Jones stormed off.

"Bollocks," said Sarah. "I really need this job."

Before Butch could say anything else, Sarah Kennedy rushed off in pursuit of her irate boss. Unintentionally, she assumed, the fire door slammed behind her. Butch considered banging on it, but thought better of it. Instead, she held her nose and walked out through the foul-smelling alley, her hundred percent record of not enjoying trips to dance schools still intact.

# CHAPTER SEVENTEEN

If he were being honest, Bunny would have to admit that he hadn't realised that blacksmiths were still a thing. He thought the job had long since gone the way of other professions such as the film projectionist, town crier or bloke who waves flags in front of an automobile to warn the locals to hide the womenfolk, or whatever the reason was for doing that in the first place. Still, here he was, not ten minutes' walk from the centre of Limerick, standing outside a working blacksmith forge. He could even hear the sound of metal pounding metal from inside.

Fitzmaurice Bros had been there for over a hundred years, according to the sign above the door. Bunny wasn't looking for any of the Fitzmaurices, though. He'd just come from visiting Bobby Walsh's family home on the Keyes Park Estate where there had been no answer. While he'd been asking around, trying to find out where to go to talk to one of the Walshes, he had received a couple of very detailed, if impractical, suggestions on where he could go and what he could do when he got there. It wasn't the kind of area that welcomed outsiders, particularly those asking questions. Eventually, an elderly neighbour had told him that Shane, the eldest of the

Walsh boys, worked here at the forge. In the absence of any other lead, here he was.

He stepped into the shop's narrow reception area and was greeted by a wave of heat. "God, 'tis lovely and warm in here."

"It is," agreed the ruddy-cheeked woman behind the counter. "That's the great advantage of having a working forge behind the door there. Not so much fun in summer, though. How can I help you today, sir?"

"I was actually hoping to have a quick word with one of your employees. Shane Walsh?"

The look on the woman's face indicated that this was neither entirely unexpected nor remotely welcome. "He's working at the minute."

"It won't take long," said Bunny, offering his most reassuring smile. "I promise. Just a quick word."

She weighed him up for a couple of seconds then pressed a buzzer under the counter. A fresh-faced teenaged boy stuck his head around the door in the back.

"Tell Shaney there is somebody here to see him – again."

The heavy emphasis on the word "again" was not lost on Bunny. As the young lad departed, Bunny studied some of the pictures on the walls. "I have to say, I actually didn't realise that blacksmiths were still going. Do you still shoe horses and stuff like that?"

"No," said the woman, trying to sound cold and distant. "We don't do that any more. It's mainly commissioned pieces for churches or private collectors."

Bunny pointed at the framed images on the wall that showed a variety of striking-looking sculptures and intricately designed gates. "Wow, these are all very impressive."

While the woman didn't want to talk, her obvious pride in the business's work won out. "The one over on the left there was for a park in France. They got an award – in France. And we all know how fussy the French are. We've another big piece going out to Germany in a couple of weeks."

Bunny nodded. "Is that right? It's great to see a family business from Limerick being acknowledged on the world stage." While it was true, it was also a shameless attempt on his part to keep the woman on side.

The door at the back opened again and in walked a muscular, broad-shouldered and black-haired man in a dirty vest. As he wiped his hands with a rag, he gave Bunny a suspicious look that verged on the hostile. "Thanks, Janet. This won't take long."

With one last glance at Bunny, the woman nodded and headed back through the door.

The man who Bunny assumed was Shane Walsh pointed towards a second door that led off reception. It took them into a small waiting room containing four chairs and more framed pictures on the wall. As soon as the door closed, Shane Walsh spun around to face Bunny and his tone changed to outright aggression. "This is full on harassment now, you realise that?"

"My name is Bunny McGarry. I just wanted a brief word."

"Yeah," said Shane, bristling, "so did your colleagues. Look how that turned out. Are you going to come at me like a man?"

Bunny held up his hands. "Whoa. Hang on there a sec, fella. I think we're seriously getting off on the wrong foot here. I'm not even here as police."

"My arse. You're a guard. Couldn't be more obvious if you were wearing a sign around your neck."

"I am a guard," confirmed Bunny, "but I have nothing to do with DI Grainger or anybody from his investigation that you might have met. To be honest with you, I'm currently suspended from the force."

"So, what the fuck are you doing here?"

"I'm just trying to get to the truth. A friend of mine, a man in his eighties, is in hospital after getting robbed up in Dublin yesterday, and my only interest is recovering what was taken from him."

A look of uncertainty flashed across Shane Walsh's face. "Good luck getting answers about anything from anyone down here after how those Italian pricks behaved."

Bunny slowly lowered one of his hands and indicated the chairs. "How about we have a quick sit-down and you explain to me what you're talking about, because I honestly have no fecking clue."

Shane Walsh bit his lower lip and considered Bunny, as if working out his options.

"Look," said Bunny, "I've already admitted I'm currently suspended, so if you want, you can easily tell me to bugger off, but I'd like to know what has got you so angry before I do."

The blacksmith sat down on the far side of the small room and folded his arms. "Alright, but let's make it quick. My employers aren't wild about these visits I keep getting from the boys in blue."

Bunny took a seat. "So, I take it Grainger has been to see you?"

"And the rest. Four of them turned up here. Grainger, some little bloke with glasses who didn't speak, a French guy and that Italian prick. Schillaci. And I told them exactly what I am telling you – I have had nothing to do with Bobby for three years. I mean, I've not laid eyes on the little arsehole and I'm happy to keep it that way."

"So, you're not close?"

"Bit of an understatement," Shane scoffed. "He put our youngest brother Felix in the hospital. Since then neither I nor my ma have seen or spoken to him. He broke her heart, not to mention poor Felix's collarbone."

"What was that all about?"

Shane's eyes flashed with anger. "It was about the fact that my brother – Bobby, I mean – is and always has been a fucking psychopath. He's like a six-tonne weight hanging around the neck of his family. Look, I did some stupid stuff when I was younger, but I'm an upstanding citizen now, married with a kid and another on the way, and for the second time in a week, I'm having to explain to my employers why I'm being dragged out of work to speak to the Gardaí."

"I'm genuinely sorry about that," said Bunny. "I'm more than happy to have a word—"

Shane Walsh waved the offer away before Bunny could finish making it. "Janet and Donal know me well enough to know what the story is, luckily. She's godmother to our little Taryn." He leaned forward and pointed a finger in Bunny's direction. "But do pass on a message to Inspector Schillaci. If his boys want to jump me again, I'll be ready the next time."

"What?" asked Bunny, genuinely confused.

"Yeah. Like I said, Grainger and the rest came to talk to me in the morning, but I guess they weren't keen on my answers because in the evening, when I'm walking home, I get jumped by a couple of his boys, and Schillaci starts slapping me about and asking the same questions a lot harder."

"That's outrageous," said Bunny. "Was Grainger there?"

Shane Walsh shook his head. "No. Plausible deniability, isn't that what they call it? I found out afterwards – I wasn't the only one on the list. A couple of other known associates of Bobby got similar treatment. Tim Martin had his nose broken and he's getting married next month."

"Did you go to the Gardaí about this?"

This elicited a bitter laugh from Shane. "Would you give over with that shit. Someone from where we are from walking into a cop shop and reporting police brutality? Yeah. That would go really well."

"Those Italian boys are not Gardaí."

"Says you," snapped Shane. "They're knocking around with your boys. What is it they say? If it looks like a duck and quacks like a duck …"

"Would you be willing to testify about this?"

Shane stood up. "Yeah, right. You're the suspended copper who's going to bring the rest to justice, are you? Don't make me laugh. Are we done here?"

"Look, you don't know me from a hole in the ground, and you've no reason to trust me. I get that. For what it's worth, I take what you told me deadly seriously and I will be trying to find some way to have it properly dealt with. In the meantime, if you could help me out, I'd really appreciate it."

"And why would I do that?"

"Because a nice old man who has never done anything to anyone is currently in hospital, and your brother put him there."

Bunny saw the wince of shame. Just because you disown

somebody doesn't stop you from feeling somehow responsible for their ill deeds.

Shane Walsh sighed and sat back down. "I am sorry to hear that."

"From what you said about your brother, I take it the idea of Bobby being violent doesn't come as a shock."

Shane shook his head gloomily. "He's my baby brother, you know? Growing up, especially with our dad dying so young and me being the eldest, from the age of about ten I was in charge, whether I wanted it or not. I tried to look out for him. All of them. I've two other brothers and a sister too. Bobby was always different, though."

"Different how?"

Shane chewed at his lip and looked down at the linoleum floor. "My ma didn't see it at first. Said he was just naughty, but our granny – God rest her – she was a lot harder to fool. I always remember her and ma arguing after she said that Bobby had the devil in him. Bit dramatic but she wasn't wrong. He could be as charming as you like – even as a young fella, the women loved him. Then, for no reason, every now and then he would just snap, and he'd do something."

"First couple of times I defended him, but once you've seen it up close yourself" – he gave a shrug – "you can't deny it. I mean, round our way, violence, fights, whatever else – not exactly unheard of. It was more the way of it." He raised his head and looked directly into Bunny's eyes. "Bobby has a pure vicious streak. Nasty. Cruel." He lowered his gaze again. "God knows where he got it from, but it's there. I think ma ignored it right up to the point when the thing with Felix happened and then – sure, there was no denying that."

Bunny nodded. "I appreciate you'd have no idea where he might be, but do you know anybody else who might do?"

Shane shook his head. "Bobby doesn't have friends, not really. Cousin Niall – he's not a bad lad, but he's a bit simple. Easily led. Gets on better with pigeons than people. I don't know if you could call Bobby and him friends. He is more of a" – Shane looked around the room as if trying to locate the word – "follower, I guess."

"So, Bobby has taken up with this Italian girl ..."

Shane sat back again. "It's a waste of time asking me about her. I only know what that arsehole Grainger told me. Yeah, Bobby always had a way with the women. Like I said, he can be very charming when he wants to be."

"It sounds like they are on a bit of a spree, though. Trying to raise a lot of money fast. Did he ever talk about going anywhere? Outside Ireland, I mean."

"Maybe. He was always full of big ideas. For a while there he was going to be an actor, despite never having acted. Then a rockstar, despite the fact he couldn't hold a note or play any kind of tune on anything. He never bothered applying himself to anything, and then had a chip on his shoulder, like somehow he'd been done wrong." Shane glanced at the clock on the wall. "Look, if there's nothing else, I really need to get back to work."

Bunny couldn't think of anything. "Thanks for your time."

Shane got to his feet. "Word of advice – I wouldn't go asking around the estate. The word is out on those Italian fellas in particular. Some poor Spanish guy caught a kicking just because somebody thought he might be one of them. Folks want to protect their own, but they're not the most choosy about who from."

Bunny stood up and offered Shane his hand. "I imagine I'll be heading back to Dublin after this, as odds on, that's where your brother and his associates are going to show up next. For what it's worth, on behalf of the vast majority of the Garda Síochána, I'm truly sorry for the shite you've been put through."

Shane Walsh brushed the apology away. "It's not the first time I've been on the receiving end of a few slaps from law enforcement. You just accept it, coming from where I come from."

Bunny tried to think of something to say in response to that, but nothing came.

Shane Walsh moved across the room, opened the door and paused. "Actually, you can do one thing for me."

"What's that?" asked Bunny.

"If you do see my brother, tell him I said that if he ever had an ounce of love for his mother or anybody else in this family, he'd stay out of Limerick and never come back. He's been nothing but a blight on us from day one."

Shane Walsh left, leaving the door open behind him.

As Bunny walked himself out, he nodded to Janet behind the counter. The cold outside hit him full in the face like jumping into a sea of icy water. Talking to Shane Walsh hadn't given him much in the way of leads and it had further dampened his mood. What Walsh had said had been right, though. For better or for worse, they had probably gleaned all they could from Limerick. It was time to head back to Dublin and get busy trying to find Bobby Walsh and Sofia Accardi before the pair either disappeared, or Schillaci and Grainger fulfilled their mission of making it look like the whole thing never happened.

The Fadden family deserved justice and come hell or high water, they were going to get it.

# CHAPTER EIGHTEEN

Bobby Walsh rolled off Sofia and gave a contented sigh. "I needed that. A good head-clearer."

He felt the mattress shift beside him and turned to see Sofia getting re-dressed.

"And where do you think you're going? I'm just getting warmed up."

She smiled back at him over her shoulder. "Niall will be back soon. I don't want him to hear us."

Bobby laughed. "Do you not reckon he heard us last night? And the night before? And the night before that?"

She giggled. "That's different."

"I'd bet you any money he's lying in bed at night, wishing he was me. Lazing there, stroking that bloody pigeon."

"Don't," she said, giving him the lightest of admonishing slaps on his bare chest.

"What? You know it's true. He's got a mad crush on you. N-N-Niall and Sofia sitting in a tree, K-I-S-S-I-N-G. In his dreams," he said with a laugh. "I'm surprised he's not named the bloody pigeon after you."

"Don't be mean. He is sweet."

"Sweet?" echoed Bobby, the joviality dropping from his voice. "Sweet?" he repeated.

"You know what I mean."

As Sofia tried to slip her bra on, Bobby grabbed her upper arm and pulled her firmly towards him. "Don't go getting soft on me."

"I'm not," she protested.

"That's not what it sounds like to me."

"I was just—"

"Just what?" he said, drawing her more firmly towards him until his mouth was a couple of inches from her cheek. "Just what?" he repeated insistently.

"Nothing," she said quickly. "I just … I didn't mean anything by it. You're hurting my arm."

He loosened his grip only slightly. "You listen to me, my girl – we can't afford you going soft. I didn't want to say this, but let's be real … Once we do this thing, there will be a lot of people looking for us and we can't afford to carry dead weight. They'll be looking for two guys and a woman. It'd be madness to take Niall with us."

She turned to face him directly. "But what will happen to him?"

"He'll have his new passport – same as you and me. I'll give him a bit of whatever is left over from the money, and he can make his own way. Maybe his stupid pigeon can fly him somewhere."

"But—"

"But nothing," Bobby interrupted. "I can't keep taking care of him his whole life. He's gotta make his own way, eventually. Now is the time."

He felt Sofia stiffen under his grip.

"Look," he whispered in a soft voice, as he let go of her arm, reached down to gently take her left hand and brought it towards him. "Do you know what this ring means?" he asked before kissing the small diamond surrounded by emeralds on her ring finger. The one they had taken from the old man. "It means you and I are going to be together for ever. You're my girl, my job is to take care of you, and that's what I'm going to do, OK?"

She nodded.

He used his free hand to tuck her long dark hair behind her ear then, leaning forward, he kissed her neck tenderly. "I love you."

"I love you, too," she said. "I just—"

They drew apart abruptly as the front door slammed. "I-I-I'm home," came Niall's shout.

Bobby shook his head. "Perfect fucking timing as always." He raised his voice. "There in a second."

Sofia quickly finished dressing and hurried out of the room. Bobby took his time before following her out and into the kitchen.

Sofia was now at the sink, washing up the dishes from the morning's breakfast and last night's late dinner. Niall, predictably, was standing beside the kettle watching it heat up. Since they'd been kids, he had been obsessed with drinking tea. It was all the big idiot ever drank, and every time he stood there like a moron, watching the bloody thing boil. Bobby's auntie was always shouting about it, something about a watched pot never boils, which never made much sense to Bobby. In fact, it made no more sense than watching the bloody thing did.

"How did the surveillance go?" he asked.

Niall nodded. "Good. P-p-pretty much the same as yesterday." He handed over his little red notepad and then turned back to the kettle. Bobby flicked through the pages and scanned today's entry. "Left the apartment almost exactly the same time as yesterday and walked the same route."

Bobby nodded. "Good. Good work. Have you had some breakfast?"

"Yeah. I g-got myself a breakfast roll from that shop across from the building."

"When did you do that?"

Niall shot him a nervous sideways look. "W-what?"

"When did you get yourself this nice big breakfast roll?"

"I-I—"

Bobby noted Sofia looking back at him. "I mean, you wouldn't have been stupid enough to go in and do that while you were on surveillance duty?"

"I could still s-see out the window."

"Ohhhh," said Bobby, in an exaggerated manner. "You could see out the window. Brilliant!"

"He got the—" started Sofia before Bobby cut her dead with a raised hand.

"Stay out of this," he said, moving towards Niall. He reached up and cupped the back of Niall's neck with his left hand. "You had one job. One job the entire plan relies on, and you wandered off. Have I got that right?"

"I just—"

Bobby moved his hand across to Niall's ear, grabbed it and twisted it, as he had done countless times before.

"Don't!" yelped Niall.

"One job." He was now tugging sharply on Niall's ear, so the bigger man had no choice but to bend down. "You had one job, and you couldn't even do that."

"It hurts," he pleaded.

"Fuck me – if you can't deal with this, how are you going to deal with prison? Because with the way you're going, that's where we're all going to end up."

"Bobby," said Sofia, placing a gentle hand on his arm before he shook her off.

"S-s-s-sorry," said Niall.

"Sorry? Sorry? Well, as long as you are sorry. That's the main thing." He yanked his ear harder, forcing Niall down onto one knee, then leaned down and shouted directly into his ear canal. "I'm so happy you're sorry."

"Bobby!" screamed Sofia. "Enough."

He whipped around to face her, and his right hand drew back. She flinched before him.

He stayed like that for a second, and then, as if a switch had been flicked, he stopped. His body relaxed and he released Niall's ear. The big man got to his feet and cowered beside the counter, cupping his ear as tears streamed down his face. Once again he stared at the kettle.

Bobby looked back and forth between Niall and Sofia. He shook his head disapprovingly. "God help us all. Am I the only one who is thinking clearly around here? We are so close. All we need is one screw-up and we are done for. Do you get that?"

He waited until they both nodded then he turned and snatched up his jacket from the back of the stool it was resting on. "Now that he's back, I'm taking the car to go see this Dermot fella – to make sure we can get what we need. Even if nobody else is sticking to their part of the plan, I'm going to make sure that I stick to mine. Try not to fuck anything else up while I'm gone."

Without another word, he snatched up the keys from the table and slammed the door behind him on his way out.

———

When Sofia heard the car pull away, she took a couple of steps towards Niall and raised her hand to touch his hair. "Are you OK?" she asked softly.

He shook her off, refusing to look in her direction. "I'm fine."

"He doesn't mean it."

"Whatever."

"He's just stressed."

Niall opened his mouth to speak, but changed his mind. He turned away, opened one of the cupboard doors and took out the same chipped mug he'd been using for the last few days. He threw a tea bag into it and then stood there, his back to Sofia, and stared intently at the whistling kettle.

After a couple of seconds, it clicked off.

# CHAPTER NINETEEN

Bunny awoke with a start. "What the ... Jesus! Who in the ...? Where the ...?"

"Eloquently put as always," said Butch, from the driver's seat. "If you have awoken from your little snooze confused, allow me to bring you up to speed. We are now back in Dublin, thanks to me driving us here. You, meanwhile, fell asleep somewhere in Kildare."

"No, I didn't," said Bunny. "I was just resting my eyes."

"Really? That being the case, I have some questions. Firstly, while you were just resting your eyes, why did you slobber all over my passenger-side window?"

Bunny glanced down at the glass and quickly wiped it with his sleeve. "I may have nodded off for a couple of minutes there."

"During which time, you did quite a lot of talking," said Butch with a wide grin.

"Oh no."

"Oh yes. You had an awful lot to say about the Kilkenny hurling team. A surprising amount of which was remarkably sexual in nature."

"It was not. You're making that up."

"That's for me and your subconscious to know, and for you to find out."

"Any more of that nonsense and you can drop me off here. I'll make my own way home."

Butch raised her eyebrows pointedly, prompting Bunny to glance outside.

"I now see that I am actually home," he conceded.

The winter's night had long since set in and the raindrops of a steady downpour were being picked out by the orange glow of the streetlights. Butch had pulled up about a hundred yards from his front door. At this time of night, parking was always at a premium and his car was already taking up the space outside his house.

"Well spotted. What did your last chauffeur die of?"

"Ara, be fair – I offered to drive."

"You did," admitted Butch. "But I'm not letting you behind the wheel of my car, and nor am I willing to risk a long-distance car journey in that God's gift to mechanics that you insist on keeping."

"'Tis a perfectly good car," said Bunny.

"Really?" asked Butch. "How about you go over to it right now and I will bet you five thousand pounds that it won't start first time?"

"I would be delighted to, but I have a hard and fast rule about never gambling with friends. It just creates ill feeling."

Butch laughed. "Yeah. Lucky for me." She drummed her fingers on the steering wheel. "So, I don't suppose that while you were having your little power nap you came up with an ingenious idea for how to find the terrible trio?"

Bunny shook his head. They had spent the first half of the journey back to Dublin going over what they had learned from DI Vanya Coyne; Sofia Accardi's flatmate, Sarah Kennedy; and Bobby Walsh's brother Shane. Sofia and Bobby seemed to have enough issues going on between them to keep a psychiatrist very busy, but any hypotheses they had formulated on the dynamic of that particular group were still only speculative. While they had gained a lot of context, there still wasn't much in the way of leads.

"No big brainwaves, I'm afraid. I've got those feelers out. Fingers crossed somebody somewhere might get a sniff of them. I've chased up anybody I can think of."

"Hey," said Butch, "you never know, Grainger might make an arrest."

Bunny made a face. "If he does, it'll be a first. More to the point, him and the goon squad will make the whole thing disappear and Sofia will be back having a nice family Christmas before you can say *arrivederci*. None of which is getting the Faddens their ring back. Seriously, thanks for everything, though. Helping out, I mean."

Butch nodded. "Don't worry about it. Assuming we are still suspended, I'm at a loose end tomorrow, if you need me."

Bunny got out of the car, pulled his coat tight against the steady rain and bent down to look back inside the vehicle. "Thanks a million. Fingers crossed something will come up or else we will both be sitting around with nothing to do."

"Oh God," said Butch. "I'm finally going to have to put those Christmas decorations up, amn't I?"

"Where's your Christmas spirit, Pamela?"

"Weren't you with me last night when Santa died?"

"Oh yeah. I forgot about that. Safe home."

"... And get yourself something to eat." As Bunny slammed the door shut, Butch raised her voice to be heard. "By which I mean – not a takeaway."

Bunny mimed not being able to hear. "Get a takeaway?" he shouted back. "That's not a bad idea."

He started to walk off up the pavement before Butch could holler any other lifestyle advice. After a few seconds she passed by in the car, flicking him the Vs as she did so. He waved cheerfully in response.

Curry? Or Chinese? He could really go for a pizza. Or he could just nip down the chipper for double sausage and chips. Ohhhh, he could really go for a nice battered sausage.

The small part of his brain that wasn't cycling through fast-food menus nudged the rest of his grey matter. Forty feet away, a man was walking down the pavement towards him. A large man. It was a free country, whatever the hell that meant, which meant that people could walk wherever they wanted. The problem with this man was that he was walking "casually".

People who were just walking somewhere, just walked. People walking casually were trying not to draw attention to themselves. It was like loitering; nobody could give you an exact definition of the term but any copper worth their salt knew it when they saw it. As this guy passed through the pools of light thrown down by the streetlights, he was staring up at the terraced houses as if there were something interesting to see. Then he'd look steadfastly into the distance like a walker on a long trek with many more miles to go. It looked as natural as tits on a donkey.

Thirty feet away. Bunny couldn't quite make out the guy's face, but the cut of his coat was smooth. Stylish. Bunny was no expert in these things, but he plumped for Italian. He felt for the keys in his pocket but thought better of it. The whole key-to-the-eye thing was a bit extreme. He'd personally recommend it to other people, and would stand by it, but he was a guard, and potentially blinding somebody for life was the kind of incident that raised questions.

Twenty feet. Bunny caught a flash of the streetlight being reflected off the guy's shiny leather shoes. The man's identity was in no real doubt before that point, but it was nice to have confirmation. This fella was big, but his size didn't bother Bunny unduly. He was a pretty big man himself, and the trick in these situations was to make yourself the jumper as opposed to the jumpee. He remembered Shane Walsh telling him earlier in the day how they had jumped him on his way home from work. Clearly this was their modus operandi.

They.

Shite.

He didn't even look around but now that he was listening for it, he could hear the set of footsteps behind him. Damn it. He should have been more alert.

Ten feet. Bunny grabbed the keys in his pocket and interlaced them between his fingers. Two on one meant all bets were off. One of these boys was going to end up enjoying 3D movies a whole lot less.

In his experience, the trick to fighting two guys was to make it so you were fighting one guy as quickly as possible. Maybe these *signori* just wanted to chat, but surrounding somebody on a dark street was page one in how not to win friends and influence people.

Five feet. The guy in front of him wasn't even pretending now. He was staring directly at Bunny, and he was close enough that Bunny could see his muscles tensing. Bunny also noticed he was wearing a tie, which was excellent news. Fashion be damned – never turn up to a fight with a rope around your neck; that's just asking for trouble.

Bunny started counting to three in his head. Feint forward. Spin around. Key to the face. Turn back. From there, there was no point having a plan. It was all jazz.

Two ...

Three ... Feint... Spin.

In hindsight, it was a perfectly decent plan for the opening stages of a fight. It relied on using what little element of surprise he had, coupled with the kind of animal cunning that had kept him alive until this point. What it hadn't factored in was the third guy. He had evidently been sneaking up out of sight, behind the parked cars to Bunny's left. He made his presence felt by shooting a Taser at Bunny just as he spun around, catching him right in the chest. If the Italians had shown this kind of tactical forethought in the Second World War, they might not have ended up having to fight on both sides.

He considered the mace to be complete overkill. Who needed three guys, a Taser and mace?

His eyes had barely started to burn as the cudgelling blow made contact with the back of his head, further scattering his senses. Bunny felt hands upon him. He attempted to lash out in the hope of making himself feel better at least, and his fist made gratifying contact with what felt a lot like a chin.

The exclamation that resulted from the blow was swiftly followed by another blow to his own head, and then everything was a blur. His eyes were burning now. Tears were streaming down his face.

Somebody definitely threw in a cheeky kick while he was on the ground, then Bunny vaguely heard the doors of a van open and multiple hands moved him in one swift operation. They'd done this before.

From very far away he could hear the voice of somebody shouting about what was going on, but by then the van was moving.

He was beginning to regather his senses when something hit him again.

His last thought before he passed out was that he probably wasn't going to get that sausage after all.

# CHAPTER TWENTY

Bunny winced as the black bag was pulled off his head and the sudden bright light dazzled his already-burning eyes. He would have shielded them, but his hands were tied behind his back and to the plastic chair he was sitting on.

"Mr McGarry," said a male voice with a distinctly Italian accent.

"Detective," responded Bunny flatly, without opening his eyes.

"I am sorry?"

"It's Detective McGarry."

"You are ... suspended, no?"

"Still a detective. You don't lose the title just because they've given you a couple of days off for good behaviour."

"Would you like to open your eyes so you can see to whom you are speaking?"

"I already know."

"But still ..."

"Not until you throw some water on my face to get rid of this bullshit mace your cowardly henchmen used to take me down. Three on one. Has your country collectively decided not to take any chances after—"

Bunny was interrupted by his wish being granted. A not inconsiderable amount of water was thrown into his face, closely followed by a cloth being wiped across his eyes. He blinked a few times then forced himself to raise his eyelids. The bright light made it difficult, but he could make out four heavyset men in suits standing around him in a rough semi-circle. In front of them was Schillaci, beaming a mocking, gold-toothed smile below his lively green eyes. Bunny ignored him entirely and looked around the room.

"Really?" he scoffed. "A warehouse? And then you did the whole putting-a-black-bag-over-my-head bit too. What a bunch of clichés. Did you lads learn how to kidnap somebody from the movies or something?"

"I'm glad to see you are in the mood to talk," said Schillaci. "That will make this easier."

"Oh, I'm always happy to talk. You could have just approached me like a man, though; instead of sending The Three Stooges here to grab me."

Schillaci shrugged. "I apologise for our methods, but it was necessary."

"Hang on." Bunny licked his lips. "Was that sparkling water you threw in my face? Jesus. You boys do everything with a bit of class, don't you?"

"You are welcome."

"Not a fan myself. It's just proper water a frog has farted in. Anyway," continued Bunny. "I hate to be the one to tell you, but in this country, we don't take kindly to people kidnapping members of the police force."

"Ah, but again, not to" – he looked back at one of the four men – "how do you say … labour the point? Yes, not to labour the point, but you are not currently a member of the police force."

"Two things there; first, I am. I definitely am. And second, we don't take kindly to the kidnapping of anybody."

Now that Bunny's eyes were adjusting, he could see more of the room. The bright light was coming from two directions, and the sources of which were the headlights of two vehicles. One was a white van, which Bunny guessed was the one that had been used to grab him. The other, from what he could see, was Schillaci's Porsche, as mentioned by Vanya Coyne.

The man himself looked back at his men and laughed again. "I think I will take my chances. You know why you are here?"

"I think I do," said Bunny, "and I'll be honest, you have entirely misunderstood how Secret Santa works."

Schillaci furrowed his brow. "I do not know what that is, but no, that is not the reason."

"In that case, I presume we're here to talk about Ray Houghton's goal when Ireland beat Italy in the 1994 World Cup?"

Schillaci leaned forward calmly and punched Bunny in the face with a sharp left hook. A southpaw, then. Bunny had seen it coming, so was able to turn away slightly, but the man still knew what he was doing. Bunny guessed there was some boxing training in his past.

He swivelled his head back around and worked his jaw up and down. "Too soon for you to see the funny side of that one, is it?"

"I grow bored of your constant chatter."

"You're not the first," admitted Bunny.

"You are here because, despite being told not to, you are interfering in my investigation."

"The problem with that ... Ehm, I don't know your first name so I'm just going to guess Luigi. Is that racist?"

Schillaci punched him in the face again. Harder this time. A right hook. Nope, definitely not a southpaw.

Bunny spat out some blood. "To be fair, I probably deserved that one."

"I am running out of patience," said Schillaci.

"You're hiding it well. Anyway, what were we talking about?"

"Why you keep interfering in my investigation. Did you think we would not know about your little trip to Limerick?"

"Right," said Bunny, nodding his head. "See, here is the problem we are having. You're apparently a member of the Italian police force, which doesn't reflect well on them if I'm honest, but – you're in Ireland. You have no jurisdiction here. You're guests – albeit ones who are using their time off to engage in extracurricular activities of a criminal nature."

Schillaci leaned in close enough that Bunny could feel the inspector's breath on his face. "I am here to do a job. Stay out of my way."

"I don't know how things work *in Italia*, but over here – if you're looking for a bit of cooperation, you fill out some forms, possibly get a round in. A box of doughnuts always goes down well. What you don't do is snatch somebody off the street and start slapping them around the place." Bunny fixed Schillaci with a stare. "It's impolite."

"I am trying to ask you nicely," said Schillaci. "If that doesn't work" – he tilted his head back towards the men standing behind him – "I will ask Mario to ask you, and he is not as polite as I am."

Bunny barked a laugh that made his head hurt. "Mario? I can't believe that's a real name. I thought they made it up for the game. You know, the computer one – with the plumbers. It's great craic. You—"

This time it was a left-right combo that thankfully was delivered with such fury that the right only glanced off him. The McGarry technique of trying to wind up your opponent in any given situation so that they don't think straight had proven effective over the years, but it certainly had its downsides.

Bunny took a moment to allow the alarm bells ringing in his ears to quieten down, then he spat out a tooth. He peered down at it. "I don't want you to feel bad about that. It's actually a replacement, if you look closely. Paidí Burke knocked out the original about ten years ago. Now that guy could hit."

Schillaci lifted Bunny's chin up. "Look me in the eye when you speak to me."

"'Tis not that easy, I'm afraid. They're a bit wonky. Well, the right one, but it sort of throws off the pair."

"I am fast coming to the conclusion that the only way you will stay out of my way is if you are in the hospital."

Bunny's face grew still. "Oh, I wouldn't be so sure about that."

"It would be terrible if you were to have some kind of accident."

Bunny laughed. "Do me a favour. Not even you would be that dumb. A member of the Garda Síochána turns up dead and several people know what I've been up to because, as you pointed out, I haven't exactly been hiding it. I'm a man with many enemies, that's true – but a fair few friends too. You take down a guard and the rest of us take it fierce personally. Always have. Grainger won't be able to protect you from that. They'll come looking for you and they won't stop. You won't even make it out of the country, buddy – even if you have diplomatic immunity, which I'm guessing you don't. And you would be surprised by the number of people in Mountjoy Prison who would want a word. A lot of them have had their heart set on killing me for years, and they'll resent you skipping the queue." He glanced to one side. "By the way, not to change the subject – but is that your Porsche?"

One of Schillaci's men laughed, which earned him a look of reproach from his boss. Schillaci stood upright and regarded the knuckles of his own right hand as he spoke. "It is. Yes."

"I own one myself. There's something we have in common."

This time it was Schillaci's turn to laugh. "That is a Porsche 911. A magnificent machine. I have seen your car. It is a piece of shit."

"Fuck you," snapped Bunny, failing to hide his irritation. "It's a grand car. It's the best Porsche you can afford on an honest policeman's salary."

"Mario?"

The biggest of the musclemen took a step forward.

"OK. OK. OK," said Bunny. "Enough is enough. I think we can come to an understanding."

Schillaci glanced at Mario then looked back down at Bunny warily. "Really?"

"Are you familiar with the phrase 'my enemy's enemy is my friend'?"

"No."

"Good," said Bunny, "because it is bullshit, as you're about to find out. Now – Ray Houghton." Bunny saw the flash of frustration in

Schillaci's eyes and drew back instinctively. "Whoa. Whoa. I'm trying to make a point."

"Make it quickly."

"Right. My point was, Ray Houghton wasn't even Irish. I mean, initially. He was Scottish but his granny was from Ireland, so he qualified. Nowadays, no matter what anyone tells you, he's as Irish as Irish can be. Never mind scoring against your lot, he scored against England. We would make him president if he wanted it."

Bunny stopped talking and Schillaci glared at him. "And what is your point?"

"That you are about to meet a second diminutive Irishman who is going to fuck up Italian plans."

Bunny had only ever been in the presence of true genius a couple of times in his life. Once, he'd been lucky enough to be sitting in a pub in Donegal while the great Davy Spillane played the uilleann pipes not five feet from where he was sitting. It had been spellbinding. Another time, he'd been sitting in an interview room with an artist who had been the victim of a robbery at knifepoint. She was waiting for a suspect to be brought in to see if she could identify him. To distract herself, she had taken an ordinary sheet of paper and a simple pencil and drawn a picture of a horse. Just a sketch. It had been unreal. It had looked as if it were about to leap off the page. Bunny had stared at it mesmerised and cringed when she casually scrunched it up and threw it away.

While it was a different experience, there was no doubting that Bunny was now, once again, in the presence of a form of genius. Gerry Lamkin was an artist, and his palette was violence, his brush a baseball bat. True, he'd had the element of surprise – Bunny having been the only one to spot him as he snuck into the warehouse. That was why Bunny had done everything in his power to keep the eyes of all the Italians on him.

Once in position, though, it was all Gerry. The first man literally didn't know what hit him, as the noise of his knee exploding was the starting gun. The second man barely had a chance to turn around before he was down, having received a home run to the face. The first thing to hit the fourth man was the third man. Bunny didn't know if it was planned or just instinct; dominos falling. Both went down within a fraction of a second of each other, and the fourth received a brief stomp in the chest to finish him off. The true magic was that Gerry Lamkin knew with the minimum amount of effort how to hit somebody so they wouldn't just go down but stay down. It was like watching a hot knife pass through butter, if the knife was wide-eyed and grinning maniacally as it moved.

Gerry took a step towards Schillaci but the sight of the gun in the other man's hand caused him to pause.

Schillaci cocked back the hammer.

"Easy," said Bunny. "Easy!"

"Who in the hell are you?" asked Schillaci.

"Gerry Lamkin," came the response. "Delighted to make your acquaintance."

"Don't do anything stupid," warned Bunny.

"I will defend myself," declared Schillaci.

"I was talking to him." Bunny had seen the look in Gerry's eyes. Gerry was not a man who feared death, and while the gun had made him pause, there was no guarantee he would stop entirely.

Given the context, Gerry then produced one of the most terrifying noises Bunny had ever heard – he giggled. Bunny looked up at Schillaci, whose eyes were swivelling between the groaning mass on the floor that had been his men, and Gerry.

"OK," said Bunny. "There is some understandable tension in the room. What I suggest we do is – myself and Gerry here leave, and let you go about the business of figuring out what the fuck just happened then probably calling an ambulance or two."

Schillaci shifted his grip on the gun.

"Before you do anything," continued Bunny, "a word to the wise. Two things, actually. One – if you kill Gerry, then obviously you're going to have to kill me. Then, remember our previous chat about how well a member of the Gardaí dying in suspicious circumstances would go down? Well, a bullet isn't even suspicious, is it? And that's assuming you manage to do that, because the second thing" – Bunny looked back at Schillaci – "is that he is about eight feet from you. I'm not sure you've got enough bullets in that gun to take him down before he reaches you because" – Bunny now looked up at Gerry – "no offence meant here, Gerry, but Gerry is clearly insane."

Gerry nodded. "I was getting better, but they didn't give me any of the good medication when I left. Cutbacks."

For what felt like an eternity but may have been only a couple of seconds, Bunny watched helplessly as the two men stared at each other. Gerry was poised like a coiled spring. Then, Schillaci took a step backwards and the angle of his gun altered by just a couple of inches. It was now aimed just to the left of Gerry and could still shoot him in half a second, but it was just enough to nudge things back from the precipice they'd been teetering on.

Still tied to the chair, Bunny shifted his weight forward and awkwardly got himself to his feet, standing in a crab-like crouch with the chair on his back. "OK. Gerry, I think you and I should be leaving now."

Gerry glanced at the groaning men on the floor and then back at Schillaci. "Are you sure?"

Bunny started to shuffle towards the door he could see on the far wall. "I've never been surer of anything in my life. Inspector, it's been fun. I'm afraid I'm going to have to take the chair with me. I'll try to return it at some point."

Reluctantly, Gerry turned and started walking beside Bunny, looking over his shoulder at Schillaci as he went. "I could have taken him."

"I don't doubt it," said Bunny. "But let's just stick to you taking the four boys down, shall we? I don't know why or how you're here but I'm extremely glad you are. I never expected to have my own fairy god ... person. I'm even more surprised to find out that it is you."

"Here, what's stopping this prick from shooting us in the back?"

"Mainly, the thought that it will be more hassle than it's worth. Having said that, let's go as quickly as we can, in case he re-does the sums and realises he forgot to carry the one."

Gerry put his hand on Bunny's arm to support him as he

stumbled. "I hope you appreciate this doesn't change our situation," he said.

"Understood. Still, thank you very much. In fact, to show my gratitude properly – how would you feel about double sausage and chips?"

# CHAPTER TWENTY-ONE

Bunny would say this for Gerry Lamkin – the man truly knew how to appreciate a battered sausage. They were sat at Bunny's kitchen table, white paper wrappings unfurled in front of them, both men chewing in slow, reverential silence. Gerry swallowed his final mouthful and nodded appreciatively. "That is nothing short of magnificent."

"I told you," said Bunny. "Didn't I tell you? That Mrs Mammadova is a true artist. It's something she does with the batter."

"There is a lightness to it and the flavour juxtaposes beautifully with the vinegary kick of the chips."

Bunny raised both eyebrows.

Gerry blushed. "I got really into watching cooking shows while I was inside. The screws like having them on the telly. They lead to fewer fights than sports or current affairs programming. Having said that, I once saw a fella get shanked after a disagreement about whether stuffing should be cooked inside or outside the turkey."

Bunny didn't know what to say to that. He was quickly coming to realise that in conversation with Gerry Lamkin, such moments were commonplace.

"Mammadova – that's a very unusual name?"

"She's from Azerbaijan."

Gerry tilted his head. "Is that right? God, fancy that. Where is Azerbaijan?"

"I'm not really sure. Would it be one of those former Soviet Union places? To be honest with you, the Berlin Wall came down after I left school and I've sort of lost my grip on geography since then."

"You reckon the battered sausage might be their national dish or something?"

Bunny shrugged. "I mean, I don't know if the battered sausage would be anybody's national dish, but in that area of the world they certainly can be a bit … unique. Even if it isn't, they might make it so after they taste Mrs Mammadova's take on it."

"True enough." Gerry popped a couple of chips into his mouth and spoke as he ate. "How's your head?"

"Not too bad, considering." Bunny's jaw ached, his mouth was sore from where he had lost the tooth, and there were some impressive swellings coming up on the left side of his face already, but, given the circumstances, it wasn't too bad a result. "I wanted to say, again – thanks very much, Gerry. You saved my arse there and no mistake."

Gerry shifted awkwardly, like a man who wasn't used to getting praise and didn't quite know how to react. "Don't worry about it."

"I mean, while I am over the moon that you were there, can I ask how you came to be so?"

"I was sitting outside your house in the car, waiting for you to come home so, you know, I could batter you." He pointed at the wrappings. "No pun intended."

"Right."

"I mean, you did not behave well last night, Bunny. You made a holy show of me – and in front of Hazel and everything."

"I'm sorry about—"

Before Bunny could go any further, Gerry waved him into silence. "Anyway, like I said, I was outside, and I saw those pricks jumping you. I mean, three on one? That's very unfair."

"That's exactly what I said," exclaimed Bunny, holding up his hands for emphasis. "It's a pure coward's move."

"A hundred percent agree. So, when they drove off, I followed the van and ... Well, you know the rest. Who were those fellas, anyway?"

"A bunch of Italians."

"What? Like the Mafia?"

"Actually, hard as this is to believe, the little fella who was doing all the talking and had the gun? He's police."

Gerry sat back in his chair. "I don't have a hard time believing that at all. In my experience, some of the worst criminals are in uniform. Present company excepted, of course."

Part of Bunny felt compelled to defend the honour of policing, but another part of him still had the memory of Schillaci smiling down at him as he was tied to a chair, so he shouted the former thought down. "They're over here looking for a girl."

"What's that got to do with you?"

"It's complicated," said Bunny. "The girl in question was involved in the robbery of a friend of mine."

"Is this to do with the young fella from last night and his granny's ring?"

"It is, yes. Sorry, I forgot you'd met Deccie. Yes, I'm trying to get the ring back. Not having much luck so far."

"Well, if people are snatching ye off the street and beating you up, you must be getting reasonably close."

Bunny shifted around the white paper in front of him, in the forlorn hope there might still be a chip left inside. "Doesn't feel that way. By the way, I have to say, Gerry – I've never seen anybody take down four big fellas like that. It was extraordinary."

He had meant it as a compliment, but Gerry looked away and pulled an expression as if he had a nasty taste in his mouth. "It's just violence. It's the only thing I have ever been good at. To be honest, when I was inside people left me alone, and they had me on the good meds, and I'd say that was weirdly the happiest I've ever been in my life. Daft as it sounds, I just want to be left alone."

Bunny lowered his voice. "I know a couple of people over at the probation service. Let me make a few phone calls first thing in the morning, see if I can find out what's going on with your medication."

Gerry's face lit up. "Really?"

"It's the very least I could do," said Bunny. "I mean, no promises now. It's only a couple of days before Christmas, and you know what the civil service are like. The people that are still there might already have one foot out the door for the holidays, but I'll do what I can."

"That's very good of you," said Gerry, looking positively cheerful. "Hazel said she was going to try to talk to somebody as well. Her lecturer. She's studying psychology at night out at UCD. Said she got interested in it because of her Creutzman Belling thing."

"That thing where she said she could only tell the truth? Is that real, then?"

Gerry nodded enthusiastically. "Oh yeah. Absolutely. She showed me the article they did about her in the *Independent*."

"God love her. That's an awful thing."

Gerry looked down at his hands as a peculiar expression dawned across his face. "I think it's wonderful. Someone you know isn't lying to you. How much easier life would be if everyone was like that." He spoke in a near whisper. "I think she's amazing."

Bunny found himself blinking a couple of times while he struggled to come up with something to say to that. The man sitting opposite him at the kitchen table had taken considerably more time over double battered sausage and chips than he had annihilating four grown men, and yet here he was with an almost childlike expression on his face, appearing suddenly very vulnerable.

Bunny drew in a breath to speak but, before he could form any words, Gerry sprang to his feet as if an alarm had gone off and clapped his hands together. "Anyway, I should let you get to bed. Thanks very much for the sausages and that."

"No problem at all. And thanks again for—"

"Right." Gerry snatched his coat up off the back of the chair. "So, I'll give you a day or two, to recover from tonight, and then I'll be back to take care of our thing properly. Won't do it now – wouldn't be fair."

"Oh," said Bunny, taken aback.

Gerry pulled his coat on and headed down the hall towards the front door. "Merry Christmas and all that bollocks."

Before Bunny could respond, Gerry was out the door, closing it firmly behind him. He rubbed a hand over the swelling that was already rising on the left side of his face.

"Well, I suppose it's always nice to have something to look forward to."

# CHAPTER TWENTY-TWO

Bunny paced up and down his kitchen with the phone pressed to his ear. Trying to do a good deed had taken up most of his morning but now, hopefully, he might be nearing the end of the near-impenetrable maze of red tape. He had started with the people he knew, who – because it wasn't their area – transferred him to people he didn't know, and he ended up going round and round while an automated voice assured him that his call was important to them. He probably should have given up, but by a certain point it almost became like he was too invested to stop. This phone call was his life now.

Finally – quite possibly by chance – he found somebody who understood the problem he was trying to solve, and actually seemed to give a shit about helping. Maureen. He was putting an awful lot of hope in the lilting Tipperary accent of the fair Maureen.

The sound of a fist being thumped against his front door prompted him to walk down the hall. "Coming," he called. Without looking, he opened the door and stepped back to allow Butch to walk in.

"Morning," she said. "Seeing as it's Christmas, I stopped at that place you like and got you one of those breakfast burritos you're always banging on about. You can—"

She broke off as she caught sight of Bunny's injuries. "What the hell happened to you?"

Bunny pointed to the side of his face as he shifted the phone to his other ear. "This? It looks a lot worse than it is. I had a bit of a run-in with the Italians."

"What?" asked Butch, incredulous. "When?"

"Last night, after you dropped me off."

"They jumped you?"

"Kidnapped, actually."

"Kidnapped?"

"'Tis alright. Gerry Lamkin saved me."

"Gerry Lamkin? Psychopathic, lunatic Gerry Lamkin? That Gerry Lamkin? The fella you pissed off a couple nights previously and who vowed bloody vengeance? Are we talking about the same Gerry Lamkin?" If Butch's voice went any higher her incredulity would soon only register with dogs.

"He's not that bad, really. I've been on the phone for most of the morning trying to get him drugs." Bunny reached out his hand towards the foil-wrapped breakfast burrito that Butch was holding, only to have it slapped away.

"Drugs?" asked Butch.

"The legal prescription kind, obviously."

"Have you reported the kidnapping?"

"I can't," said Bunny. "I mean, I'm pretty sure it'd count as a violation of Gerry's parole. I can't put the poor lad back in prison for Christmas."

"And when were you going to tell me all of this?"

"Sure, amn't I telling you now?"

"Telling me now?" echoed Butch in disbelief. "We're supposed to be a team. Last night you got kidnapped by a couple of Italian thugs—"

"There was actually five of them."

"Five? How did you get away from five guys?"

"Gerry Lamkin is an absolute beast with a baseball bat—" Bunny winced. "Oh, hello, Maureen. No, I wasn't talking to you. A friend of mine has just popped round. We are ... planning on starting a baseball team in the new year." He cringed at Butch while Maureen spoke. "... Are you?" Bunny moved the phone away from his mouth slightly. "Good news, Pamela – Maureen here is a big fan of baseball, and she says she'd be up for joining our team."

She rolled her eyes at his pleading look. "Great," she said. "The more the merrier."

"Absolutely," chimed Bunny, before changing tack. "And how are we doing on getting Gerry sorted out?"

Bunny listened for a few seconds, then pumped his fist. "Maureen, you're an angel. You are an absolute angel. Thank you so much. I will be in touch about the team, have a great Christmas."

He hung up and looked down at Butch.

"So," she said, "since I dropped you off last night, you've been kidnapped by Italian thugs, saved by the local uber-thug – who you are now acting as a social worker for – and, oh yes, you're starting a baseball team now, too?"

"Technically, *we* are starting a baseball team."

"I'm not sure that's going to work," said Butch, "seeing as we're supposed to be a team already and you are not communicating well."

"I sent you a text earlier."

"You did," confirmed Butch, pulling out her phone and opening the aforementioned message. "And it says ... 'I've had an idea. If you're free, drop round as I'd love to get your opinion.'"

"See?" he said. "I'm asking your opinion because we are a team and I respect and value your input."

Butch noticed Bunny's eyes wandering down to a certain something. "Yeah," she said. "Pull the other one. And before you ask, no, you cannot have the breakfast burrito. I'm annoyed with you. No burrito until you tell me this brainwave of yours."

"OK. We – and, I assume, Grainger – have been trying to find Sofia and the dynamic duo and are having feck-all luck."

"I'm aware."

"How about we take a different approach? We know they're grabbing cash and any valuables, jewellery, et cetera. Maybe we should start asking what they need all that money for?"

"And have you come up with an answer for that?"

"No," admitted Bunny. "But what I did realise is, if they do need money, they're going to need to find a way to turn the jewellery and watches into cash."

Butch considered this and nodded begrudgingly. "Alright, that does make sense."

"So, rather than trying to follow them, we need to follow the money."

"And how exactly do we do that?"

"That's where my idea comes in. Now, you might not like it, but hear me out."

Butch stood there in silence for the next two minutes and listened to his idea. When Bunny had finally finished speaking, she bobbed her head a couple of times before saying, "I'll be honest, I had a sneaking suspicion from the way you introduced this idea that I was going to not like it. But that doesn't do it justice. I hate this idea. It is a terrible idea. Do not do this idea."

Bunny attempted to give her an endearing smile.

"You are going to do the stupid idea, aren't you?"

"I am," admitted Bunny. "Unless you have any better ideas?"

"My only better idea than the one you just suggested, is to do nothing."

"That's not an option."

"And all that stuff about respecting my opinion?"

"I do. I just ..."

"You're just not going to pay any attention to it," finished Butch.

"But only this time," he said. "Honestly, next time there is every chance I am going to do exactly what you tell me to do."

"Now, where have I heard that before? Oh yeah – every other time."

"That's unfair," said Bunny.

"So, if you're going full steam ahead with this idea regardless of what I think, then why am I ..." Butch thumped the heel of her hand into her forehead theatrically. "I just got it. Has the mechanic come to pick up your useless car that never works yet?"

"My car is working fine."

Butch stared and, after a few seconds, Bunny hung his head in shame. "Alright, it isn't. But he did say he reckoned this problem would probably be pretty easy to fix."

Butch sighed. "Screw it. I have nothing else on today anyway. Come on and I'll drive you to your monumentally bad idea which will undoubtedly end your career." She turned and headed back out the door.

"You're a wonderful friend, Pamela," Bunny shouted after her.

"Yeah," she responded without turning around. "And I'll tell you something else for nothing – there's no way you're getting this breakfast burrito."

# CHAPTER TWENTY-THREE

DI Fintan O'Rourke entered the outer office of the Garda Commissioner to find his long-suffering personal assistant, Carol Willis, in the midst of wrapping a large pile of presents.

"Excuse me," said Fintan, "I seem to have mistakenly wandered into Santa's grotto."

As soon as Carol looked up at him, he realised that his attempt at bonhomie had been ill judged. Her normally impeccable hair was askew, she had pieces of Sellotape attached to three different fingers of one hand, and her facial expression would have been better suited to accosting a home intruder than greeting a work colleague attempting to be jovial.

"What?" she snapped.

"Nothing," he said. "Can I help at all?"

"Has crime in this country been so thoroughly thwarted that a detective inspector in the Garda Síochána has time to take out of his busy day to assist in Christmas wrapping?"

Coming into Commissioner Ferguson's office, anybody in their right mind would mentally prepare themselves for the strong possibility of a dressing-down, but for it to come from Carol was an unpleasant surprise.

"Sorry," he mumbled. "I was just ..."

Carol sat back in her chair. "No, I'm sorry. That was very rude of me. I apologise." She indicated the pile of unwrapped boxes beside her desk. "This is not a good use of my time, and it certainly would not be a good use of yours. The Commissioner needs it done and, apparently, he is unable to do it himself." As soon as the words popped out of her mouth, Carol looked embarrassed, as if she had crossed some invisible line by openly criticising her boss. "Happy to help, of course." She snatched up a roll of tape from the desk and looked around her.

"Is he—" started O'Rourke.

"Yes," she said firmly, happy to be on more solid ground. "He is on a call, but he said to go straight in."

"Should I wait until the call is over?"

Carol looked at the roll of Sellotape and then at the individual pieces she had already stuck on her fingers. "He's the head of the Irish police force. Let's assume he understands the implications of saying go straight in."

"Right." O'Rourke headed towards the door, hoping that the rest of his visit would go better than that part just had.

He knocked, waited a couple of seconds and then, in the absence of any response, entered.

Commissioner Ferguson was sitting behind his desk, with the phone held to his ear and a rather exasperated expression on his face. O'Rourke hovered in the doorway and the Commissioner gestured for him to come inside. He got halfway to the desk when Ferguson jabbed a meaty finger in the direction of the door he had just come through. For a moment, O'Rourke wondered if he was being thrown out, but then he turned around and realised that he was being instructed to close the door behind him. He duly obliged.

"Yes, Minister. I fully appreciate that we are members of the European Union and, as such, getting on well with our European neighbours is of the utmost importance to the country. I assure you, I was not trying to offend anybody, but it is in the nature of my job ..."

He paused. The person on the other end of the line had evidently interrupted him. This was not something Ferguson would be particularly used to, and, judging by his facial expression, he didn't appear to like it either. The Commissioner scratched under his chin irritably as he waited for his turn to speak again. Eventually it came.

"I am more than happy to drop around to see Marcel Ricard with a nice bottle of wine and—"

He was interrupted again. The experience did not appear to be growing on him. He listened for another full minute while the person at the other end continued to talk. Halfway through, Ferguson started to use his free hand like a snapping crocodile to mimic the other person's yapping.

Ferguson threw a hand up in the air and shook his head in exasperation. "Yes, Minister. I don't agree, but if you'd rather have him go over and deal with the situation, that is entirely your prerogative."

The response to this was mercifully brief.

"Very well, and to you, too. Goodbye." And with that, Commissioner Ferguson slammed down the receiver. Then he picked it up again and slammed it down twice more, to the point where it looked seriously in danger of breaking. He only stopped when the intercom on his desk buzzed.

"Are you having a problem placing a call, Commissioner?"

Ferguson winced and set the handset back in its cradle gently. "No. Thank you, Carol." He glanced at O'Rourke and waved him into the chair opposite him.

"Is everything alright, Commissioner?"

"As always, Fintan, your ability to read body language boggles the mind. No, everything is not alright. Far from it. The repercussions of my dereliction of my Santa Clausing duties of a couple of evenings ago have been more extensive than I feared. Don't get me wrong – the anticipated issues in the Ferguson homestead have indeed emerged, and the temperature is

· · ·

currently hovering just above absolute zero. While that is the worst of it, it now seems that certain members of our government are taking the view that I have also insulted the French."

"Really?"

"Really. The travelling picture show from the Louvre is France's idea of sending cultural aid to barbaric outposts such as ourselves, and apparently, my abscondment while being the guest of honour they graciously agreed to host – in our museum, I might add – has been taken as a slight. A gentleman by the name of Marcel Ricard is the head whatever. Incidentally, how's this for a stereotype fulfilling itself – he wears a beret and has a pet chihuahua. I mean, I ask you. Anyway, it is considered that I offended him, and it seems the corridors of power have been all aquiver talking about little else."

"That seems like a rather big overreaction," offered O'Rourke.

"That was very much the case I tried to make. Quite aside from anything else – let's be honest, you can insult the French by using the wrong fork at dinner or pairing the wrong wine with fish. Why all of a sudden we're getting so sensitive about the French being upset is entirely beyond me. Umbrage is one of their leading imports – they take it at the drop of a garlicky snail. Nevertheless, being a good soldier, I of course offered to go over and make nice, but I have now been informed that the assistant commissioner will be doing so instead, as he is seen as more of a 'safe pair of hands'."

"Oh dear."

"Yes," agreed Ferguson. "It seems that while we are all terribly afraid of offending the French, nobody seems that bothered about offending me."

O'Rourke said nothing to this, reasoning that there was nothing that he could add to make it better, and every chance he could make it worse.

"Anyway," said Ferguson, sitting back in his chair, "none of this is of your concern. Do you have good news for me?"

"I don't know if it's good, sir, but I certainly have news."

"I'll take what I can get," offered the Commissioner, before tipping forward suddenly and lowering his voice. "Before we get to that – did Carol seem a bit off to you?"

"Your Secretary?"

"Executive Assistant," he corrected.

"Right," said O'Rourke. "Of course. Sorry. I mean … I don't know her well, so I'm probably not the best person to judge, but …"

"But what?"

"She did seem a tad … grumpy. On my way in."

Ferguson slammed a meaty hand down on the desk and threw himself back in his chair again. "I knew it. I gave her a Christmas present this morning and, despite assurances to the contrary, I don't think it's gone down well. Normally, Mrs Ferguson deals with this kind of thing, but present-buying is just one of the many services that have now been withdrawn following what one of us is referring to as 'when I let all the orphans down'."

"I see," said O'Rourke. "Can I ask what you got Carol?"

Ferguson pulled a face. "A bottle of Bushmills whiskey."

"I see."

"And now I have a sneaking suspicion that she doesn't drink."

"Ah."

"For goodness' sake, though – it's Ireland. It's not like she won't know someone who does. It was one of the really good bottles as well." He held his head in his hands. "I am not having an enjoyable week. Any suggestions?"

"Well, what has your wife got her in previous years?"

Ferguson shrugged. "They're always nicely wrapped objects of between six inches and two foot in size." Highly unusually for him, the Commissioner looked embarrassed. "I always wrote something very sincere and personal in the cards," he added plaintively. He stared up at the ceiling. "Oh God. I'm going to have to go home and beg for mercy. I'm guessing my wife already has an appropriate present for Carol. She usually starts the Christmas shopping in April." He shook his head mournfully. "I'm honestly in the shit here, but I have been utterly outplayed by a vastly superior foe. Thank God

my beloved doesn't want to be Commissioner of the Garda Síochána
– she'd have the gig in a week."

He let out a heavy sigh before leaning forward to face O'Rourke
again. "Anyway, on to lighter matters. I take it your subtle watching
brief on the ongoing adventures of DI Grainger and his little
international task force is the reason you are here?"

"Yes, sir," said O'Rourke, delighted to have moved on to matters of
policing. "It appears four Italian men were dropped off at accident
and emergency in the Mater Hospital last night, having sustained
injuries."

Ferguson raised his large eyebrows. "Injuries?"

"The main ones being a shattered kneecap, a broken jaw, a
fractured collarbone and a couple of broken ribs, which I believe
were spread out amongst the quartet."

"Shit the bed. And we believe these gentlemen to be the squad of
unattached 'independent contractors' working for our friend
Inspector Schillaci?"

"I'm assuming so."

"That is interesting," Ferguson mused, rubbing his hands
together excitedly. "What reason did they give for these injuries?"

"They said they were attacked by a baseball-bat-wielding
madman in a balaclava who they could not identify, while out on an
evening stroll."

Ferguson nodded. "Well, that passes the smell test." He placed
one elbow on the desk and scratched his chin. "Do we think this is
McGarry?"

"I mean ... It's hard to say. As we know, he is not ..." O'Rourke
paused as he tried to find a diplomatic way of phrasing things.

"Fundamentally opposed to the use of force if he deems it
necessary?" suggested Ferguson.

"Yes," agreed O'Rourke. "But this does seem a little much. I mean,
a baseball bat? If it had been a hurling stick, perhaps, but ..."

"In which case, is it possible that this was the result of a run-in
with Mr Walsh and his cousin?"

O'Rourke shrugged. "It could be, but that seems a tad unlikely, doesn't it? I mean, if they knew where they were, surely DI Grainger would at least attempt to make an arrest."

"One would assume so, but it is possible at this point that he has completely forgotten that it is part of his job description."

"Has there been any update on the investigation?"

Ferguson shook his head. "No, but then it's all running through the office of our newly crowned diplomatic liaison – my esteemed assistant commissioner. There's every chance I will only get to read about it in the paper. That's assuming they don't manage to keep it out of the papers entirely. Still, though, it appears the Italian muscle came off worse in a tussle with the natives?"

"It would seem that way," confirmed O'Rourke.

"While, of course, officially I am appalled at any violent crime ..."

"Of course," repeated O'Rourke.

"Is it wrong that I feel a weird little piece of nationalistic pride?"

"If that's what it is, then I'm right there with you."

"Should we check McGarry's alright? I mean, we're assuming he wasn't involved, but if he was, we should check that things haven't escalated to a point of no return."

"While I appreciate your concern, sir, I don't know how we could enquire about his well-being without acknowledging an awareness of his involvement in affairs. Affairs, need we be reminded, he has no business being involved in."

"Hmmmm, that is a pickle," agreed Ferguson. "Although, as an old friend of his, you could pop over and drop off a little Christmas present?"

"We haven't been that close for quite some time, sir."

"Exactly," said Ferguson. "Should anyone ask, you've decided that, this being the season of goodwill, it was time to mend some bridges. Here, you can give him this." He reached down to open the bottom drawer of his desk and produced an expensive-looking bottle of Bushmills whiskey, which he placed on the desk.

"Is that—" began O'Rourke.

"No," interrupted Ferguson. "I actually got two, but it felt weird when I went to give them both to her, so I only went with one. I still can't figure out if doing so would have made her twice or half as much annoyed as she is now. God, I bloody hate Christmas."

# CHAPTER TWENTY-FOUR

Adrian Murphy kept his eyes glued on the stage and resisted the overwhelming temptation to reach into the pocket of his suit to check his phone. His wife, Katie, who in reality was a woman of only five foot two, was metaphorically looming over him from the next seat. They had argued in the car. The main thrust of it had been that he had not been paying enough attention to the children or to her. Quite how him forgetting to bring the camcorder with him equated to this was anyone's guess, but apparently it did.

This was his second marriage, and it was starting to feel an awful lot like his first one. Divorce had only been legal in Ireland for the last few years. He was beginning to worry he might be in serious danger of being the first person to collect two of them. He also had a sneaking suspicion he was bad at being a husband. The accusation that he was hyper-focused on work was accurate, but what it didn't take into account was that if any of the lawyers, bankers, doctors, developers or whoever else were seated around them had a bad day at work, it probably resulted in a deal falling through, an investment going south or, all right, perhaps somebody dying, which presumably led to paperwork. If Adrian had a bad day, he could end up in jail for a very long time.

Katie told people he worked in import/export, but she was smarter than that. She was also seventeen years younger than him, and he didn't delude himself that she was with him for his looks or charm. The problem with that was, if somebody loved you for your money, they could get possession of that in the courts and amputate the bit they didn't like in the process – i.e., you.

It didn't help his case that the other families around them had evidently not forgotten the camcorder. People were recording this nativity play with the kind of fevered zeal that would be more appropriate for the second coming of the actual Jesus Christ, rather than what would turn out to be a Cabbage Patch doll when it was eventually delivered a painful seventy-eight minutes from now.

At that moment, a young girl was on stage belting out a rendition of the song 'Tomorrow' from the musical *Annie*. She was, even to Adrian's untrained ear, a shockingly bad singer. Nobody could fault the amount of welly she was giving it, but amongst the audience of a couple of hundred parents, grandparents, nannies, and people who couldn't think of a good enough reason to get out of the invitation, there was an unmistakable collective wince every time she went for a high note in a song brim-full of them. He took a deep breath. It was time to suck it up. This thing was scheduled to go on for two hours, and if the first fifteen minutes were anything to go by, nobody was willing to stop it on the grounds of quality control.

Attracted by the sound of a kerfuffle, Adrian turned his head to the left. Amidst an array of tuts and dirty looks, a large man in a brown sheepskin coat was shuffling his way along the row towards him. Adrian took consolation in the fact that while he'd forgotten the bloody camera, at least he hadn't been late. Their eldest, Tom, was only in senior infants, but from reports he received from Katie, it seemed the favourite activity amongst the parents at this eye-wateringly expensive school was judging their counterparts and bitching remorselessly about anyone who was found wanting. This poor bastard was ...

Adrian felt as if he had just been punched in the stomach.

He recognised the poor bastard. The poor bastard was heading straight for him. The poor bastard in question was Detective Bunny McGarry. Except him being Bunny McGarry meant that the true poor bastard was about to be Adrian Murphy.

Sure enough, Bunny reached him, stopped, and then sparked a second, escalated wave of tutting and grumbling as he orchestrated moving six people up one seat to create an opening for himself to sit down beside Adrian. While Bunny was doing this, Adrian awkwardly attempted to convey "sorry", "not my fault" and, despite all available evidence, "this guy is not with me", all through the medium of embarrassed smiles, nods and grimaces. He didn't dare look at Katie directly, but he could feel the bubbling hatred of her stare burning into the right side of his face.

Eventually. Finally. Bunny sat down.

"Howerya, Adrian."

His words were greeted with a shush from behind.

At this point, the singer on stage was reaching what could technically be called a finale. Substituting volume for the idea of constraining herself to one key, she was assuring her audience that tomorrow was only a day away, while simultaneously making it feel so much longer. Her final note was greeted with the kind of rapturous applause you might receive from a room full of people who had just been informed that their participation in a world-record attempt at the most root canal surgeries performed simultaneously was no longer required.

Adrian took the opportunity to grab Bunny by the arm. "What the hell are you doing here?"

"I've always been a big fan of the theatre."

As the applause died away, a teacher came on stage and gently guided away the young girl, who was still bowing.

"Leave. Now."

Another shush came from somewhere behind them.

Bunny lowered his voice. "I was hoping you could assist me with something, Adrian."

"I can't help you. I am a legitimate businessman."

"Who happens to know an awful lot about any dodgy high-value goods in Dublin."

The shush was repeated.

"Why the fuck would I help you?" he hissed through gritted teeth.

"'Tis the season of goodwill, Adrian."

"Get out of here. Now."

Adrian felt Katie's hand on his knee. To the unknowing observer it might look like an act of affection, but he knew better. It was a warning.

"Isn't this supposed to be a nativity?" asked Bunny.

"Yes," whispered Adrian.

"I'm no Biblical expert but why are a dozen Teenage Mutant Ninja Turtles coming on stage, then?"

A nervous-looking young child was ushered up to a microphone at the side of the stage into which he read a couple of lines that presumably offered some form of explanation to cover this unexpected twist in the story of the birth of our Lord and Saviour. Whatever it was was sadly lost for ever as the microphone had not been turned on. Another teacher rushed up to try to remedy this, but by this point the Teenage Mutant Ninja Turtles had started fighting each other. The "fight" consisted of one half of the turtles standing still with one arm held out, while the other half inexpertly executed an Aikido throw.

Adrian ignored Bunny's question for many reasons, one of them being that nobody had an answer to it. "You need to leave."

"There's a bloke called Bobby Walsh, who will be trying to shift a load of dodgy jewellery."

The shush sounded somehow sharper this time.

Meanwhile, an air of furiously suppressed tittering started to fill the hall, as everyone's attention was drawn to an unfortunate duo on the stage. While the other turtle pairings had by now executed somewhere between three and four throws, the smallest boy in the class had somehow drawn the short straw and been paired up with the fattest child, and he was still stuck on throw number one, furiously endeavouring to drag his heftier classmate over his shoulder, his exasperation growing with every failed attempt.

"My lawyer is going to have a fantastic case for harassment with this," muttered Adrian.

Bunny dipped his hand into his coat pocket and withdrew something which he held face down in the palm of his hand. He shifted it so that only Adrian could see what it was – a set of handcuffs. "You're not wrong."

"You wouldn't dare."

"Adrian Murphy, I'm arresting you for—"

"You've got nothing on me. You'll never make this trumped-up bullshit stick."

Katie's nails had started digging into his thigh now.

"You're right," conceded Bunny. "If you like, I'll even come back to next year's show and explain that to all these people."

This shush was louder and had real venom behind it.

"I will have your badge for this."

Eventually, clearly frustrated with not getting his turn, the fat child took it upon himself to throw himself down on the ground. He then got to his feet and hurled his opponent over his shoulder with more force than was absolutely necessary.

Bunny shrugged. "I've been wanting to travel."

Adrian turned and pulled his wife's hand away from his leg, where it was about to draw blood. He met her glare with a pained smile and spoke through gritted teeth. "I am dealing with this!"

There was an audible gasp as a quick-thinking teacher intervened in the nick of time to stop an overexcited Teenage Mutant Ninja Turtle, who had fallen out of formation, from accidentally throwing one of his brethren off the stage.

The turtles were hurriedly shepherded into a line and took a bow to a smattering of applause. The child who it was hard not to think of as the fat turtle threw up his hands in exasperation and stomped off stage. Adrian could sympathise. He turned back to Bunny.

"Look, I've never heard of any Bobby Walsh."

"No. But I bet you can point me to who has."

*Shush.*

As the rest of the turtles were being guided off stage, Adrian was aware that more and more sets of eyes were now focused on him and his unwanted guest. He attempted an increasingly desperate-looking smile and spoke under his breath. "We can discuss this after the show."

Bunny reached his free hand into the inside of his coat and produced his business card, held between two fingers. "You can text me the details now."

Adrian winced as the woman he was pretty sure was about to divorce him dug her elbow into his ribs with more force than should be possible for such a small woman from a seated position. A whimper escaped his lips.

With actual tears in his eyes, he gave her a pained look before turning to Bunny and snatching the card out of his fingers. He pulled his mobile out of his inside jacket pocket and started texting.

On the stage, a gaggle of five-year-olds in Santa hats were being herded into an approximate formation.

"And don't skimp on the details," said Bunny.

At this point, the woman behind them, apparently having run out of shush, leaned forward and tapped Bunny on the shoulder aggressively. "Would you mind being quiet?"

"No problem at all."

"What are you even doing here? You're not a parent."

Bunny nodded. "I'm reviewing the show for *The Irish Times.*"

This led to the woman's severe expression falling away as her face seemed to run through various options for how to react to this piece of news, before it settled on an approximation of a smile. "My daughter is in the ABBA tribute section, and they are very good."

"Is that right? Are they doing 'Dancing Queen'?"

The woman shook her head. "No, and I too said that was a mistake."

Someone from behind them took it upon themselves to shush her and the woman's head spun around so fast that there was a hint of an audible whipping noise.

Adrian re-read the text he had just composed, double-checked the number on the card in front of him and then hit "send".

Ten seconds later, just as the nervous-looking five-year-old who had been separated from the herd and led forward towards the mic opened his mouth to sing, the air was rent asunder by the piercing fanfare of someone receiving a text.

Bunny gave the rest of the hall an apologetic wave.

"For fuck's sake," hissed Adrian, "turn your ringer off."

# CHAPTER TWENTY-FIVE

Bunny squinted out the front window. "I think this is the place."

"You thought the last two places were also the place," responded Butch.

"It's not my fault none of these people have house numbers that you can see in the dark and all the street signs are covered in leaves. It must be a nightmare being a pizza delivery driver out here."

The "here" in question was one of the fancier parts of Lusk, in north County Dublin. It had been a frustrating day. Adrian Murphy had given Bunny a list of three names of people who fenced jewellery in Dublin. As far as Bunny and Butch could tell, the information had been good, it just hadn't led them anywhere useful.

They had spent a frustrating three hours tracking down the first name on the list only to be informed that the individual was currently in Barbados on a second honeymoon. If crime didn't pay, it would appear that fencing the results of it certainly did. The second lead took them to an electrical shop in Malahide. Bunny and Butch attempted to do their very best to good cop/bad cop the guy behind the counter, but he was either one of Ireland's great undiscovered acting talents or he seemed genuinely mystified as to what they were driving at. Eventually, he'd admitted that he only normally worked there on Saturdays, but the boss had headed off early for Christmas with his in-laws up in Donegal, so he was filling in. The trip wasn't a total waste as Bunny had remembered to buy himself a new kettle.

Chasing down the first two leads had taken up so much time that Bunny had been forced to call in a couple more favours to get the home address of the owner of the shop up in Stoneybatter that had been closed when they finally reached it through the rush-hour traffic. All of that had led them here – to a large, detached house behind an imposing set of wooden gates amidst tall, wrought-iron fences buttressed by neatly maintained hedges. Everything about the place was designed to convey the message that the owner had a few quid and valued their privacy, so please bugger off.

The individual in question was one Harry Jacobs. He had a trio of convictions from his earlier days, but had managed to keep his nose clean for the last couple of decades. He seemed to do an excellent job of keeping his jewellery business in that grey area where it was mostly legit, or could at least appear that way. The friend Bunny had asked for the info had noted that while Harry had not been in trouble with the law recently, there was plenty of information there about his current and previous business interests. He would lay good money on the fact that Harry had either appeared tangentially in a few investigations or had possibly been open to quiet chats with certain members of the Garda Síochána in exchange for keeping his name out of things.

Bunny got out of the car and walked up to the gates. He pointed to the stone column on the left. "Look, it's number twelve. It's got it written in black paint. Black Paint! How fecking useful is that?"

Butch parked the car up just to the right of the gates and joined him.

"Is there a buzzer or something?"

Butch pointed to the other column. "Intercom."

"Ah, I hate these fucking things."

Bunny's opinion of intercoms did not improve over the course of the next seven minutes as he attempted to get a response by whacking various combinations of buttons in an increasingly futile operation.

"I'm going to go out on a limb here," said Butch, "and suggest they are either not home or not wishing to receive visitors at this time."

"Or this bloody thing could be broken?"

"If it wasn't when you started, there's every chance it is now."

"'Tis a shame to come all this way and not be able to wish Harry a merry Christmas."

Butch gave Bunny a wary look. "And what exactly do you mean by that?"

Before she could say anything else, Bunny took a few steps back towards the car, braced himself for his run-up and sprinted at the tall wooden gates to clear them nimbly like a gymnast vaulting over one of those wooden horses. At least, that had been the plan he had in mind. In reality, he lost his footing on a patch of wet leaves and his attempt to clear the structures in a single bound ended with him stumbling into an awkward shoulder-charge that left him lying crumpled on the ground.

Butch offered him her hand to get back up. "Did that go how you hoped?"

"Not exactly, no."

"Maybe you should—"

Again, before Butch could say any more, Bunny grabbed the top of the gate and, this time from a standing start, attempted to drag himself up and throw his leg over the top. He sort of managed it, but didn't have quite enough momentum to get the rest of him up. After dangling there for about half a minute, straining unsuccessfully in his endeavour to mount the gate, he tumbled gracelessly back to the ground.

On this occasion Butch didn't help him up. That was because she was sitting on top of one of the stone columns to the side of the gate, looking down at him. Instantly, Bunny felt even more of a fool when he could see how she had used a handy foothold to get herself up there.

"Do you remember how only this morning we had a discussion

about communication in our relationship, and how I felt you didn't listen to me?" she asked.

"This is starting to feel a lot like a marriage without the good bits."

"There are good bits?"

Bunny looked up at her. "Are you enjoying yourself?"

She took a disposable camera out of the pocket of her coat and snapped a quick picture of Bunny sitting on the ground. "I am now. I might get that framed."

"Ha ha," he said, picking himself up and dusting himself off. "Budge over."

A minute later, when they had both successfully scaled the wall, they started walking up the drive towards the large detached house that sat in the middle of a plot about an acre in size.

"For a house where nobody is at home," commented Butch, "they've left an awful lot of lights on."

"If you can afford to live somewhere this big, maybe you're not overly worried about the electricity bill." Bunny pointed towards the roof where smoke was coming out of the chimney. "Having said that, you'd have to be very blasé about health and safety to leave a fire roaring away while you go out for the evening."

When they were close enough, they peered in the windows. While lights were on in several rooms, there was no immediate sign of life. At the front door, Bunny progressed through his knocking repertoire – starting with polite tapping, moving on to more vigorous banging before reaching a crescendo with some wood-shaking thumping – all to no avail.

"So, we try around the back?" asked Butch.

"Might as well," said Bunny. "We are here now, after all."

They started to walk around the building.

Butch stopped and swore.

"Problem?"

"Well," she said, examining the bottom of her shoe, "I can confirm that Mr Jacobs owns a large dog, and he isn't particularly good at cleaning up after him."

"Either that," said Bunny, "or he has all this privacy because he occasionally likes to take a shit on his own lawn."

"Ah, gross," said Butch, wiping her shoe vigorously on the grass. "Thank you for that lovely image. That's going to stay with me all evening."

"You're welcome," said Bunny, moving on.

He looked in the side windows of the house. "Not that I'm trying to prove my theory, but it seems particularly odd that we haven't heard any barking, given the evidence you just stepped in."

They both made their way towards the back of the house with slightly more urgency. A light was on in the kitchen, but again, no sign of life.

Bunny pressed up against the glass. "There are plates and half-finished glasses of wine on the table," he reported. "Like somebody was interrupted in the middle of a meal."

Butch held up a hand. "Shush. Do you hear something?"

They both held their breath. There was something. It was hard to make out, but it sounded like a voice in distress. Butch pointed towards the other side of the house, and they rushed around. It was easier to hear from there. A voice. A male voice. Crying out in anguish.

"Please. I'll do anything you want. Please – I'm begging you."

Bunny rushed to try the back door. Upon finding it locked, he stepped back and shoulder-charged it. It gave on the second attempt. As he crashed into the kitchen, he confirmed the evidence of a recently consumed meal on the kitchen table, and the empty crate belonging to a very large dog in the far corner.

They could hear the voice more clearly now. "I'm sorry. I'll give you anything you want."

Bunny rushed down the hall, with Butch following directly behind him. The noise seemed to be coming from the right side of the hallway. They stopped, confused.

"Upstairs?" asked Butch.

Bunny shook his head and, after another second, pointed at a large panel of wood where a framed portrait of a rather dour-looking woman was glaring at them.

"I'm sorry!" screamed the voice. "I have been so bad."

Bunny ran his hand around the painting and located a latch underneath it that popped open a concealed door. He pushed through it to reveal a set of carpeted stairs leading down to a basement.

"Oh God," wailed the voice. "Please help me. Oh God. I'm sorry, mistress."

Only when he was halfway down the stairs did the use of the word "mistress" register with Bunny. It happened at the very same moment that a woman clad in black leather with knee-high boots and an outfit that offered precious little cover from the elements leaped back and started screaming at the sight of them. If she was distressed, it was nothing compared to the man bent over an elaborate and terrifying-looking contraption, with something equally elaborate and terrifying sticking out of somewhere it patently didn't fit.

Bunny took in the room. The display cabinet was full of things that had very definitely not been designed with comfort in mind. The woman looked terrified as she stood with her back to the wall, holding one of the devices out in front of her like a weapon. To be fair, it looked like it could do an awful lot of damage.

"Who the fuck are you?" she screeched.

Bunny held up his hands. "It's OK. We are the police."

"What the hell are you doing here?"

"We were looking for Harry Jacobs and then we heard ..."

"Oh God," said the woman.

"Oh God," said Bunny.

"Oh God," said Butch.

"Oh God!" screamed the man, who, noticing at that moment that a lot of the action had suddenly stopped, turned his head. Seeing as he was wearing an elaborate-looking leather mask, he obviously couldn't hear much and was unaware that they had guests. "Why have you stopped, Fiona? I mean, mistress."

Bunny noted a large sign on the wall that proclaimed in gold lettering 'THE SAFE WORD IS MARMALADE'.

"I didn't say the safe word. I thought you were doing a great job."

"Shut up!" screeched the woman, who was now transitioning from terror to pure mortification. She rushed over and slapped him on the back of the head.

"Oh yes, mistress. I've been a bad boy. I've been ..."

He trailed off as the woman unzipped the back of the mask, causing it to fall to the floor. Harry Jacobs looked up to see a man he didn't recognise standing over him.

"Hello, Harry. My name is Bunny McGarry. I'm here because you have indeed been a very bad boy."


The woman, who it turned out was Mrs Jacobs, departed quickly after untying her husband. Her closing remarks indicated that what had been going on was the Christmas present Harry himself had requested. She also told him in no uncertain terms where he could shove any similar request in the future. Ironically enough, the suggestion was very similar to what had been happening when Bunny and Butch had barged in.

Bunny gave Harry Jacobs credit for at least trying to rally, given the circumstances.

"What the hell are you doing here?" he demanded. "This is a gross invasion of privacy."

"No, it isn't," said Bunny.

"We heard sounds of someone in distress," continued Butch, "and in that circumstance, we are allowed to take reasonable steps to ensure their safety. We were unaware of ..." She wrinkled her nose and waved a hand in the general direction of the rest of the room.

"But the front gate was locked, and there was no way you heard anything from the road. I've had this place specially soundproofed."

"Out of curiosity," said Bunny, "what did you tell the builders it was for?"

"That," snapped Harry Jacobs, "like everything else that is happening here this evening, is none of your business."

"Alright," he said. "Relax. It was a simple misunderstanding."

"You'll be hearing from my lawyers – you can be sure of that."

"Really?" asked Butch. "You're really going to file a report about this? What a fun day in court that will be."

"I ..." He hesitated.

"That's what I thought."

Harry Jacobs folded his arms and stared daggers at them both. Now that Bunny could see him from the front, what was notable about Harry Jacobs was just how unnotable he was. He was a very ordinary-looking man in his late forties or early fifties. Well, bar the outfit. That was made up of an awful lot of leather and chains, not to mention almost fifty percent of the garment seemed to consist of zips. It must be a right pain to get into, but then that was probably the point.

Bunny picked up a towel from a nearby bench and tossed it to him.

"What's this for?" snapped Jacobs.

In lieu of an answer, Bunny simply pointed down south. Jacobs belatedly realised what he meant and, blushing, covered up his modesty. Ironically, it was one of the few areas not covered in leather. The garment was clearly not designed for everyday use.

While Jacobs was busy with the towel, Bunny looked away, which is how he came to scan the rest of the room. He noticed the two shelves laden with implements. "Oh, shite!"

"What?" asked Butch.

"Nothing." What Bunny didn't want to admit was that he had just remembered the device he had taken away from Phil Nellis a couple of days ago. It was still in a carrier bag in the boot of his car. The one the mechanic had collected that morning. The car required a couple of specialist tools that lived in the boot with the spare tyre. That bag was sitting directly above it. A judder of embarrassment passed down his spine.

"You still haven't told me why you're here," said the now-covered-up Jacobs.

"I'm looking for information about a gentleman called Bobby Walsh. We believe you may have been in contact with him."

"You break into my house and upset my wife. Why on earth would I tell you anything?"

Bunny turned and raised an eyebrow at Butch.

After a couple of seconds, she pulled a face. "Really?"

Bunny nodded.

"Gross." Butch pulled the disposable camera from her pocket and snapped a quick picture of Harry Jacobs.

"What the hell are you doing?" he wailed.

"You tell us what we need to know," said Bunny, "and the camera is yours" – he looked around the room – "to do with as you wish. The mind boggles."

"Ahhhh," said Butch, "I've got pictures on here from my nephew's birthday party." She folded her arms. "On second thoughts, fine. I can't see myself picking this up from the chemist."

"So, you're blackmailing me?"

"Think of it as also putting the screws on you," said Bunny. "I thought you'd enjoy that."

Despite herself, Butch smirked and had to turn away.

"Is this funny to you?" growled Harry Jacobs.

"I'm trying to track down a serious criminal," said Bunny. "And that's as serious as I take anything. Bobby Walsh."

"I don't know what you've heard, but I don't have any dealings with criminals."

"Would you like eight-by-ten copies or the full poster-sized ones?"

Jacobs bit his tongue and exhaled heavily through his nostrils before adopting a more conciliatory tone. "The name means nothing to me."

"That's a shame," said Bunny, before turning to Butch. "Do you reckon that one-hour photo place on O'Connell Street might still be open?"

"I meet a lot of people," said Jacobs. "How would I know this fella?"

"He's a scrote from Limerick who's trying to move a load of hot jewellery and watches."

Jacobs's face lit up. "Had a big fella and some foreign girl with him?"

Butch and Bunny shared a look. "That's them, alright," he said. "Any idea where we can find them?"

Jacobs shook his head. "No."

"I'm going to need a sight more than that or else I'm off to the one-hour photo."

"Listen to me," said Harry Jacobs, exasperated. "He came to me, alright, but I wouldn't deal with him."

"And why was that?" asked Butch.

"I had a bad feeling about the guy."

"A bad feeling?"

"You don't do what I do for a living," he said, before looking at them both. "Not that I'm saying anything about what I do for a living, but – you develop a highly honed instinct on these things and the fella was bad news."

"So, all we've got is you having a bad feeling?"

"I didn't want to deal with them," said Jacobs. "But I also couldn't give him what he was looking for."

"You mean money?"

Jacobs shook his head. "He wasn't looking for money. He was looking for a lot more than money."

Bunny and Butch exchanged another glance before Bunny spoke. "Like what exactly?"

# CHAPTER TWENTY-SIX

Bobby Walsh rocked up and down on the balls of his feet anxiously. He looked at his watch again. It was still 9:22pm, the same time it had been when he'd last checked. They were standing in a car park in the Wicklow Mountains that on summer days was chock-full of cars as people brought their underwhelmed kids to see some glorious nature at one of the designated beauty spots. On the night before Christmas Eve, however, it was dark, empty, and the surrounding trees were making Bobby antsy. One of the things they never tell you about nature is that it is never silent. It's always whispering away to itself, like it's planning something.

Standing beside him, Niall shifted his feet and kicked a pebble.

"They'll be here," said Bobby, staring straight ahead.

"I didn't say n-n-nothing."

Bobby looked up at him and then glanced back at the car that was parked behind them, its headlights offering the only illumination in the car park save for the moon, which was skittering in and out of cloud cover. Sofia was seated in the passenger seat where he had instructed her to stay.

"Have you got my back?" asked Bobby.

"Course," replied Niall.

"I don't just mean tonight. We're family. We have to look after each other because nobody else is going to."

From the corner of his eye he could see Niall nod, but with that all-too-familiar blank expression on his face.

"What I mean is ... we can't trust Sofia."

"I th-think she's nice."

"Oh, she's great," agreed Bobby, "but never forget she's a little rich girl. Anything goes wrong here, she can just run off home to daddy. She's not going to see the inside of a prison cell, whereas you and me ..." He turned to look directly at his cousin. "If it comes down to it, we need to remember that all we have is each other, alright? I'm not going to prison, and you wouldn't last five minutes in there."

"It's not too late to—"

The rest of Niall's sentence was lost as an Audi pulled into the car park and stopped about twenty feet from them. Dermot, no second name given or asked for, got out on the driver's side, leaving the engine running and the interior lights on. He was an older lad with long hair and a beard of a similar length, both of which looked like unruly steel wool. There was something going on with his mouth, which made it look like the left side was always chewing something.

"You're late," said Bobby. "We said 9pm."

"No," said Dermot in his Northern drawl, "I said you had to be here at 9pm. I never said I would be." Dermot looked at Niall and then back at the car. "And why have you got so many people with you?"

"It's just my cousin and my girlfriend."

"Should I be happy you didn't bring your ma, and a load of nieces and nephews? This is a private transaction, not a day out for all the family."

Bobby rolled his eyes. "Are we doing this or not?"

Dermot took one long last look around him. "Did you bring what we agreed?"

"I did. Did you?"

Dermot patted a sports bag he had swung over his shoulder. "I wouldn't be here without it." He nodded to the far side of the Audi's bonnet. "Step into my office."

The two of them moved forward until Dermot raised his hand. "That's far enough."

He unzipped the sports bag, took out a thick brown envelope and held it up. "As requested, three brand-new Irish passports."

The envelope landed on the bonnet in front of Bobby. He turned to Niall and nodded. Niall picked it up and took out each of the passports in turn, leaning forward to examine them in the weak light coming from inside the Audi. His forehead creased in concentration until eventually he nodded.

"Seal of approval from the big man," said Dermot. "That's what I like to see. As I said, they'll get you anywhere in Europe and a few places beyond, but I'd stay out of North America."

"They won't work for the States?" asked Bobby.

Dermot tilted his head and narrowed his eyes. "I told you that. Day one. You want something that will get past the Americans, that's a whole other kettle of fish."

"Sure, don't we have free travel in Europe, anyway?"

"We do, but you still need a passport. If you don't want those, give me them back and our business here is done."

"Alright," said Bobby. "Calm down. I'm just saying."

"Saying what?"

"Never mind. Have you got the guns?"

"I do," he confirmed, patting the sports bag. "Money first."

"I already gave you those three watches and all that jewellery. They're worth way more than the five grand we agreed."

"No," said Dermot, the irritation growing in his voice, "they were worth a lot more than that to the people you stole them from, or to the insurance company that has to cover them. It's not like I'm going to get market value for them when I sell them on."

"Thing is, though – those passports are a bit basic, and I've already paid you a lot. Fair is fair, I think you give us the guns and we call it even."

"Even?" echoed Dermot. "We call it even? Are you out of your fucking mind? We have an agreement. The watches and the jewellery were a down payment. Five grand right now or I walk away, and I'm taking everything with me." He shook his head in disbelief. "Fucking amateurs."

"Mind your manners."

"Mind my manners? Son, have you any idea who you're talking to?"

"Do you?" countered Bobby. He could feel Niall tense beside him as, in one swift movement, he flicked out his knife and pointed it across the bonnet at Dermot. "Now, old-timer, how about you give me those guns, apologise for being disrespectful and then piss off?"

Dermot sighed, took a step back and held up his hands in surrender. "Alright. Just calm down."

"Yeah," said Bobby with a sneer. "Not so full of it now, are you?"

Bobby was surprised when Dermot laughed. "Look at you – the Big Bad Wolf. Puffing your chest out. Do yourself a favour, son – while you're doing that, maybe take a quick look-see at your chest?"

Bobby did so and felt a horrible sinking feeling in his stomach.

"There is a red d-d-dot on your—" started Niall.

"I know, you moron," snapped Bobby.

Dermot lowered his hands. "I wouldn't go calling him a moron, you're the clever boy who pulled a knife on a guy who sells guns for a living. Have you not seen *The Untouchables*?"

"What?"

"The film?"

Bobby looked at him blankly.

Dermot shook his head. "Unbelievable. This is everything that's wrong with the current generation."

"What are you talking about?"

Niall cleared his throat. "You b-b-brought a knife to a gunfight."

Dermot applauded sarcastically. "See? I knew the big boy was really the brains of the outfit. You should let him do the talking next time. Now, drop the knife, reach a hand into your pocket ... slowly, and toss me the money. If anything else other than money makes an appearance, or if the money isn't in there in the first place – take comfort in the fact that I know the last rites. I've given them to several people before."

Bobby glanced around.

Dermot gave another exaggerated sigh. "And if you're thinking of diving for cover, you would want to be very sure that the red dot currently dancing on your chest is the only one. I've been doing this for a long time and I'm still alive. Ask yourself, does a man who has that kind of CV really only bring one back-up with him? A lot of people I deal with are dangerous and, unlike you, not just to themselves. Now, are you paying or do I have to book myself a physio appointment in the morning because I'm gonna mess up my back carrying your body?"

Bobby reached a hand inside his coat pocket and, extremely slowly, withdrew the wad of notes held together with an elastic band.

"Good boy. Toss it over here."

Bobby did so. Dermot caught it and examined it. "Next time use an envelope. It's just a little bit of class. Tell me now if it isn't all here, because if I count it and you're short, even by a fiver, so help me God, I'm having one of my friends shoot you in one of your extremities, just on principle."

"It's all there. You have my word."

Dermot roared with laughter. "We have his word, lads. And clearly, he's a man of honour."

"Alright," said Bobby. "Do I get my guns now?"

Dermot's face settled into a grin. "'Do I get my guns now?' I tell you what, you've no shortage of balls. Brains – yes, barely any, but you've got balls for days, son. Here's what we'll do." He reached a hand into the sports bag. "I'll give you one of the guns."

"But—"

Dermot's head snapped up. "Seriously, I would be very careful about choosing the words that are about to come out of your mouth, because if you're about to say what I think you're about to say, they might be the last words you ever speak."

"It's just ... We need two guns. Please."

"And you should have thought of that before you started playing silly buggers, then, shouldn't you? I did enjoy the please, though." He reached into the bag, pulled out a handgun wrapped in cellophane and tossed it across the bonnet. Bobby caught it awkwardly.

"Bullets?"

"He wants bullets now as well. It's always take, take, take." Dermot pointed to the far side of the car park. "You'll find them under the bench over there. Try not to shoot yourself in the bollocks."

"But—"

"Not another word from either of you. Here's what's gonna happen now – you're both going to take five steps back and hold your hands in the air. They are going to stay there until my car is out of this car park. Don't follow those instructions to the letter and see what happens."

They meekly complied.

And with that, Dermot got into his car and drove away.

Bobby turned to Niall with a snarl. "Fat lot of use you were."

# CHAPTER TWENTY-SEVEN

Laurence Toussaint watched as the doors to the lift closed. He propped himself against the lift's rear wall, lifted his head up towards the ceiling and exhaled loudly.

It was almost over. Thank God, it was almost over.

He would be delighted to get out of this hotel and back on a flight to Paris tomorrow. Unless there were any significant travel disasters, he would be home in time to see his grandchildren open their Christmas presents. More importantly, his part in this ridiculous charade would finally come to an end and he could get back to doing his job. His superiors had strong-armed him into coming here, and he had loathed every single second of it.

Detective Inspector Grainger was an empty shirt, a politician in the very worst sense of the word, and far more interested in people's perception of him than he was in solving any crimes. Inspector Schillaci – well, he was something far more problematic. He and Toussaint had erupted into a full-blown row on his third day here, only the second time he could recall raising his voice to anyone in the last ten years. Since then, he had been left without a voice. Grainger hadn't turned a blind eye to Schillaci's outrages so much as he had shoved his head in a bucket and la, la, la-ed loudly like a stubborn child refusing to eat his greens.

Toussaint was supposedly here to lend his expertise, and yet from day one he had been sidelined while Schillaci led Grainger around like a dim-witted poodle on a lead. The only reason Toussaint had not got on a flight before now was that he had sensed his presence was one of the few things keeping Schillaci somewhat in check.

The doors pinged open on the fourth floor and Toussaint trudged down the corridor towards his room. He was cheered by the thought that this was the last time he would have to do this. Normally, he hated packing, but he would savour it this time. After tomorrow, he would do his best to wash the memory of sitting in the corner of the off-site task force operations centre, as Grainger had grandly titled it, from his mind entirely. It was the low point of his career as a *juge d'instruction*. He took pride in not just doing what he did, but also what it stood for. Justice. In these cynical times, the belief in the importance of such things may seem naive, but Toussaint was happy to be so. Imperfect, unwieldy and infuriating as it can often be, he believed in the importance of a legal system that worked. One that worked for everybody, not just for those who could afford it.

He slipped his room key into the electronic lock and, on the third attempt, the light turned green and he opened the door. He missed his own front door, his whole apartment, and his bed in particular. He had reached the age where the human body responds badly to any change in routine. In Paris lay a mattress that knew him well, and he was looking forward to becoming reacquainted with it.

It said something for his oft-commented-upon unflappable nature that he didn't scream when he turned on the light. A man was sitting in the armchair beside the window.

"*Putain!*" exclaimed Toussaint.

"Who? The Russian fella?" asked Bunny McGarry. "I look nothing like him."

"No, not ... What are you doing here?"

"Sorry," said Bunny, reaching out a hand in apology. "I didn't mean to startle you."

"Really? In that case, may I suggest that in future you do not sit in somebody's hotel room in the dark."

"I apologise, but this is the only way I could think of for you and I to have a quiet chat."

"For your information, I had a heart operation eighteen months ago. What would you be doing right now if I'd collapsed when you sprang out at me?"

"Be fair," said Bunny. "I didn't jump out like a jack-in-the-box."

"I'm sure that quote would look very good on my death certificate."

"Besides, I did a half-day CPR course there a couple of years ago. I just need to push down on your chest while singing an ABBA song." Bunny paused and crinkled his forehead. "Hang on, that's not right. Gloria Gaynor? No. Earth, Wind & Fire? No ..."

Toussaint folded his arms. "It appears I may have died with an Irishman pumping my chest while performing a medley of disco hits."

Bunny clicked his fingers excitedly. "The Bee Gees! It was the Bee Gees."

"Do you happen to know which song?"

"It would have to be 'Stayin' Alive', wouldn't it?"

Toussaint shrugged. "That makes sense. So, to come back to the issue of you being in my room – why are you in my room? Actually, no – forget that. First things first, how are you in my room?"

"I knew they'd have put you up in a hotel. It was just a matter of ringing around to find out which one."

"That would be a good explanation if we were meeting in the lobby. Should I repeat my question?"

Bunny sat back. "No offence, but you can definitely tell from the way you talk that you're a member of the legal profession."

"And you can definitely tell from the way you talk, Detective, that you are trying to avoid the question."

Toussaint's deduction was greeted with a smile. "No flies on you, judge." Bunny nodded towards the phone on the desk. "If you'd like to ring down to reception and get them to call the Gardaí,

I will happily sit here and wait for them to come. That's your prerogative."

"But you won't tell me how you got into the room?"

"I know quite a few people in this town. And they know even more people. I pulled in a favour, but I won't be getting anybody in trouble for being willing to help me out. Besides, I don't think you are calling the police."

Toussaint rested his shoulder against the wall, the still-open door of the room just a few feet behind him. "And why is that, exactly?"

"Because I'm betting that you're the only person in that entire clown show of a task force Grainger is running that's actually police."

"I am not a policeman at all. As you said, I'm a judge."

"You're still more police than anybody else in that room," countered Bunny, "and if you are, I'm guessing you're appalled at what's been going on."

Toussaint paused then jutted his chin forward. "How did you get all that bruising on your face?"

"I had a run-in with Inspector Schillaci and his band of merry men."

"Are you the reason why four of them look as if they got hit by a truck?"

"Not directly."

"Not directly?" repeated Toussaint.

"Like I said, I know quite a few people in this town."

"And it certainly looks as if one of those people drives a truck." Toussaint's eyes narrowed and he gave Bunny a long, assessing look. Finally, he nodded his head. "Alright, seeing as you have had to deal with Schillaci's little militia, I think it's only fair that you and I have a talk." He turned around and closed the door, before moving into the room and sitting down on the edge of the bed. "I'm only doing this because Grainger vouches for you."

Bunny raised his eyebrows in disbelief. "Excuse me?"

"Maybe I'm saying that wrong. Grainger is the worst kind of idiot, and the fact that he hates you so much is a ... How would you put it? An excellent reference!"

Bunny laughed. "I suppose I can stick that on my CV if he gets his wish and gets me booted off the force for good."

"I should tell you – the task force has had something of a breakthrough this evening."

"Is that right?"

Toussaint nodded. "Schillaci, as well as whatever else he was up to, has been out offering an unofficial reward to the criminal elements for any information that leads to the location of Sofia Accardi. An hour ago, a man gave us the names on three fake Irish passports that he sold to her, Walsh and Duggan."

Bunny nodded. "Part of what I was going to tell you was that they were in the market for passports."

"Well, they have them now. Two of the three names in question are booked onto a ferry, leaving tomorrow from Dublin Port for Holyhead."

"Only two?"

"Yes. Sofia and one of the men. We don't know which one, but the obvious guess is Bobby Walsh. As we speak, Grainger and Schillaci are organising a welcoming committee at the port. It would have been far more useful if we'd been able to arrest the trio when they went to get the forgeries, but I suppose this way, the seller believes he is covering his own ass and getting paid twice in the bargain. Seeing as we're not exactly working within the law, he can do that."

"It also means he didn't need to tell you the other items they wanted," said Bunny.

Toussaint tilted his head. "The other items?"

"According to my sources, they were looking for two things. One – passports, and two – guns."

It was now the Frenchman's turn to look surprised. "Really?"

"Really," Bunny confirmed.

"What for?"

"Your guess is as good as mine, but it's a worrying development. That's why I'm here."

Toussaint scratched at his tightly trimmed goatee. "That is ... unexpected. Schillaci's contact mentioned nothing about guns."

"Which is a bit of a worry, isn't it? It might mean they no longer want them ..."

"Or they already have them," finished Toussaint. "Why are you telling me this?"

"Because it'd be irresponsible not to tell someone, and who else could I talk to?" said Bunny. "Grainger? His response would be to try to get me locked up. Schillaci and I have not exactly hit it off. Despite all that, Bobby Walsh's a nasty piece of work and now there's a good chance he's armed. Somebody needs to do something about that, and fast." Bunny hesitated and looked away before speaking again. "I lost a good friend in the line of duty not that long ago. I'm not sitting on information that could put a guard or a member of the public in danger."

"I will raise it with Grainger. Then, when he inevitably does not do very much about it, you can be certain I will go looking for somebody who will."

"I appreciate that. I can give you a few names of people you might want to call."

"Thank you."

"Doing so will piss off Grainger."

Toussaint smiled. "Let us consider that a bonus."

Bunny laughed. "A man after my own heart." He leaned forward and rubbed his hands together. "Can I ask, and no offence in case this doesn't translate correctly, but what the hell are you doing here?"

"I have been asking myself the same question."

"But I mean," said Bunny, "Schillaci, piece of shit that he is – I understand why he's here. He's been sent by the parents and their political cronies to get Sofia back, no questions asked. It doesn't explain what a Frenchman is doing here."

Toussaint smoothed out a crease in the bedspread beside him then gave Bunny a piercing look. "She has done it before."

"Excuse me?"

"Sofia Accardi. Just over two years ago in Paris, while she was studying there, she disappeared. We had reports that she was last seen with an Algerian immigrant by the name of Farid Zekkal, and that the duo had robbed several individuals."

"You're kidding?"

He shook his head. "No. A similar modus operandi to what has been going on over here for the last couple of weeks. Maybe she has refined her technique a little, but the same general idea. Back in Paris, I wanted a full investigation, but it all got hushed up. Sofia Accardi, in the official version of events, was an unwilling accomplice to Zekkal, who went to prison after accepting a rather unusual plea deal. I cannot prove it, but I shall go to my grave believing that the Accardi family paid him off to confirm their story. Sofia went home and I thought that would be the end of it." He shrugged. "I thought wrong."

"So, this is all her?" asked Bunny.

"This is what she does to get attention in their messed-up family. I met them – the parents – the first time she was supposedly kidnapped. The mother appeared to be stoned and the father, he was quite something. Doing what we do, you and I have both met a lot of concerned parents in our time. Believe me when I say he was ... unusual. Far more concerned with the publicity than the safety of his youngest daughter. He spoke about the whole thing as if he were negotiating some business deal."

"Jesus. So, this is all some little girl working out her daddy issues?"

"Indeed. And the worst thing about it is, the same thing will happen this time as last time. Walsh and Duggan will be arrested, and she will be on the first flight back to Italy, never having to face up to the consequences of her actions."

"'Tis a disgrace."

Toussaint stood up and walked towards the door. "What it is is politics. Flavio Accardi is an incredibly powerful man, and it seems the governments of three countries now, including your own, will do whatever it takes to keep him happy. And if justice has to burn in the process, well, that is just the price of doing business." He opened the door to the room and stepped to one side. "Now, if you'll excuse me, I will give you a couple of minutes to clear the building then I need to inform my so-called colleagues we are now dealing with an armed individual." He nodded at Bunny as the big man got to his feet. "For what it is worth, Detective McGarry, I wish we had met under better circumstances."

"Likewise. Before I go, though ..."

"Yes?" asked Toussaint.

"There is a ring."

"Ah," said Toussaint, "the one they took off your poor friend. You have my word. I will do everything to make sure it is returned to him if Walsh and Accardi still have it, or if we can find out who it was sold to if they do not."

Bunny extended his hand. "'Twas a pleasure to make your acquaintance, sir."

They shook hands amicably. "Likewise, Detective. Although next time, please knock on my door. I am really far too old for surprises in the bedroom."

# CHAPTER TWENTY-EIGHT

Bobby Walsh lay in bed and stared up at the ceiling. This was it. It was now the very early hours of Christmas Eve. He should be sleeping, but his mind was firing on all cylinders, working its way through all possibilities. The morning would bring the culmination of everything they had been working towards. Two weeks ago, this had all seemed like a mad idea, but it was real now. Very real. Sofia was in the bed beside him, always so quiet when she slept. As he lay there, the thoughts that had swirled around his head for the last couple of weeks coalesced into something hard and sharp. This was his big chance and, come what may, nobody but nobody was going to get in his way.

———

Sofia lay there, staring at the wall. She kept running things over in her mind, again and again. The plan relied on one man sticking to his routine. If, for some reason, he didn't, everything would be for nothing. All that she had gone through would have been a total waste of time. More than anything, she wanted to show her bastard of a father that she was not the screw-up he thought her to be. In one day, she could be free of her family for ever and he would go to his grave knowing that he had been wrong.

She could hear Bobby breathing beside her. Sleep would not come, but she didn't want to go to the sink for a glass of water because then he'd know she was awake and, inevitably, he would want to have sex again. That particular activity was beginning to lose its appeal. So was Bobby. He was a means to an end, but he had become utterly tedious. Still, in a few hours, it wouldn't matter any more. She would have what she needed, what she deserved – and Bobby would no longer be necessary.

———

Niall Duggan lay in his small single bed and stared into the eyes of Björn the pigeon. Maybe he should never have let himself get dragged into all this, but it was too late now. He could never go home again. He knew that for certain. Björn could. Going home was what Björn did. From here, he could make it back to the loft in Limerick in about two and a half hours, all going well.

Niall ran the tips of his fingers along Björn's feathers. Niall didn't want to be here. None of this was his idea – not that it mattered now. He was in too deep. All he could do was look after what was important to him. He eased himself out of the bed, its frame creaking alarmingly under his weight as he did so, and opened the window. Holding Björn close to him, he whispered, "You go home now. Good birdie." And then he released him. He stood at the window, as he had done many times before, and imagined his birds flying through the air, the wind rushing around them, the ground scrolling by beneath their wings. The freedom of it all.

# CHAPTER TWENTY-NINE

Marcel Ricard was a creature of habit. So was Trixie.

The advantage of the exhibit being in Europe was that Marcel could bring Trixie with him. The North Americans were positively beastly with all their ridiculous rules, as if a tiny little chihuahua could be a danger to anybody. True, Trixie occasionally took a little nibble out of people, one customs agent in particular, but he really considered that to be her way of expressing her displeasure at bad manners. Neither she nor Marcel could abide bad manners.

Habit was an indicator of a tidy mind. They left the apartment at the same time every day, stopped at the same little shop for the morning coffee, and then walked the same route to the gallery. Seventeen minutes all in; sixteen if the traffic lights went their way. That and the same route home was enough walking for Trixie, who was not as young as she had once been. Who was, though?

As a younger man, Marcel might have taken the opportunity to fly home for Christmas but, nowadays, it felt like too much bother. Besides, travel made Trixie cranky. It wasn't worth the effort only to have to come back again in a couple of days when the exhibit reopened. What's more, the manager of the gallery was going to be off for the holidays and so Marcel was going to take the opportunity to rearrange the paintings as he saw fit. While the cat is away ...

They had been butting heads ever since he'd got here. On the first day, she had curtly informed him that dogs were not allowed in the building. There had nearly not been a second day. After some negotiation, an accommodation had been reached. Now they abided each other, nothing more. The woman did not like dogs. If there was ever a preference that showed a flawed personality, surely that was it.

Marcel had been pleasantly surprised to find himself growing fond of Dublin. He hadn't expected to. It helped that the apartment they had put he and Trixie up in was really quite nice considering, and it was such a short walk from the gallery. The city was certainly not Paris, but it had its own provincial charm. It was also nice that across the road from the gallery was the delightful Merrion Square Park. At lunchtime he would take Trixie there for her daily movement, and then they would swing by the Oscar Wilde memorial to pay their respects. He was not a fan of statues in general, but that one had an undeniable personality to it.

He held on to Trixie's lead tightly as he joined the throng of people waiting at the pedestrian lights that took them from Ely Place on to Merrion Street Upper. He had to be particularly careful here, as experience had shown him that when pedestrians were rushing, they did not pay enough attention to the ground and any poor little doggies that might get in their way.

When the lights allowed, they crossed. Marcel adjusted his sunglasses as they weaved their way towards the gallery gates in the dazzlingly bright early morning sunshine. Given the time of year, the weather was surprisingly good. He had been led to believe that Ireland in the winter would be terribly wet and dreary.

"Marcel?"

He was busy rearranging paintings in his mind as they walked, which was why the voice didn't register at first.

"Uncle Marcel?"

He broke from his reverie with a start as a face he recognised appeared before him. A young woman with long dark hair was standing on the pavement and giving him a quizzical look accompanied by a brilliant smile. "Do you not remember me?"

He rushed forward and grabbed the young woman's forearms. "My God, little Sofia, is that you?"

"So you do remember me!" she said with a grin.

Marcel threw his head back and laughed. "My darling girl, how could I forget you? I am just so shocked to see you here."

"Did Papa not tell you? I am studying in Limerick now."

"No, I did not know this at all. How did I not know this? All I knew was you were in Paris and then you were gone. My favourite little songbird." He slapped her hand playfully. "You disappeared on me. I should be very cross with you."

"I am terrible," she said. "You have no idea." She looked down. "And is that the wonderful Mademoiselle Trixie I see?"

"But of course. As you well know, she is the one true love of my life."

Sofia bent down to pet the dog, who begrudgingly allowed her to do so.

As she did, Marcel noticed the two men in suits standing awkwardly behind her. The short, handsome one looked all the more tiny compared to his great lumbering colleague. "And who are these fine gentlemen?"

Sofia waved a hand dismissively. "Security."

"Security?" he asked, taken aback. "Is everything OK?"

Having paid the appropriate amount of attention to Trixie, Sofia stood back up. "Everything is fine. Daddy worries."

Marcel patted her hand again. "As well he should. You are the most precious of all of his treasures."

"Oh, I don't know about that." She turned to speak to the smaller of the two security guards. "Uncle Marcel is a wizard. He has found so many wonderful pieces for my father's collection."

"Stop it, you embarrass me," Marcel said, beaming. "Your father is so generous. Without people like Flavio Accardi, so much of the world's most beautiful art would be locked away in dreadful bank vaults. He believes these treasures should be shared with the world."

He pointed at the National Gallery. "Why, I am here with an exhibit that features a certain painting he has been kind enough to lend to the Louvre."

"I know," said Sofia. "I'm in Dublin doing some last-minute shopping, and I was hoping to go in and see them, but unfortunately you are closed today."

"Little bird! We are closed to other people, but we are never closed to you." He linked his free arm through hers and started walking towards the gates of the gallery, the two-man security team falling into step behind them. "Come, Cinderella," he said. "You shall go to the ball."

# CHAPTER THIRTY

Security guards could be such a chore.

There was something about putting somebody, anybody, into a uniform that brought out the worst in them. Marcel Ricard had been embarrassed when the female security guard on the staff entrance to the gallery had made such a big deal out of him having guests.

"You can't bring in three guests without approval," she had repeated several times, like a particularly irksome parrot.

"I am not bringing three guests in. I am bringing one."

"But what about the other two fellas?"

"They are with her. She has security because she is a member of the Accardi family" – he leaned in and placed heavy emphasis on the end of the sentence – "who own one of the paintings in the exhibit."

The guard looked at the list again and then back at Marcel. "I was told that I could only let in people that are on the list."

Marcel had found himself about to utter the immortal words "do you know who I am?" but he realised that might make him look bad. Instead, he went for "are you new here?"

The security guard wound her neck in to reveal an unflattering double chin as she gave him an affronted look. "I'm not new, but I've never worked the desk before. I'm covering for Christmas. I know the rules, though."

"If it is a problem ..." started Sofia.

"No, no, not at all, darling girl. Just a little bit of red tape." Marcel held up his badge and showed it to the security guard. "This says that I am the curator of the collection currently on display in the Beit Wing, so, according to the almighty rules, I have the power to add names to the list." That sounded as if it might be true. For all Marcel knew, it was. If it wasn't, it certainly should be. Before the guard could say anything else, he grabbed the clipboard, snatched up a pen and wrote "Sofia Accardi +2" at the end of the list. He then spun it around and showed it to her. "See. There it is. Problem solved."

"Ah, but—"

Marcel had already swept away down the corridor, with Trixie trotting primly beside him and the other three following close behind.

The voice of the defeated guardian of the gate trailed in their wake. "Are you allowed to have a dog in here?"


Marcel had heard people describe empty galleries as being eerie, spooky, somehow lesser for the absence of people. Personally, he found that to be utter drivel. While he knew better than to say it out loud, galleries looked so much better to him without people wandering around, cluttering up the place, gawping at things. He knew the official message was that art must be brought to the public and the public must learn to appreciate art, et cetera, et cetera. He toed the party line but, deep down, all that was nonsense to him. Art existed because he saw it and it was good because he said it was. Everyone is entitled to their opinion, of course, but why must we pretend all opinions are equal? He had worked so very hard, fought tooth and nail, to get where he was today – a curator at the Louvre. That meant he knew better. Knowing better was almost in his job title.

He turned the lights on as he went. He loved that brief moment.

As if a wave of his hand magicked a room full of treasures into existence.

As he guided the trio through the gallery, their footsteps echoing around the large and largely empty rooms, he glanced at Sofia Accardi, who walked beside him. "So, any exciting news you'd like to share with me, my dear?"

"Nothing in particular."

"Really?" he asked, arching an eyebrow. "It's just that I've noticed that ring on your finger."

Sofia Accardi looked down at her left hand and blushed. "It is nothing."

Marcel laughed. "I think she's keeping something from us, Trixie. We shall have to delve further."

The sound of her laugh tinkled around the gallery as they walked. "You are an awful gossip, Marcel."

"All the best people are."

"And where are all the staff?" asked Sofia, neatly changing the subject. "It is so empty."

"As we are closed today, the cleaners have been and gone, and most of the staff are already on holidays." He patted her hand, their arms entwined. "You are receiving a very special tour. Nothing but the best for you, my darling."

"So, why are you still here?"

He laughed again. "Darling girl, I am always here. I am like the walls. As long as the paintings I am in charge of are here, I will roam these halls like a little guard dog, protecting the treasures that your family and others have given me to mind."

It was her turn to pat him on the arm. "Poor sweet Marcel. We need to get you a hobby or a hubby."

He laughed uproariously at this. "I have always so enjoyed you. What a wonderful little Christmas present you are. Please tell me you will have time for us to get some lunch later on?"

"Sadly not." He noticed her glancing back at the handsome man. "We have very definite plans."

They turned a corner into another slightly smaller wing of the gallery where the walls were painted a light blue. "Well, then," said Marcel, releasing her arm so that he could make a particularly dramatic hand gesture, as he waved up at the painting on the wall, "may I present a masterpiece by the genius Caravaggio, once thought lost but now brought to you by the ever so wonderful Accardi family, the magnificent *I Gioielli di Famiglia*" – he glanced at the two security guards – "which translates as 'the family jewels'."

The portrait showed a finely dressed middle-aged woman looking into a mirror, her hands gently caressing the jewelled necklace that hung around her neck. In the mirror, the reflection wore simpler clothes and no jewellery, but looked younger and happier than the subject. Academic papers had been written about the subtle message of the composition. Marcel Ricard did not care. It was beautiful. It was valuable. And, while not technically true, it was his.

Sofia looked up at the portrait, her eyes wide. "I forgot how breathtaking it is."

The handsome security guard spoke for the first time. "Yeah, I love it."

It was then that Marcel saw the gun.

"We'll take it."

# CHAPTER THIRTY-ONE

Bunny walked down the hallway towards his front door. "You can stop pounding on it. I'm coming."

He opened it to reveal the unexpected sight of DI Fintan O'Rourke standing on his doorstep.

Bunny leaned against the frame and folded his arms. "Bit early in the morning for carol singers, but go on, so – give us a few bars of 'Silent Night'."

O'Rourke smiled awkwardly. "Morning, Bunny. Do you know your doorbell isn't working?"

"It's not that it isn't working, more that it's been unfairly suspended. It made a ding-dong noise which some prick objected to, despite the fact it was just doing its job."

"I see."

"That's one of them metaphors."

"Yes," replied O'Rourke. "It was very subtle, but I think I got it. By the way, what happened to your face?"

Bunny self-consciously ran the back of his hand over the bruising on the left side of his jaw. "I walked into a door."

"Did you? Was it Italian-made, by any chance?"

Bunny ignored the knowing question. "So, what are you doing here?"

O'Rourke shifted awkwardly then held up the bag that was in his left hand. "I brought you a Christmas present."

"Bullshit."

"No, actually – it's a rather nice bottle of Bushmills. If I'd have known you wanted bullshit, I would have got you that instead."

"Are you sure you didn't, because I definitely smell it?"

"Any chance I could come in?"

"Have you got a search warrant?"

O'Rourke simply raised an eyebrow at this.

"Now that I've been indefinitely suspended from the Garda Síochána," continued Bunny, "I may or may not have turned my abode into a house of ill repute. Now isn't a good time – I'm installing all the mirrors and the love swing. Also, quite a lot of lino, as you want it to be wipe clean, for obvious reasons."

"While that is a lovely image, I'm afraid I am the bearer of bad news – your suspension has been rescinded, with immediate effect."

"That seems unlikely," said Bunny. "Seeing as I have it from a very good source that it was signed off by the second-highest-ranking guard in the country."

O'Rourke nodded. "Turns out somebody outranks him."

Bunny bowed his head theatrically. "Is that so? And where was this person three days ago when me and Pamela Cassidy were booted off his force for no good reason and Grainger was running roughshod over the Irish justice system?"

O'Rourke looked around. "Could we discuss this inside?"

"No," said Bunny.

"Only it isn't terribly private here. I'm pretty sure your next-door neighbour is listening in on our conversation."

"How dare you," came the instant response of Cynthia Doyle from behind her front door, which sat a few feet to Bunny's left. "I'm here minding my own business, polishing this doorknob as I'm expecting my son and his wife for Christmas. I don't have time to listen to other people's conversations."

Bunny raised his voice. "Don't mind him, Cynthia. It's an appalling trend in the modern Garda Síochána that senior officers are allowed to make all sorts of allegations without having any proof to back them up."

"It is shocking. Did you get that Christmas pudding I left for you?" asked the unseen Cynthia.

"I did," replied Bunny. "Thanks very much. It was absolutely gorgeous." As he said it, he looked O'Rourke in the eye and shook his head to indicate that may not have been the case.

"Don't mention it," she said. "Anyway, I can't stay chatting all day. I've to regrout the bathroom." Her pronouncement was quickly followed by the sound of loud, some would say overly emphasised, heavy footsteps going upstairs.

"I see you have a very active neighbourhood watch around here," observed O'Rourke.

"We do. People who look out for their friends. Not enough of it about."

"By the way, I thought you might like to know there have been developments in the Sofia Accardi case."

"Who's that?" asked Bunny. "The name is like my doorbell – doesn't ring any bells."

O'Rourke smiled. "Sorry, how would it? We believe she and two other individuals were involved in the robbery of your friend Declan Fadden."

"Is that right?"

"Yes," said O'Rourke, playing along. "She and two gentlemen by the name of Bobby Walsh and Niall Duggan have been implicated in a series of robberies. Detective Inspector Grainger has been leading a task force to deal with the issue."

"No better man," said Bunny, before spitting on his own doorstep.

"Although there was a development last night. I got a phone call at midnight from a Judge Toussaint, a Frenchman who has been seconded to the investigation for some very interesting reasons I and other parties were previously unaware of."

"Perhaps somebody should have asked him before now?"

"Perhaps," agreed O'Rourke. "Regardless, he said he had it from a rock-solid source that the trio had been attempting to acquire firearms. He informed me he had shared this information with DI Grainger and felt it was not being taken as seriously as it should. I passed this new information up the chain of command, and it led to a re-evaluation of the softly-softly approach the task force had been taking. Two of the trio, under their newly obtained identities, are booked onto a ferry that leaves Dublin in a couple of hours, and when they arrive at the port, they will have the unpleasant surprise of being met by the Garda armed response unit."

"The Gardaí are back in the arresting-people business, then?"

"It would seem so. I asked the good judge who his source for this information was, but he refused to reveal it."

"Good to see the concept of loyalty is at least still alive and well in France."

O'Rourke raised a hand in surrender. "Look, I get that you're annoyed, and frankly, you've got every right to be, but I'm just the messenger here. Certain people want you to know that your part in this will not be forgotten. Same goes for Cassidy."

"Oh, I'm sure Grainger and his highly ranked amigo will see to that."

O'Rourke shrugged. "OK, well, I said I would deliver the message and I have."

"Next time maybe just go for the Christmas card."

"Fair enough." O'Rourke held up the bag containing the bottle of whiskey. "Do you want this or not?"

Bunny snatched the bag out of his hand. "Merry bloody Christmas." And then he slammed the door shut.

"And to you, too," shouted O'Rourke through the door.

Nobody was more surprised than DI O'Rourke when, after getting in his car and driving away, he found himself back at Bunny's front door fifteen minutes later, having received a rather alarming phone call. He pounded on it with a greater sense of urgency this time.

"Alright, alright, alright," shouted Bunny, opening the door. "Keep your fecking hair on. I'm—" He gave O'Rourke a bewildered look. "If you want the whiskey back, you can feck off."

"No," said O'Rourke. "Grab your coat. There's been a development."

# CHAPTER THIRTY-TWO

Marcel Ricard looked up into the corner of the room at the infuriatingly unmoving security camera. He couldn't be certain, but it seemed likely that the internal CCTV was currently off. That would not come as a surprise to anyone who had worked in a building such as this. It was a curse of publicly owned museums and galleries that the drive to keep down costs was never-ending, which was why not having security systems running when the building was "empty" during the day is the kind of thing that made perfect sense in bureaucratic logic.

He turned his eyes back to the floor, where the big burly bodyguard now had *I Gioielli di Famiglia* laid out and was using a knife and a screwdriver to remove it from its frame. "Does that buffoon know what he's doing?"

The other bodyguard – the one that Marcel had considered handsome up until the point he had pulled a gun on him – smirked back from where he was standing lookout. "Yeah. He watched a video."

Marcel rolled his eyes. "Barbarians. That is a priceless work of art."

"We will definitely put a price on it. Now shut up."

Trixie growled at him.

"And shut that dog up and all."

"I cannot help it if she is an excellent judge of character."

This prompted an ugly sneer. "If she starts to bark I'm gonna boot her clear across this gallery."

"Beast," hissed Marcel. He turned to Sofia, who was standing quietly a few feet from him. "Lovely friends you have."

She gave him a frightened look and spoke in a whisper. "I am so sorry."

This prompted a laugh from the man with the gun. "She's always really sorry." He nudged his colleague with his foot. "Is this going to take much longer?"

"N-n-no."

On cue, he removed the backing from the frame then gently rolled up the canvas. In hindsight, a man walking into a gallery with one of those cylindrical document-carrying tubes should have aroused suspicion, but he was a big enough man to have comfortably hidden it about his person. Marcel winced as he watched the man's ham-hock-like hands guiding the canvas into the tube.

"Right," said the other man, taking some cable ties from his jacket pocket then nodding to the public toilets on the far side of the room, "let's go tie you to a cistern and then we can get the hell out of here."

"Absolutely not," said Marcel.

"Did you think I was asking?" said Bobby, walking towards him.

People make assumptions about dogs. Trixie, for example, had an unexpected history. When people see a small chihuahua, they assume that they have been pampered throughout their entire existence. Trixie was certainly very pampered now, but that had not always been the case.

She had been found abandoned on the streets of Marseille, near death, having been starved and attacked several times by bigger, brutish animals if the wounds were anything to go by. You could still see the scars on her belly. The kindly vet she had been left with had nursed her back to health and then offered her to a dear friend from her childhood, one Marcel Ricard.

This traumatic experience had left Trixie with a ferocious protective instinct when it came to her owner, which is why Bobby Walsh now felt sharp teeth digging into his ankle. Trixie, heedless to her own safety, would happily die in defence of her owner. On a primal level, she enjoyed the howl of anguish from her foe immensely.

Marcel had an unexpected history of his own, too. People looked at him and saw what they expected to see. He was the curator of a gallery – an effete man in a beret and sunglasses who wore a purple cravat with an immaculately tailored three-piece suit. His nails were perfectly manicured, his hair tightly trimmed. He was fully aware of the stereotypes he was fulfilling. The reason Marcel tried so hard to live up to those expectations is that it was less what he was, and more what he had consciously determined to mould himself into.

He had grown up in Marseille on the wrong side of the tracks and had become razor sharp out of necessity. Not only had he learned how to take a beating, but he had also learned how to make sure there would not be another. He had lived in the gutter and reached for the stars – but you could never forget what you learned while you were down there, even if you wanted to. All he needed was the momentary distraction of Trixie's bite. His vicious left hook caught Bobby Walsh so completely off guard that it spun him around before he fell to the ground. The gun flew from his hand and skittered across the floor.

Momentarily dazed, Bobby had the presence of mind to at least grab the leg of the Frenchman as he tried to pass by him to get the gun. Almost simultaneously, Bobby shrieked as the bastard little dog dug its teeth into his other ankle. As he maintained his grip on its owner's leg, he swung his own leg around and made satisfying contact with the canine. Its plaintive yelp echoed around the gallery as it skidded off across the floor.

A barrage of frantic punches began to rain down on Bobby from above, accompanied by some swearing in French. It was all he could do to hold on. He shifted his body weight, preparing to drag the man to the ground.

"Enough!"

This shout came from Sofia. He looked up to see her holding the gun.

"Marcel, move away from him," she ordered.

"Songbird, you don't have to—" started Marcel.

"Stop calling me that," she snapped, "and move. Now!"

He stepped away. "I see we are done playing the little victim."

Something in her eyes looked very different now. There was a hunger there. "Shut up! That painting belongs to me. It is just a fraction of what those bastards owe me."

"But—"

"But nothing." She pointed at the cable ties lying on the floor in front of Bobby. "Put one of those on your wrists, tightly." She watched as he did so. "And now use the other one to tie yourself to that pipe on the wall." Once he had done as instructed, using his teeth to tighten it, she turned to look at Niall. "Are you ready to go?"

He nodded.

Bobby spat out some blood and began to get up off the floor. "Before we go, I want to have a little word with this prick."

He stopped in his tracks as Sofia swung the gun towards him. "You'll have plenty of time to get acquainted. You're staying."

"What the fuck are you talking about?"

"Get back down on the ground."

"What?"

"This is where we part company. I would say it has been fun but, mostly, I'd be lying. You're a nasty, spiteful little man, a bully, and nowhere near as good in bed as you think you are."

Bobby glared at her and then turned to Niall. "I told you she would betray us."

This prompted a bitter laugh from Sofia. "*I* would betray you?" She looked at Niall. "The tickets for the ferry are in his pocket. Would you like to guess how many people he's booked for?"

Niall turned to Bobby, his mouth hanging open in shock.

"It's not like that. I was just … I just thought we should split up for a little bit. So you'd be safe."

"Oh, please," said Sofia, shaking her head. She reached across and laid a hand on Niall's shoulder tenderly. It's OK now. He can't hurt you any more. You and I can get out of here, just like we agreed."

"We agreed?" repeated Bobby in disbelief. "Niall, you bastard! After all I did for you."

Niall went to speak, but Sofia cut him off and pushed him gently away. "Come on, we have to get moving."

Marcel laughed and looked across at Bobby. "So sad. No honour amongst thieves."

"Shut up," snapped Sofia. "I am not a thief. I am taking what is rightfully mine. This is the least I deserve for putting up with the bastards God gave me as a family. My sainted father – you have no idea. None." Her voice was nearing a screech now. She took a breath and calmed herself. "You'll know exactly what I mean when you see him, the real him – which you will, believe me. He will have someone do things to you like he did to my first love because he did not approve. Like the husband of our sweet nanny, because he thought he had stolen from him. Poor Nanny, she cried for days because she thought Paulo ran away. He hadn't. I know what my father did, because he told me. Who tells a ten-year-old girl that?"

With her free hand she slapped at the single tear that had slipped from her eye.

"The man is a monster and the people who displease him either disappear or wish they had. You should know that for when he finds out you lost something that he treasures." She laughed bitterly. "Not me. I mean the painting. Tell him, though – tell him that I said I will disappear now, just as he always wanted. But let him know that I won, and he lost." She turned back to look directly at Bobby. "I am done with being pushed around."

Bobby met Sofia's eye. "You're not going to do this."

"I already am."

He took a step towards her and held out his hand. "Come on, now. If you give me the gun back, I promise I won't be mad."

"Don't take another step."

He took another step. "How are you going to get out of the country?"

"Please," she said, mockery in her voice. "You think that is your ace card? Tickets for a ferry? There is a reason nobody has ever escaped from a robbery via a ferry. You're a moron."

Bobby felt the anger swell in his chest now as he took another step. "You ungrateful bitch."

"One more step and—"

"And what?" said Bobby, before pointedly taking another step.

Which is when she shot him.

# CHAPTER THIRTY-THREE

Laurence Toussaint sat in the corner of the room and attempted the crossword in *The Irish Times*. He wasn't doing very well, for the joint reasons of him not being very good at crosswords and this one being in English. Still, it passed the time and, seeing as everyone else in the room was determined not to speak to him, he had time to fill.

He wasn't bothered by being shunned by the rest of the laughably titled task force. He had previously scraped things off the bottom of his shoe for which he had more respect. No, that was a little harsh – the dozen or so more junior members of the Garda Síochána present were just doing what they were told. The battered and bruised Italians in the other corner, though, seemed determined to spend every last minute of their time glaring at him. Seeing as they looked like a well-dressed field hospital, glaring was probably all they were currently capable of.

Their unhappy little group had not been getting along for quite some time, but Toussaint's phone call last night to a Detective Inspector O'Rourke, informing him of developments in this case, had gone down particularly badly. Inspector Schillaci had to be held back from striking him. While he wouldn't admit it, Toussaint was a little disappointed about that. Before he became a *juge d'instruction* he had held several other jobs, including that of soldier. Some reckless part of him would have enjoyed seeing what he could do with the element of surprise on the younger man.

Instead, he sat in the corner, with his packed suitcase beside him, and struggled to get a second clue. As far as he could tell, Schillaci and Grainger were finalising the travel arrangements for flying Sofia Accardi back to Italy that evening, after what sounded like it was going to be a tremendously brief and superficial police interview. Toussaint ignored them. For better or for worse, he had played his part here, and it was up to others to determine if Ms Accardi would finally face the repercussions of her actions. This was not his country.

If nothing else, the door flying open and three people striding in provided a welcome break from the monotony. Two of them he recognised as Detectives McGarry and Cassidy, although he had never been formally introduced to her.

Grainger shot up from his chair and addressed the man in the centre of the trio. "Detective Inspector O'Rourke, what are you doing here?"

"Taking over. You are relieved of command."

Fintan O'Rourke. Toussaint had never met him either, but he recognised the voice.

Grainger wore a facial expression appropriate for an unexpected rectal examination. "On whose authority?"

With perfect timing, the door swung open again and a very large man marched in. "Mine!"

"Commissioner," said Grainger, in a near squeal that implied the medical professional conducting the exam had not warmed their hands first. "I must protest."

Every other member of the Garda Síochána in the room quickly leaped to their feet.

"I couldn't give two shits what you feel you must do. You are suspended. And as for everyone else in this room who works for me – Fintan O'Rourke is now your commanding officer. Anyone has a problem with that, consider yourself suspended too."

Grainger, showing a survival instinct that would have caused lemmings to wince, said, "I will have to take this up with—"

Commissioner Ferguson cut him off by taking several steps towards him until he towered over the man. "You can take it up later with whomever the hell you like, but right now, you are going to sit down and shut up. Sofia Accardi and her chums robbed the National Gallery forty-two minutes ago. This shameful debacle is at an end. Not unlike your career."

Grainger sat back down, his facial expression now indicating that the results had come back from the medical professional, and they were extremely bad.

Inspector Schillaci, on the other hand, was not a man so easily fazed. "Commissioner, Sofia is a vulnerable girl who should be considered a hostage."

"Well, the good news is she appears to have freed herself from her captivity, seeing as she shot Bobby Walsh in the leg before making off with a painting that her family apparently already owns. Still, call me old fashioned but I'm going to believe there is a crime in there somewhere and she committed it. Now, sit down."

"I do not work for you."

"Have it your way," said Ferguson, before raising his voice unnecessarily further and pointing at Schillaci. "If this man or any of his associates attempts to leave this room or communicate with somebody outside of it in any way, you are all instructed to arrest him for interfering with an active investigation."

Schillaci waved his hand dismissively before stomping towards the door.

"I said ..." started Ferguson.

Detective Pamela Cassidy stepped in Schillaci's way, and he went to push her aside. What happened next happened so fast that every time Toussaint thought of it afterwards, he was never quite sure if he was remembering it exactly right. Still, he thought of it often. The glorious sight of Schillaci flying through the air as a diminutive woman took him out in a flawless judo throw that left the Italian face down on the floor, having bounced off a table on the way to the ground, was a memory to warm an old man's heart on the coldest of nights. Before anyone in the room had a chance to draw breath, Cassidy pinned down the inspector with her knee buried in his back and his arm locked behind him in a textbook armbar.

"Jesus," said Ferguson, sounding awestruck. "The last time I saw an Italian take that bad a beating was—"

"Ray Houghton, 1994 World Cup," finished Bunny.

"Sounds about right," agreed Ferguson. "Magnificent work, Cassidy. Magnificent."

By this point, Schillaci had had just enough time to re-master the art of breathing as he hissed something in Italian. In response, his four countrymen got to their feet. Bunny took an immediate step towards them, as did several other officers in the room.

"Gentlemen," said Ferguson, "while I appreciate you would have been rightfully impressed by your first contact with the Irish medical services, are you that keen to meet our delightful nurses again?"

The four men looked at each other then retook their seats.

"A wise choice," he said, before turning towards O'Rourke. "Fintan?"

"Right," said O'Rourke. "We want a full description of Sofia Accardi and Niall Duggan put out to every police officer in the country. Ports. Airports. Train stations. It being Christmas Eve, there will be an awful lot of travellers everywhere, so we need to make sure the message gets out there and they don't get lost in the rush."

Grainger, looking slightly dazed, chirped, "They are booked on the Irish Ferries' sailing to Holyhead at 3pm."

"Yes," said O'Rourke. "However, seeing as Sofia Accardi made reference to that in front of the curator from the Louvre – judging from the brief highlights of his statement relayed to me on the drive over here – let's not be lazy enough to assume that's their only escape route."

Grainger slumped back in his chair, the last of the air now gone out of his balloon.

"We need to work fast," continued O'Rourke. "We need to work smart and, to be crystal clear, we are no longer worried about being quiet. Sofia Accardi's face is about to go out on the *One O'Clock News*."

"Shit," exclaimed Butch, causing the room to turn momentarily in her direction.

"I believe Detective Cassidy has a further contribution to make," observed Ferguson drily.

"Yes, sir. Sorry, sir." While she spoke to the Commissioner, she was looking pointedly at Bunny. "Another escape route."

Bunny clapped his hands together.

"Jesus, Butch. You're a fecking genius!" He snatched up a phone from one of the nearby desks. "How the hell do I get hold of the phone number for a ballet school in Limerick?"

# CHAPTER THIRTY-FOUR

Sofia Accardi held on to the railing and watched the bow of the yacht as it cut through the waves. If she turned her head, she would have an excellent view of the Irish coast, but she had no desire to see it. She was thoroughly sick of the backward little country. It hadn't been her idea to come here in the first place. She had tried to make the best of it, only for her interfering father to intervene again and ruin everything. She would show him. She would show them all. Sofia drew in a deep lungful of sea air and tried to calm her anger.

She flinched as a pair of hands was laid on her waist. "Enjoying the view, darling?"

Terry was something in IT. Or possibly real estate. Come to think of it, he might have been a trader. She had definite memories of him banging on about some stock or other, but then a lot of people with money did that. It was what many of them did in lieu of having a personality.

He kissed the back of her neck. "Feeling any better?"

As soon as she had come aboard, he had wanted to "start their little voyage off with a bang". She had explained that she wasn't feeling well. To be fair, that wasn't even technically a lie. She felt sick in a way.

She laughed, despite Terry not having said anything funny. It always amazed her that it didn't seem to matter. "A little, thank you."

"You will love Guernsey. It's still really authentic. That's so my thing."

She noted his love of authenticity didn't extend to his teeth, hair, or the new nose he'd acquired since last year. Still, he was convenient. He had also been pathetically easy to manoeuvre into unwittingly providing her with a handy escape route. She had rung him from a payphone ten days ago, claiming that she had lost her mobile. In reality, Bobby had taken it and she had let him. He was the type that was easier to manipulate if they thought they were in charge. It had been a risk assuming Terry would stick to the plan that they would "have Christmas on the high seas", as he had grandly referred to it, but not much of one. She had bet on him being a horny idiot. Banking on such things hadn't let her down so far. People were so disappointingly predictable. Being useful didn't make Terry any more palatable, though. As he stood with his arms around her, a part of her brain imagined turning around too fast and him falling into the Irish Sea. What a tragedy that would be.

Failing that, she still had the gun. One of the major things she had learned today was that she was capable of shooting a man. It had been rather thrilling. Unfortunately, she had run out of bullets. The original plan, at least her version of it, had involved them going into the gallery – or rather being escorted in – stealing the painting, and then her losing the other two later on. When she'd found herself with the gun in her hand, she had improvised and removed the problem of Bobby while the chance had presented itself.

Then, in a moment of quick-thinking she was a little bit proud of, she had emptied the gun into the ceiling before running past the security station in tears, screaming that there was a madman in there shooting indiscriminately. A good idea, but just two or three additional shots would have been enough. If they couldn't sneak out quietly, then covering their escape in chaos would do nicely.

Terry moved closer. She could feel something unimpressive but insistent poking in her back.

"Do you think we will have lunch soon?" she asked.

He chuckled. "It's good to see you're getting your appetite back."

There was a crew of three people. Conceivably, if she killed Terry and threw him overboard, could she convince them to take her wherever she wanted to go in the world? They didn't know the gun wasn't loaded. While it was a lovely plan, it relied on her not falling asleep for several weeks. She was sure there would be some drugs on board, but not that much.

"I could definitely do with—"

They were interrupted by the captain shouting down at them. "Mr Blake."

Terry tried to turn around without fully turning around, to protect his modesty. "Not now, captain."

"Sorry, sir, but we are being hailed."

Terry, his mouth uncomfortably close to Sofia's ear, shouted back, "It's probably somebody wanting to see if we fancy some Christmas drinks. We're not in the mood."

"No, sir," said the captain, pointing off to the starboard side. "I'm afraid it's the coastguard."


Bunny beamed across the boat at Butch as it bucked back and forth over the waves. "Come on, this is fun!"

She held her hand in front of her mouth. "This is not fun. This is the opposite of fun."

"We get to board somebody. When do you ever get to board somebody on the high seas?"

"I could live without it."

"I was having a quick chat with one of the armed-response lads in the other boat before we left. They're buzzing. They train for this, but they never get to do it. It's going to be a right laugh." He slapped his life jacket. "And I like these. Do you reckon they'll let me keep it?"

"No."

"I tell you something, Butch – you're a lot better craic on land than you are at sea."

"I hate you so much right now."

"You could have stayed back at the dock, or whatever they call it, if you liked."

She shook her head and pursed her lips before saying, "No way, José. I worked too hard on this—"

The rest of her sentence was lost as she whipped around and threw up over the side.

Bunny turned to the nice woman from the coastguard who was sitting beside him. "She's not great on boats. You're not seeing her at her best. An hour ago she figured out how the fugitive we're pursuing was going to attempt to flee the country, while simultaneously smashing a corrupt Italian cop into the floor. She is having a great day" – Butch retched again and threw up more food than Bunny could believe she had ever eaten – "overall."

The actual boarding bit was somewhat of an anti-climax. The yacht heaved to and everybody on board complied with the instructions that were shouted at them over the loudhailer. Sofia Accardi had attempted to come up with some story about fleeing in fear of her life, but Bunny could tell that even she didn't think anybody was buying it. She, the three-person crew, and the boat's owner, who seemed confused about who he should vent his rage at as he simultaneously tried to hide the effects of some poorly timed Viagra, were all handcuffed and left sitting on the deck under the watchful eyes of the Garda armed response unit.

The yacht wasn't that big, so the search didn't take that long. What did take a long time was the search being conducted for a second time, as it didn't produce the result everyone had been expecting the first time. It didn't look like things were going to change on this occasion, and if they didn't, the boat would be brought ashore and ripped apart entirely.

While all this was going on, Bunny and Butch stood on the deck, in the odd position of having nothing to do.

"Have you got a mint?" asked Butch.

"I don't. But you're fine. If anything, your breath has improved."

"You're hilarious. And …"

Butch trailed off as she noticed Bunny's body language suddenly stiffen.

"Joanna," said Bunny. "Quick word, please."

Joanna was one of the tech-bureau bods currently conducting the search. She looked up from the inflatable lifeboat cabinet she was searching for the second time. "I'm a wee bit busy right now."

"Just a second of your time, please, Jo."

She gave him a suspicious look before making her way over. There then followed a quick, whispered conference that broke apart with Bunny clapping his hands together as he stepped forward.

"Right, folks," he announced, "seeing as it's Christmas, while we're waiting, who fancies a bit of a sing-song?"

It was hard to say who looked less keen on this – the men carrying the semi-automatic machine guns or the people who had just been put under caution for either assisting a fugitive or being the fugitive in question. Sofia Accardi's sneer might just have won her the award.

"I demand to speak to my lawyer," barked Terry Blake, the owner of a boat that was being ripped apart and an erection that was being studiously ignored.

"I'm afraid I don't know that one," said Bunny, entirely unfazed by the lack of enthusiasm for his idea. "I'd love to take a crack at the one about the bells, where everything overlaps, but let's not run before we can walk. Let's go with 'Jingle Bells'." He pointed at the armed-response boys. "And none of you go adding in the alternative lyrics about Batman farting. I know what you're like. OK, here we go …"

He then began to sing while throwing in a bit of a soft-shoe shuffle and waving his hands about. "Jingle bells, jingle bells, jingle all the way. C'mon, everybody! Oh, what fun it is to ride on a one-horse open sleigh. Anybody?" He threw in a twirl. "Ohhhh, jingle bells, jingle bells— NOW!"

At the signal, Butch and Joanna, who had been nudging

themselves out of the way in either direction, leaped forward and grabbed Sofia Accardi's hands.

"Get off me!"

Butch restrained Sofia by the arms as Joanna removed from her finger the ring that Bunny had spotted glinting in the sunlight.

Bunny leaned in. "Well?"

Joanna held up her bounty. "Is this it?" She turned it around carefully in her blue-gloved hands. Bunny noticed the tell-tale glint of the green emeralds.

"Oh yes," he said gleefully, "that's it alright."

"Frank!" shouted Joanna. "I need an evidence bag and a camera to process this asap." She moved off to complete her task.

As Sofia Accardi ranted at Bunny in furious Italian that he couldn't understand, he smiled down at her. "Yeah, you probably should've thrown that in the sea while you had the chance, but luckily, you're not nearly as clever as you think you are."

She turned her head away, and then, when she turned around again, the mask was back in place. "That was a gift. I don't know where it came from."

"Sure," said Bunny. "And let me guess," he said, bending down to look her in the eyes, "you're so sorry and you need my help?"

Sofia said nothing to this. Instead, she stared into the sea as if waiting for a salvation that wasn't going to come sailing in.

Eventually, DI O'Rourke re-emerged from below decks and stood in front of her. "OK, I have a lot of people with families here working Christmas Eve, so let's not drag this out. Where is it?"

"Where is what?" Sofia asked blithely.

"There really is no point trying to play the innocent. Marcel Ricard has given a very extensive and damning statement about your involvement in the robbery. While the main cameras may not have been on in the gallery, we already have footage of you shooting a gun into the air several times and fleeing the scene. Bobby Walsh is also very keen to explain to anyone who will listen how you shot him. Now, where is Niall Duggan and where is the painting?"

They all saw it – the unmistakable visceral rage as it flashed across her face. "I wish I knew. The bastard! We were running away from the gallery. One moment he was there, and then the next ..."

O'Rourke looked at her, and then back at Bunny and Butch. Despite the situation, he couldn't hold back the smile that played across his lips. "Are you telling me you got played by the big soft lad?"

––––––

Mark Dillon nudged the van forward. He was the next one up to the booth. He was trying not to look nervous. He wasn't great at meeting people at the best of times, and now that he had three broken fingers on his right hand, he felt even more nervous. It wasn't like most people understood sign language, but he felt even more vulnerable knowing it wasn't really an option. He had a notepad and pen on the seat of the van beside him and a pre-prepared note written out, with the details of his booking on it.

It was a week since Anna had flown home to the coop and changed his life.

It was amazing how much detail you could fit on a note in a canister attached to a pigeon's leg if you could write small enough. Niall had proposed a plan. In the past, while the pair of them had quietly worked away on the pigeons, Niall had often talked about how nice it would be to be somewhere else. Mark had agreed, never thinking a chance to actually do it would present itself. And then, here it was. He had withdrawn from the bank the money his granny had left him and used a little of it to buy Rio Doyle's van off him. Then he had got to work customising it. Even then, he'd thought he wasn't going to go through with it. Not really. It was just a nice dream.

Ironically, he'd been on the fence until that arsehole Schillaci and his goons had broken three of his fingers. That had made his mind up for him. He felt weirdly proud. He had stood his ground and told them nothing of Niall's suggested plan. He'd been bullied his whole life. It felt good to finally get one over on his tormentors.

By the time Björn had flown home that morning, delivering the second message from Niall, with the exact details of where to meet later that day, Mark already had everything booked and ready to go. He locked up the house, put all the birds into the van and drove up to Dublin, parking and waiting in Phoenix Park, at the exact spot where he had been told to. He'd been starting to worry that Niall wasn't going to show, when the big fella had appeared, out of breath and smiling, with a document tube strapped across his back. They had spoken only briefly before Niall had slipped into the compartment in the van under all the cages full of birds.

In the queue for the ferry, the car in front drove off and Mark nudged the van up to the ticket booth.

"Merry Christmas," said the lady behind the glass, who was wearing a green Santa hat.

Mark nodded and handed her the note.

*Hello, my name is Mark Dillon – I am profoundly deaf and unable to speak. I can read lips and use sign language or write a note!*

*My van is full of pigeons scheduled to be released on Christmas Day for a race run by the St Thomas's Pigeon Racing Club. My booking reference is A3421869.*

*Thank you.*

The lady read it and her eyes widened. "Oh, right," she said, leaning forward to make sure he could see her. "I will ring through, make sure Customs know about ..." She held up the note. "You know ..."

She typed away at her computer then handed him a ticket and a sign to hang off the rearview mirror indicating he was a priority customer. "Lane thirty-two," she said, over-pronouncing the words. "And I hope your pigeon wins."

It didn't. In fact, none of those pigeons ever went back to Limerick. It takes quite some time, but birds, not unlike people, can get used to living somewhere else. In fact, they can be a lot happier there.

# CHAPTER THIRTY-FIVE

It being Christmas Eve, O'Hagan's public house was particularly busy. Packed to the rafters with people getting in one last quick one before heading back home to their families. In contrast to the celebratory mood, Bunny sat alone in the snug, contemplating the empty pint of Guinness in front of him.

As days went, it had certainly been eventful. Sofia Accardi had been arrested and was spending her Christmas behind bars because even her father's influence had its limits. Inevitably, things were going to get political. Bunny honestly didn't care. His job had been to get Bridie Fadden's ring back and he had. Proving who had done what and why was someone else's problem. He didn't even give much of a damn about Niall Duggan and the painting. The thing belonged to the Accardi family, and them losing it seemed like a result to Bunny. Besides, it wasn't as if they couldn't afford it. Butch had posed the question whether insurance would cover a theft if it was carried out by a member of the owner's family. No doubt some serious legal fees would be burned through deciding that one.

Bunny had just come from the Fadden household, where the news that arrests had been made had been well received, but it was nothing compared to the moment when Bunny had asked Declan

Fadden Senior, discharged from hospital just that morning, for a quiet word. Without saying anything, he had pressed the ring into the older man's palm. Grandad Fadden's eyes had welled up and he had struggled to speak. Instead, he'd just patted Bunny on the arm and gave him a cheerful smile. It made getting slapped around a bit by an Italian gobshite feel like a very small price to pay.

Bunny had politely explained how he couldn't stay long as he'd somewhere to be, and he'd also deflected the invitation to join them for Christmas dinner with the assertion that he already had plans.

All of which should have left him in a good mood, but then this meeting had been there, like a ghost at the feast, hanging over him.

Tara Flynn, a pint of Guinness in her hand, appeared in front of him. "I thought you might need a fresh one." She set it down on the table.

"Much appreciated."

"Don't mention it." She stood there for a couple of seconds, smiling awkwardly, unsure of what to say next. She nodded at the large, wrapped present beside him. "Did you get something nice?"

"'Tis not for me."

"Oh. Right." She looked around the bar and then back at Bunny. "Look, are you OK?"

He gave her that wonky-eyed look that she knew so well. "Why wouldn't I be OK?"

"Because it's Christmas Eve and the world is one massive conga line except for you, sitting here like the Grim Reaper who's just been told the taxman is going to audit him."

"Can I not have a quiet drink?"

"Of course you can. You could do that at home, though, which makes me think that maybe you'd like to talk to somebody?"

Bunny tapped the side of the pint glass. "I don't have Guinness on tap at home."

"Fair enough. You know how I don't like to interfere."

Bunny raised his eyebrows at this statement.

"There's no need to be like that about—"

"Bunny."

Tara spun around towards the source of the voice and found an attractive red-haired woman standing behind her.

"Oh," she said, embarrassed. She looked back at Bunny. "I didn't realise you were expecting company." She turned to address the woman. "Can I get you a drink?"

"I'm OK just at the minute," the woman said, pulling off her scarf.

"Right," said Tara. "Good. Well, if you change your mind ... we are a pub."

"Thank you, Tara," said Bunny.

Tara shot Bunny a wink before heading off to deal with the backlog of thirsty punters at the bar. Bunny indicated the seat opposite.

"Thanks for coming, Jane. Grab yourself a pew."

Jane sat down and sighed. "It's madness out there. I can't stay long. My husband forgot to get a present for his mother, of all people, and I need to sort that and catch a bus while the getting is good." She nodded at the present beside him. "Speaking of which, you shouldn't have."

Bunny shifted awkwardly. "Actually, no, I—"

"Relax," she said. "I know who it's for. What is it?"

"I got him one of those PlayStations. I asked a couple of the lads and they said they were the big thing everybody wanted."

Jane nodded. "Whom am I supposed to tell Paul it's come from?"

Bunny looked down at his pint. "Christ, I didn't really think of that. He's a bit old to go with Santa as an answer, isn't he?"

"Yes," she said, not unkindly. "Don't worry, I'll come up with something. We often get unusual donations around Christmas time. It's not that unlikely a thing."

"Great. Thanks. How's he getting on?"

She shrugged. "Look, Paul Mulchrone is a thirteen-year-old boy who unfortunately has spent most of his life in care. Yeah, he's angry because his adoption fell through, but he'll get over it. Kids can be surprisingly resilient."

Bunny nodded and ran his finger along the rim of his glass.

Jane lowered her voice and leaned in. "Only you, me and your partner know the truth about why you interfered. If it bothers you that much, I'm happy to go to Paul and we can both tell him the truth."

Bunny shook his head firmly. "No. I haven't changed my mind about that. I'd rather he be angry at me than know that the only people who'd ever wanted him beside his poor late mother were ... what those people are."

Jane rubbed a hand across her neck. "OK. If that's what you want, then I'll respect it."

"Have they ..."

"Yes. They've withdrawn completely from attempting to adopt. Your quiet word saw to that. He was described as appearing positively terrified."

"With good reason."

Jane nodded. "I can imagine."

Bunny shifted nervously in his seat. "Did you ask your boss about the other thing?"

Jane puffed out her cheeks and nodded. "It is what I told you it would be. Adoption in this country is infuriatingly difficult as it is. A single person on their own ..." She shrugged and gave him a kindly smile. "I mean, if you were related to Paul, that'd be something, but unfortunately, you're not. And I'll be honest, your job – it's not exactly conducive to raising a kid."

"I can get another job."

"Doing what exactly?" She reached across and patted his hand. "I know better than anybody that your heart is in the right place, but you can't fix everything, Bunny. We're doing the best we can for the lad, and who knows, something may change in the future."

Bunny nodded glumly. "Just doesn't seem fair."

She arched her back and groaned, suddenly looking years older. "The one thing you quickly learn in this job – things are very rarely ever fair in this life. All things considered, he's in the best place he can be, and you need to stop beating yourself up about this. You did the right thing."

"Why does it feel so fecking miserable, then?"

"Take it from somebody who does what I do for a living. That's all too common. You should look around my office sometime. Nobody looks like they've had a decent night's sleep in a decade. Look, I'm sorry the news isn't better, but I'm afraid I have to get going."

"No problem," said Bunny. "Thanks for taking the time. Let me know if there's anything ..."

"Don't worry," she said, reaching across the table to pick up the present, "I will. Merry Christmas."

"Merry Christmas."


Five minutes later, Tara Flynn "dropped over" and was disappointed to see Bunny sitting on his own once again, an empty pint in front of him. She set the new one down. "Has your lady friend gone?"

Bunny nodded. "If you could keep these coming, that would be much appreciated."

"Like that, is it?"

He nodded as he picked up the fresh pint. "It is. Merry Christmas."

# CHAPTER THIRTY-SIX

"Boss."

Bunny was seated in a boat, alone in the middle of the ocean. It wasn't a yacht, like the one he had spent a while on yesterday, just a small wooden rowing boat.

"Boss."

Even as some part of his mind realised he was in a dream, he started to look around him. There was no paddle. Nothing. He was stranded.

"Boss!"

In the dream, he heard a noise and turned to find a massive tidal wave heading straight for him. His heart began to race.

He tried to open his mouth to speak, and then ...

Bunny's eyes shot open as the contents of a glass of water hit him straight in the face.

"Jesus Christ on a tandem bike!" he hollered as he flew out of bed and ended up on the floor. He turned to see Deccie Fadden peering down at him.

"You shouldn't be taking the Lord's name in vain, boss. Not with this being Christmas morning and all."

Bunny ran a hand over his soaking-wet face. "Did you throw water over me, Deccie?"

"I did, boss. I tried shouting at you, but it wasn't working."

"Did you consider maybe shaking me?"

Deccie shook his head. "Absolutely not. That would be a terrible violation of your personal space."

Bunny looked down at the pyjamas he was surprised but thankful to realise he was wearing. "Hang on a second. Let's back up the bus here. What the hell are you doing in my house, Declan?"

"It was Granny's idea."

"Your granny thought it was a good idea for you to break into my house?"

"She didn't exactly put it like that, boss. She found out that you saying you had plans for Christmas was bollocks."

"I'm going to assume she didn't phrase it quite like that."

"Not far off."

Hungover as he was, it was taking his senses a little bit of time to come online. He now noticed the sounds of activity downstairs.

"Stall the ball," Bunny said, closing his eyes for a long moment, as if hoping that would dispel the throbbing headache that had now also decided to put in an appearance. "Forget why you're here for a second. How did you get into my house?"

Bunny opened his eyes again to look at Deccie. The young lad wasn't speaking and this was a rare enough occurrence to warrant someone's full attention. "Declan?"

"I'm trying to phrase this diplomatically, boss – out of respect for you being a pig and all."

"Thank you, as always, for your tact and subtlety, Deccie. Much appreciated."

"You're welcome. Now, Phil's uncle Paddy may have ... unexpectedly found your front door to be open?" Deccie put his hands out as he spoke, as if to say, "Does this sound remotely believable?"

Bunny nodded. "Well, that was certainly a collection of words that approximately formed a sentence. I suppose my follow-up question would be, what the hell is Paddy Nellis doing here *not* breaking into my house?"

"Phil decided to surprise his auntie for Christmas by supercharging her cooker."

"Oh God," said Bunny.

"Yeah. Luckily, the fire brigade got there fast, so there wasn't that much damage done. So, they were coming to ours, but now everyone's come to yours instead."

"But what ..." Bunny stopped talking again. Another of his senses had now clicked in. "What the hell am I smelling?"

"Granny is downstairs cooking dinner. Well, supervising other people cooking dinner. They're also cooking breakfast, y'know – to keep us all going until the dinner is ready."

"My God, that smells incredible."

"Full Irish. None of that English breakfast nonsense."

"What's the difference?" asked Bunny.

Deccie gave him a look of disbelief. "Ours is better, of course."

"Right. Obviously. I'm sorry I asked."

They were interrupted by somebody thumping on the bedroom door. "Are you coming downstairs or what?"

"Butch? What are you doing here?"

"I didn't want you to be alone at Christmas."

"Chance would be a fine thing."

"So, get dressed and showered – not in that order. Pre-dinner dinner – aka breakfast – is almost ready."

Bunny stood up, his addled brain ignoring the reports of protest from the other areas of his body. "Hang on a second. What happened to vegetarian Christmas with your ex?"

The question was met with silence.

"Pamela?" he asked. "Are you still there?"

"I am. I'm just not dignifying that with a response."

"But you were all being so mature about it," said Bunny, smirking to himself. "You and the ex, the girlfriend, your pre-prepared collection of jokes, whatever you were having instead of a turkey and—"

"Hey, Deccie," interrupted Butch, "why don't you ask Bunny what we caught a man and his wife doing in their basement a couple of nights ago? You'll love it."

Deccie's face lit up. "What was it?"

"Ehm ..."

Bunny had never been more relieved to hear his name shouted than when Deccie Fadden Senior called, "Bunny?"

"I'll be down in a second," he shouted back in response.

"No rush. Only you've got a visitor."


Three minutes later, now fully dressed, teeth brushed and hair vigorously shown a comb, Bunny was running down the stairs. Despite himself, his mind had excitedly come up with a couple of possibilities for who could be at the door. He was trying not to get his hopes up, but it was Christmas, after all.

Gerry Lamkin on your doorstep was nobody's idea of a happy surprise.

Bunny tried to smile. "Gerry. Merry Christmas. I know we said you were going to drop over in a couple of days but is there any chance we could not do this on Christmas Day? There are kids here and ..."

Gerry gave him a confused look. "What are you talking about?"

"I mean, I appreciate you already helped me out greatly this week and you feel there are matters to be settled, but if we could deal with our little problem maybe in a few days' time?"

Gerry cut him off by waving both his hands in the air. "Oh, no, no, no. I'm not here to batter you."

"Oh, right," said Bunny. "Well, that is good news."

"Yeah. I've given up on violence entirely."

"Have you?"

"Indeed, I have. I'm back on my meds. Thanks very much for your help with that, by the way."

"You're very welcome," said Bunny. "It seems it has worked out great for both of us."

"It has. I'm a new man. In fact, I'm getting married."

Bunny blinked a couple of times then shook his head. "Sorry, hang on a mo, Gerry. I'm only out of bed and I think I'm a little bit behind the run of play here. You're getting married?"

He nodded excitedly as an enormous grin spread across his face. "I know it's sudden, but when you know, you know."

"Right. And I hate to be the one to ask this, but is the lady in question aware of this plan?"

"Of course she is," beamed Gerry. "Sure, didn't she drive me here?"

Bunny looked down the end of the garden path and saw the car parked in front of his house. The woman in the front seat waved happily at him. "Is that Hazel? The barmaid from the snooker club?"

"Actually, bar manager," corrected Gerry. "But yes. After I helped you out with your thing— Oh, how is that going, by the way?"

"Great," answered Bunny. "Deccie's granny got her ring back."

"Ah, isn't that brilliant? Anyway, I went back to Shotz after I left you, and Hazel and I got to talking and now we are getting married."

"It feels like you're leaving out a few steps there, but nevertheless, congratulations, Gerry. Will the two of you come in for a drink?"

"Thanks, but we have no time. We're off to tell Hazel's family, but I just wanted to talk to you first." He stopped and straightened himself up. "Bunny McGarry," he said in a solemn voice, "would you do me the honour of walking me down the aisle?"

Bunny paused for a second. "Walking you down the aisle?"

Gerry suddenly looked unsure. "Shit. Have I said that wrong? I just meant, would you be my best man?"

"Oh, right. Absolutely. I mean – I'd be honoured to."

"Great," said Gerry. "We've not done much planning yet."

"I can imagine."

"But we will let you know. It'll be a small affair because Hazel hasn't got much family, and all of mine are pricks who are mostly in prison. We should still have a stag do, though."

"Of course," said Bunny, who was now actively considering the idea that he might still be asleep and the events of the past few minutes were part of some very weird dream. He had probably eaten cheese before going to bed again.

Hazel honked the horn.

"Coming, sweetheart," shouted Gerry, before grabbing Bunny's hand and pumping it up and down several times. "Thanks for everything. Have yourself a very merry Christmas."

Once he'd waved the newly betrothed off, Bunny walked down the hall and into what he was pretty sure had once been his front room. It now contained a very long table, made up of at least three tables, with mismatching chairs placed all around it. All of his furniture had also disappeared.

"Where's me sofa gone?"

"We put it outside in your back garden to create some room," said Cynthia Doyle from next door, who was busy repositioning a centrepiece that appeared to be a large swan attacking a block of cheese. "Luckily, it doesn't look like it's going to rain. Would you like some cheese?"

"I think I'm OK for the minute," he said, still feeling rather confused by everything. "Good to see you, Cynthia."

"You too. That lovely Lynn lady knocked on the door earlier and asked me if I had any spare chairs, and when she found out that I was alone for Christmas ..." Cynthia paused, and a slightly awkward look passed across her face. "My son had to change his plans at the last minute. He's very busy with work."

"That's a shame," said Bunny.

"Yes, so, anyway – Lynn asked if I'd like to drop in." She looked suddenly nervous. "Is that OK?"

"Of course it is. You're very welcome."

"Thanks very much. You should get into the kitchen. Your breakfast will be going cold."

. . .

In one corner of Bunny's kitchen, Paddy Nellis and Butch were making an unsuccessful attempt at resolving a dispute that Paddy's nephew and Deccie Fadden Junior were having over a board game, while in the other, Bridie Fadden was supervising Lynn Nellis and Deccie Fadden Senior as they took an enormous turkey out of the cooker and poured something over it.

"I wasn't even sure that oven worked," said Bunny.

Bridie Fadden was only a small woman, but the ferocity of the bearhug she gave Bunny when she grabbed him took his breath away. At the point he thought there was a very real possibility he might pass out from a lack of oxygen, Bridie released him and took a step back. She patted herself down then pointed to the counter at a plate that was heaped with the fullest of Irish breakfasts.

"It's about time you were out of bed," she scolded. "Eat your breakfast. It'll be dinner soon."

As she pointed, Bunny couldn't help but catch the green glint on her finger as the morning sun streaming through the window caught a diamond surrounded by green emeralds.

"Merry Christmas," she said, before turning back to the turkey.

"And to you, too," said Bunny.

Behind him, he heard the unmistakable sound of young Deccie Fadden raising his voice. "You know what your problem is, Phil ..."

In a moment of unexpected perfect unison, Bunny, Deccie Fadden Senior and Phil all spoke simultaneously. "You've no appreciation of the fundamentals of the game."

# EPILOGUE

Detective Inspector Eduardo Schillaci could not wait to get home. Since the Sofia Accardi debacle that had ended with her being arrested for stealing from her own family and shooting her co-conspirator, his life had been chaotic. The last week had been full of awkward questions, none of which he had answers to. He had gone from running the investigation to being part of it, as the Gardaí had gone from treating him like an honoured guest to a possible suspect. They had seriously run with the idea that he could have been somehow aiding Sofia Accardi in her lunatic plan.

After a couple of days, the useless bunch of buffoons they had sent to assist him had been allowed to return to Italy, but Schillaci had only been cleared to do so now, on New Year's Eve. He would spend it on a ferry to France before driving back to Italy. This might be the final straw to end his relationship with Tanya. In truth, he was starting to think that just having the one girlfriend might be simpler anyway. His life was over-complicated.

As well as his day job, for the last eight years Schillaci had been a troubleshooter for the Accardi family. It had been a profitable position, but it was fair to say that association was now at an end. Flavio Accardi had made it extremely clear that he was holding him responsible for the mountain of trouble Sofia now faced. While Schillaci would miss the money and the influence, he would certainly not miss the Accardis. Sofia was a deranged nightmare to deal with, trapped in a never-ending battle with her father. The only good thing that he could say about her was she was less of a flaming car wreck than her brother.

His last discussion with Flavio had been interesting, more so for what was not said. Flavio was an undoubtedly smart man. He knew enough to know that Schillaci knew where the bodies were buried, and so, while their relationship was at an end, there would be no recriminations. Schillaci was savvy enough to realise that what he knew would need to go with him to his grave. Any suggestion to the contrary and he would meet the grave in question sooner rather than later. He more than anyone knew that Accardi was a man of means with a willingness to do what he deemed necessary.

He was leaving Garda Headquarters in Phoenix Park, having had an informal chat with Fintan O'Rourke, the new head of the investigation. It had been made clear to him that he would not be welcome back. He was fine with that. He had absolutely no intention of ever returning. Let the whole stinking country sink into the Atlantic Ocean and he would not shed a tear. If it took Sofia Accardi with it, so much the better.

As he finished descending the stairs and laid his hand on the door to exit, he lurched backwards as he recognised the man standing outside.

Bunny McGarry held the door open for him. "Inspector Schillaci – small world."

Schillaci regarded him carefully then looked behind him. They were alone except for the two women behind the reception desk who were now looking at him.

"Are you OK?" asked McGarry. "You seem a little jumpy?"

"It's been a long couple of weeks."

"I can imagine. Still, all over now. All's well that ends well, as they say. I mean, your alleged victim is going to jail and one of her alleged captors has disappeared with an incredibly expensive painting belonging to her daddy, but still – we found most of the criminals, and sure, isn't that the main thing?"

Schillaci nodded. The man wasn't going to jump him in broad daylight right in front of the police headquarters. He seemed a tad unhinged but nobody was that stupid.

"Yes," he said, deciding that styling it out was the way to go. "I hope one day we can meet again."

"Oh, absolutely," replied Bunny. "For the evening that's in it, should old acquaintance be forgot? I think not."

Schillaci had no idea what he was talking about, but he nodded before moving swiftly by.

As he walked to his car, he looked over his shoulder a couple of times. Nothing to be seen.

Nothing to …

The thing he noticed first was the chair. It was a plastic chair. The chair that McGarry had been tied to while he had worked him over. He wouldn't have recognised it on its own, but in the context it was obvious.

Schillaci screamed the foulest words in Italian that he could summon as he raced towards his car.

His Porsche.

His lovely Porsche.

His perfect, beautiful Porsche.

He collapsed to his knees beside it.

The roof was down and the plastic chair was placed on the bonnet. The rest of the car was filled to the brim with the foulest-smelling horseshit. In the middle of it sat a framed photo of Ray Houghton lobbing the ball over the Italian goalkeeper in the 1994 World Cup.

# FREE BOOK

Hello again lovely reader-person,

I hope you enjoyed The Family Jewels. Thanks for buying it and taking the time to read it. There'll be more Bunny and co in 2023. If you need a Caimh fix before then make sure you've signed up for my monthly newsletter for free short stories, audio, and the latest goings on in the Bunnyverse.

You'll also get a copy of my short fiction collection called *How To Send A Message*, which features several stories featuring characters from my books. To sign up go to my website:

*www.WhiteHairedIrishman.com*

The paperback costs $10.99/£7.99/€8.99 in the shops but you can get the e-book for free just by signing up to my newsletter.

Cheers muchly and thanks for reading,
Caimh

# ALSO BY CAIMH MCDONNELL

Visit www.WhiteHairedIrishman.com to find out more.

Made in the USA
Las Vegas, NV
15 December 2022

62931725R00162